THE LAS PUERTAS TALES
LOS CUENTOS DE LAS PUERTAS

THE LAS PUERTAS TALES
LOS CUENTOS DE LAS PUERTAS

David Dexter Correa

SUNSTONE
PRESS
SANTA FE

Sunstone books may be purchased for educational, business, or sales promotional use. For information please write: Special Markets Department, Sunstone Press, P.O. Box 2321, Santa Fe, New Mexico 87504-2321.
Printed on acid-free paper
⊗
eBook: 978-1-61139-756-7

Library of Congress Cataloging-in-Publication Data

Names: Correa, David Dexter, 1946- author. | Correa, David Dexter, 1946-
   Gordo. | Correa, David Dexter, 1946- Boxing game. | Correa, David
   Dexter, 1946- Strangers. | Correa, David Dexter, 1946- Land of
   enchantment.
Title: The Las Puertas tales = Los cuentos de Las Puertas / David Dexter
   Correa.
Other titles: Cuentos de Las Puertas
Description: Santa Fe : Sunstone Press, 2024. | Summary: "Four novellas
   detail the people who live in Northeast New Mexico and the challenges
   faced by the county sheriff in his efforts to maintain the peace during
   some trying times"-- Provided by publisher.
Identifiers: LCCN 2024038047 | ISBN 9781632936875 (paperback ; acid-free
   paper) | ISBN 9781611397567 (epub)
Subjects: LCSH: New Mexico--Fiction. | LCGFT: Novellas.
Classification: LCC PS3603.O77186 L37 2024 | DDC 813/.6--dc23/eng/20240819
LC record available at https://lccn.loc.gov/2024038047

WWW.SUNSTONEPRESS.COM
SUNSTONE PRESS / POST OFFICE BOX 2321 / SANTA FE, NM 87504-2321 /USA
(505) 988-4418

PREFACE

It was the wild west. Las Puertas was a small city in northeast New Mexico where most of the families were descendants of the Spanish, Mestizo or Indigenous peoples who have been living in the area for centuries. The townsfolk worked hard to make a living in the frontier town. Their efforts were made harder by poverty, outlaws, con-men, politicians, and alcohol. The local sheriff, an honest man, tried his best to keep his community safe for everyone. But Las Puertas had the reputation of being as wicked a city as Dodge City, Kansas. The locals were used to visitors like Doc Holliday, Big-Nose Kate, Jesse James, Billy the Kid and Vicente Silva, and his gang. There was frequent violence and crime, sometimes local, but usually caused by outsiders and opportunists.

Las Puertas is still the wild west, but it is now the latter half of the twentieth century, the turbulent 1970s. The stories are set in the town, the surrounding mystical Sangre de Cristo mountains and the pristine, rugged Pecos Wilderness. Once the center of commerce in the heady days of the Santa Fe Trail, it is still the local business hub for the region's ranchers, land barons, merchants and the tightly knit working class. But modern times have not been good for the area. No longer prosperous, it remains the ancestral home for a people whose spiritual connection to the land is unbroken. It is their deep love for this beautiful, unforgiving landscape, the powerful energy that permeates its mesas, mountains and high desert and its colored history that has inspired the four stories in this collection.

My life there was like living in another time, in a distant country. The people and families I knew were warm and giving. I was never treated like an outsider, quite the opposite. I was welcomed into the community. Living in that magical place, in Atzlan, became a permanent part of my being. It was only fate and misfortune that forced me to leave.

Although fictional, the town and characters are based on real places and real people. The stories are derived from true events that I experienced in my years in New Mexico. The character *Gordo* was a fugitive laying low for crimes in Santa Rosa. Johnny Abeyta, the central character in *The Boxing Game*, was inspired by the students I knew while I was teaching at the local, primarily Chicano high school. Rachel, Mother Sun, in *The Strangers*, is an amalgamation of various wealthy hippies and new age refugees who came to New Mexico for a boost to their spiritual needs. And Mike O'Farrell of *Land of Enchantment*, is based on an artist and close friend of mine who came to New Mexico in search of a muse to inspire his drawing and painting. Real people, real places in very tall tales that I hope will be enjoyed by all.

CONTENTS

GORDO

Sadly, this wasn't the first time Francisco Ramirez woke up in the cell of the cop shop in Las Puertas. He was a regular "guest" and had often been held there on a variety of minor charges...drunk and disorderly, petty theft, under the influence...the usual.

As he struggled to open his eyes, the bright shaft of sunlight from the small window illuminated the concrete floor of the ten-by-ten-foot cell. It helped him focus on the wet spot below his bunk.

"Gabby's not going to be happy about this" thinking of the cantankerous housekeeper of the sheriff's office.

With some difficulty, he managed to lift himself up into a sitting position. He rubbed more of the bleariness out of his eyes and then swung his legs over the edge of the bed. Looking around the cell, on the other bunk he saw he had a roommate.

"Who the Hell is that? This is my cell." He mumbled. He managed to stand up and take a closer look at his cellmate. The young man was big, maybe six three or four. Looked like he weighed about two fifty. He was sleeping facing the wall and breathing heavily.

Francisco, or Frank as his few friends called him, went over to the cell door. He could see that someone was in the office out front and let out a whistle.

"Hey sheriff! Anybody there? Oyé." He kept his voice low so as not to wake up the other man. Didn't want to cause a ruckus if his cellmate had violent tendencies. He could hear the desk chair rolling back. Footsteps. Sheriff Joe Lujan appeared at the door leading to the cells.

"Well, well. Morning Frank. Sleep okay?" The sheriff was also a big man. His weathered face reflected the many years he had been keeping the peace in Las Puertas as best he could. "Are you about ready to go home?"

"Yeah, I guess so. Sorry about last night. Guess I passed out again in La Casita."

"You're lucky you didn't crack your skull or anything falling backwards off the bar stool. Your head okay?"

Frank felt the large bump on the back of his head and grinned. "I'd have to fall a lot further than that to..." Behind him he heard some movement. The other man had rolled over and was glaring at the sheriff. He sat up and stared at Frank, then at the Joe.

"When can I get out of here? You got nothing on me."

Joe's face got stern looking. "You caused me a lot of grief, friend." He moved past Frank and focused on the big man. "I'm going to need some ID and info about you. You didn't give me much of a chance last night."

The big man mumbled something under his breath and lay back down. "Sure, whatever you need. I'm not going anywhere."

"You're lucky nobody wants to press charges. The car you kicked in was so beat up they figured it wasn't worth the hassle." Joe unlocked the cell door and swung it open. "Frank, you go on home. You, Mister. Come on out to the office. We'll do a little paperwork and then you can go too." Joe stood aside as Frank walked out and headed for the office. The big man got up and ambled by Joe, giving him a once over as he passed.

"Let's get this over with," he said.

Frank went through the office and headed for the door leading to the street. He opened it and walked out onto Bridge Street. It was another beautiful crisp autumn day in northeast New Mexico.

§

Las Puertas, in northeast New Mexico, was a place where in many ways, time stopped. Sure, there were 20th century houses, cars and stores... but the place itself held the strong sense of another time and place. The occasionally dry, occasionally flooded, Caballos River divided the town into two parts. There was East Las Puertas which had been settled in the late 19th Century primarily by Anglos, white folks from back East and down in Texas. Then there was west Las Puertas, where the long history of the Spanish conquerors and the heritage of the indigenous peoples lingered. Intermingled with wooden buildings and houses, one could still find long houses made of adobe on the central plaza and back streets. The dust of the colonial past still blew in through the cracks of the windows and doors of the centuries old buildings.

If you drove out of town to the nearby smaller settlements, some were just ten or twelve ancient adobe houses and outbuildings that had families who dated back to the 1600s still living there. Scratching a living out of the red earth. Growing corn, chiles and pinto beans like their ancestors had before them.

The landscape was high desert. Cactus, scrub oak, piñon and thistle dotted the landscape. Water was precious and wells were deep. The gullies and arroyos often had the weathered remains of old cars and other discarded remnants of no longer useful items half buried in the soil. When it rained, the dirt back roads became treacherous, slick and muddy. Many of them ended at long abandoned "ghost towns" where the melting adobe structures were reminiscent of better times.

The tarmac narrow county roads led into the nearby Sangre de Cristo mountains. Dry, high country forests with pine trees and the occasional aspens. The roads would be straight until the foothills and then turn into winding narrow mountain lanes. No guardrails to keep the inattentive driver from plummeting down the steep embankments.

The painted center lines started out straight, then turned into twisted markings and finally disappeared altogether. No shoulders, no turn offs. Most of the roads ended up at some lonely cabin or a wall of pine trees. The high desert and dry mountains offered solitude and quiet, hard to find anywhere in the modern age.

This quality of the landscape attracted many looking for escape from the crowded centers of population. No cars to be seen for days at a time. Folks who come into town for supplies once or twice a month. People living close to the earth; some in poverty, some in isolation, some in hiding.

For the citizens of Las Puertas, the edge of town is truly, the edge of town. One hundred miles of empty highway to Colorado. One hundred miles to Santa Fe. One hundred fifty miles to Albuquerque. The hard times of the last few decades of the 20th Century had taken its toll. The area was no longer prosperous or even adequate as in the past. The county was one of the poorest in the nation.

Throughout the town were abandoned storefronts and empty buildings that used to house the dry goods stores, restaurants, and supermarkets. Banks were closed, businesses shuttered and the drug store that had a lunch counter and soda fountain was neglected and empty.

In the beginning, Las Puertas was a thriving settlement in the most northern part of what was then Mexico. It later became a major stop on the Santa Fe Trail. In the 19th Century, it became a rowdy commercial center. A lawless but thriving community where Jewish merchants from the East opened their stores and the Santa Fe Railroad served great, old hotels, stockyards and tanneries. In East Las Puertas, wealthy merchants built large Victorian houses on tree lined streets. There was even a small state university. In West Las Puertas, the original plaza was still the center of town where fiestas, political events and other celebrations were held on a regular basis.

There was only one problem. If you lived in East Las Puertas you stayed in East Las Puertas. In West Las Puertas, it was the same.

This separation, this schism in this small town, led to frequent confrontations. The contentious relationship between East and West manifested itself in barroom brawls, high school fights and the occasional gunfight and shooting.

West Las Puertas, like much of northeast New Mexico, identified itself with Atzlan, the mythical homeland in the north of Mexico. A place where the descendants of the earliest peoples, the Chicanos of today, could be empowered and free of the oppression and discrimination they had been facing for decades.

East Las Puertas was the home of the interlopers, the oppressors. The home of the wealthier, whiter residents who did not feel as close to the land. They came to enjoy the commercial rewards of the better days and remained, unbound to the ancient heritage of the land.

So, when Frank walked out onto the sidewalk of Bridge Street, he felt at home. His family had been living in Las Puertas for generations. And his little house on Chavez Street, one of west's side streets, was his sanctuary. Nothing could have suggested to him that his life of drinking, semi poverty and petty crime was about to change very much for the worse.

§

Frank headed west toward the plaza. He saw Gabby coming down the street to begin her day keeping the Sheriff's office tidy.

"Morning, Gabby. Looks like it should be a nice day."

"If you're coming from the Sheriff's I better not find a mess there," she scolded. "I'll make you clean it up if I do."

"Yeah, I was there but the other guy left the mess."

"Other guy? Must have been a hard case for Joe to lock him up with you," she said over her shoulder and walked by muttering. "No good barracho..."

Frank shrugged and headed for Duran's Liquor store. He still had a couple of bucks so he could get a tamale or two from the pot Duran's wife kept on a hotplate on the counter of the store and a pint of Old Overholt.

To Felix Duran, Frank was a regular customer. He had many customers like Frank. A pint, a six pack, sometimes just a quart of beer. They started coming in as soon as he opened at eight. The breakfast of champions. He never ran a tab in case one of them didn't make it through the day.

Usually, they headed up to the plaza where they settled in on one of the park benches for the day. Most got disability or some sort of government aid. Some would persuade Felix to take food stamps, though they weren't worth full value at his store. Others would head back down Bridge Street toward the river and drop down into the underbrush beneath the cottonwoods. A quiet place to drink and watch the day pass by through their glassy, bloodshot eyes.

Frank headed for the plaza. He had a favorite spot in the sun next to the gazebo in the center. When he was younger, he brought his wife there before they married. It was a nice place to have a picnic and hold hands.

After they married, his drinking became a problem, his beautiful wife became depressed and overweight. He lost his job with the highway crew and grew sullen and brooding. His wife left him and moved to Albuquerque. He began to spend all his money on booze and drugs. Shoplifting and breaking into cars. He became just another pobrecito in town, getting by and counting on the mercy of the sympathetic sheriff to keep him out of state prison.

He crossed Valencia Street and headed for his bench. Settling in, he took a pull on the whiskey and ate a tamale, the sun was warm on his face even though the chill of the morning was still in the air.

"Hey, Bato," a voice from behind him said.

Frank ignored it. They must mean someone else.

"Oyé, cabrón! I'm talking to you." The man came around in front of Frank and he saw it was the big guy from the jail.

He stood in the sun and his shadow covered Frank, the man was so big. He sat down next to Frank and looked at his bottle and the other tamale on the bench. "Lemme have some of that, and I'll take a swig of your whiskey too."

"Get your own damn whiskey," Frank said. "I've got to make this last."

"Hey, amigo. I'm your roommate. You have to share." He snatched the bottle out of Frank's hands and took a long drink. Holding onto the bottle, he reached across and took the other tamale.

Frank started to feel nervous. He was not very strong anymore and didn't like to fight. He usually lost any scuffle, and this guy was much too big to resist. "Okay, okay! I don't want any trouble. Just give me my whiskey and leave me alone."

"I don't think so." A nasty smile was on the big man's face. "The sheriff told me you live around here. I could use a shower. Let's go to your place."

"What the Hell are you talking about. I don't know who you are and so far, I don't like you much."

The nasty smile turned to a glare. "I'm Gordo. That's all you need to know. And we're roommates, so let's head to your place before I decide I don't like *you* very much." He paused. "You wouldn't want that, believe me."

He stood up, still holding Frank's whiskey. "Let's go."

Frank was scared. He looked around but there was no one anywhere nearby. The man grabbed his arm and pulled Frank up off the bench. "Yeah, I could really use a shower," he said.

Still holding Frank by the arm, they headed toward South Pacific Avenue at the other end of the plaza. "We're going to be great friends... amigos. I think I'm going to like it here."

§

Frank's little house on Chavez Street wasn't much to look at. Not a whole lot of curb appeal. It had a low adobe wall around the small front yard with the stucco coating peeling off in many places exposing the brown mud bricks underneath. The yard was rough, full of weeds and debris. Some empty beer cans and whiskey bottles as well as the wrappers from chips and other cheap snacks. The gate was half off its hinges and the concrete walkway leading to the front porch was cracked and crumbling in spots. The porch was not in much better shape than the wall. Frank kept an old couch there for nicer days where he could sit and drink, watching the cars go by until he passed out.

The front door had an old screen door hanging by some rusted hinges. The door was worn with flaking paint and a loose, rusty doorknob. Frank wasn't worried about being robbed. Everybody knew he had nothing worth stealing inside.

The Big Man, Gordo, kept a hold on Frank as they walked up the one block hill from South Pacific Avenue, the main southbound street off the plaza, to Chavez Street.

As they approached Frank's house and stopped at the gate, Gordo laughed. "What a dump! You live here?

"It's my place," said Frank. "I like it. It's mine."

Gordo shoved Frank through the gate and followed him to the front door. "I hope you got hot water." He glared at Frank.

"Yeah, I've got indoor plumbing, hot water, even a toilet."

"Let's get inside, hope you don't have any nosey neighbors." The big man looked around the street, making sure there was nobody around. He let Frank open the door then followed him inside.

The inside of the house was just as neglected as the front yard. Another old beat-up couch. A television. A small, well used painted table with two mismatched rickety wooden chairs was near the archway leading to the kitchen. "Why don't you just sit down while I have a look around... Don't go anywhere."

Gordo went into the kitchen. Frank could hear him open the refrigerator door. He came back out and went into the short hall, looked into both little bedrooms and then went into the bathroom. "Dios mio. What a shit hole." He came back to the living room and stood over Frank.

"I'm going to try to clean up. That jail stunk. This place stinks too. But we're roommates now. Like when we were cell mates. I'm going to stay here awhile." He looked around the living room. "You got any rope around here? Maybe out back?"

"Rope? What the Hell do you need rope for?" Frank was worried now.

"Rope, wire, anything like that. Let's go look." He grabbed Frank by the shoulder and pushed him through the kitchen out the back door. Frank's old truck was parked in the backyard off the alley that ran behind the houses on Chavez Street. There was some worn out rope in the back of the pickup. Gordo grabbed the rope and dragged Frank back into the house.

He pulled Frank into the front room and sat him down on one of the chairs at the kitchen table. "What are you doing? I'm not going anywhere. I'm not going to leave you alone here in my house. Just leave me alone. Get out of here..."

Gordo knocked Frank down with the back of his hand. "Damn right you're not. Empty your pockets. Give me your money." He picked him up and sat him down in the chair. Frank put his money, a jackknife and his driver's license on the table. Gordo tied Frank's hands and feet to the chair and made sure the rope was tight. Frank winced in pain. "Hope you've got a clean towel," he said over his shoulder as he headed for the bathroom.

"What the Hell?" Frank thought to himself. "Who is this guy? What is he going to do?"

He heard the shower running in the bathroom. He tried to loosen his hands. No luck. He struggled to get his feet loose, but the rope was too tight. Gordo was taking a long shower. Probably couldn't hear much from the living room. Frank took a deep beath, threw his body backwards and could hear the chair start to creak. Another push and the chair went over and broke into pieces. The ropes around his feet came loose. Standing, Frank broke off the piece of chair that was tied to his hands. He was free.

Just then, the water stopped running in the bathroom. Frank scrambled to his feet and headed toward the front door. As he opened it he looked over his shoulder and he saw Gordo coming back into the living room. He was naked, rubbing himself down with a ragged towel. Frank ran out of the front door, through the yard and back down Chavez Street. From behind him he heard Gordo shouting, 'Come back here! ¡Traviesillo!"

Frank had a head start. Gordo couldn't come after him naked. Had to get dressed first. Frank ran as best he could. Heading down the street, back toward the plaza, then down a side street toward the river where it runs behind the High School. He knew the town. He knew where he could hide. But somehow, he had to find a way to stop the Big Man, this "Gordo". The guy was trouble, if not for Frank, then for the rest of the folks in Las Puertas. As long as the guy was around, the vulnerable people in town, the people like himself, were not going to be safe.

§

Santa Rosa was about one hundred miles southeast of Las Puertas. It was in the flatter, drier part of the state along Interstate 40. Surrounded by ranches and rugged, dry terrain, the town was a tough place where most folks worked hard for a living. But like any southwest, semi-rural community, there were always the few bad eggs. Those who were less likely to do honest work and more likely to see how they could get by with the least amount of effort.

Growing up in Santa Rosa, Gordo's family lived in the less prosperous part of town, south of the tracks. The streets were dirt. The houses were small. The yards were also pretty much bare dirt. Cars up on jacks and spare tires lying nearby were the lawn ornaments.

His parents were not happy. His father was a functional alcoholic who worked for the railroad and was gone for days at a time. His mother cooked for a local restaurant, breakfast mainly, and was out of the house at 5:00AM seven days a week. When she came home, Gordo was usually not around and she went to bed for a few hours. Waking up later in the afternoon, she made posole, green chile or pinto beans so there would be food for her son and husband to eat whenever they were hungry. They never had dinner together. If his father was home he'd start drinking and eat whatever was available in front of the television. His mother just passed time reading the local paper or watching television. She went to bed early. His dad stayed up and drank, falling asleep in front of the tube. There wasn't a lot of conversation. Gordo would come and go as he pleased even when he was only six or seven years old.

Some of the neighborhood kids only went to school occasionally. Young Gordo hardly ever went. He liked sitting on the front porch, thinking about what kind of mischief he could get into...how he could pick up a few extra bucks for spending money. Most of the day he wandered around town.

He was always a big kid. Taller than kids his age, and always a little overweight, he found it easy to lord it over the other kids. Most of them were afraid of him since he was quick to shove them around if they disagreed with him or said something he didn't like. At first, they called him Gordo behind his back, but he heard about it and decided he was *Gordo*, the big guy.

As a hulking teenager, he started to graduate from hitting up kids his age to looking in unlocked cars for something he could turn into cash. Sometimes he would wait until people would leave their houses and he would go in, wearing a bandana, and see if there was anything he could grab. If someone caught him, he would use his size and weight to frighten someone off. Telling them to "Fuck off." He was smart enough to not steal from the same part of town too often. That way people would leave their doors unlocked since it didn't seem to be a real problem.

Gordo wasn't a normal bully. He was not a coward who picked on kids smaller than him. He got into fights with some of the older, bigger boys and got a reputation for holding his own. Nobody bothered him much. The funny thing was that Gordo enjoyed getting into trouble, getting into fights. He liked the danger of slipping into people's houses and breaking into cars. His parents didn't much care. They paid no attention to what he was doing. They had no close friends and nobody had much to do with them. The local cops had their hands full with oil workers, ranch hands and trouble in the bars and saloons. Nobody had time to deal with a local punk kid doing things that kids do.

Santa Rosa was easy pickings for many years. Getting restless, and too well known in his hometown...when Gordo was about seventeen he decided to try his luck in the city...in Albuquerque. Adiós Santa Rosa

§

Hitchhiking to Albuquerque was easy. Just get on the on-ramp at the edge of town and stick his thumb out. Interstate 40 went straight into the city and there weren't many places to stop in between.

He got a ride from a heavy-set man with a Pancho Villa moustache. The guy didn't have much concern about giving a lift to the big kid. He looked like he could handle himself and besides, this was just a kid. He thumped his fist on his chest when Gordo got in and said, "Ortega."

Gordo smiled at him, "Me llamo Gordo."

"Where you headed?"

"Just going to Albuquerque to see my primo" even though Gordo didn't really know anybody in the city, he figured a cousin was good cover. His mother had family in the southeast part of town and he had gone there with her once or twice. Usually, to get some hand me down clothes or borrow some money when things got tight at home. He didn't want to answer a lot of questions. He had a gym bag with some clothes and a couple of hundred dollars. He figured he could find a cheap place to stay and then start looking for some big city action.

Ortega looked at him, sizing him up. "I'm headed down Central toward Old Town. Where do you want me to drop you?"

"Central and Broadway. My Tia lives near Broadway and Coal."

Ortega reached up under his hat and pulled out a good-sized joint. He lit it and inhaled deeply. "You want a hit, kid?"

"Sure. Thanks." Gordo took the joint and took a nice long toke. "Looks like this will be a nice ride" he thought to himself. "Hey, Ortega, maybe we should pull over at Clines Corners and get a six pack. I'll buy."

Ortega looked over at the boy and laughed. "They start you early in Santa Rosa. Sure. I'll buy you lunch."

They rode on in silence for the next few miles. Ortega had some Norteña and Tejano tapes and the music was good. "I'm on my way" thought Gordo. "This is a good start."

After an hour or so they got to Clines Corners, a combination truck stop, souvenir shop, travel center and restaurant. There were several semi's parked in the truckers' areas and quite a few tourists with campers and RV's. Ortega parked his truck and he and Gordo went into the store. There were lots of folks buying snacks, trinkets and drinks.

They walked through the store to the Cocina Restaurant and grabbed a booth. The waitress tossed some menus on the table and asked, "You want anything to drink?"

Ortega ordered a beer and Gordo just got a Coke.

"I'll be right back with your drinks," she said.

The food was good TexMex and when they were heading out, Gordo gave Ortega a ten, "You better buy the beer. I'm going to have a look around. Meet you out by the truck."

Ortega waved him off.

Gordo went back into the store. He looked around to see if there were any cameras and if anybody was watching him. When he was comfortable that nobody was paying any attention to him, he managed to slip a few items into his pockets. He picked the easy stuff, disposable cameras, bolo ties, sunglasses, anything that would fit into his baggy jeans and that would be a quick sale on the streets or near New Mexico University. Looking around again, he noticed the woman behind the register giving him the eye. He went right up to her at the counter and bought a pack of gum." He could feel her eyes on the back of his head as he slowly walked out. When he got to Ortega's truck, he turned around. She was still looking at him but then turned away to take care of another customer. Ortega was waiting for him, a nice cold six pack on the seat. "Here's your change. Let's go."

They pulled back onto the highway.

Gordo smiled to himself, "Yeah, this is a good start." Reached over, pulled the tab on a can of Lone Star and took a long, cold drink. Hola Albuquerque.

§

A kid of eighteen, dropped off in the center of a city one hundred times as big as his hometown. Wide streets, six or eight lanes, many stoplights. Traffic. Cars and trucks racing to get through the intersections before the lights changed. To anyone else, this would be intimidating. But not to Gordo.

He felt confident, eager to begin a new life. Walking south on Broadway he headed into the grittier part of Albuquerque. The southeast part of town. He got to Coal Avenue and turned East, looking for a house or building with a "Room for Rent" sign. Most of the houses and apartments were pretty run down...peeling paint, cracked glass. He'd only walked a block or two when he came to a large white house with a "Cuarto para rentar" sign in the window. He went up to the front door and knocked on the old wooden screen door.

"Quien es?" An old gray head called to him from the window by the door. "Who's there?"

"Hola Abuela," said Gordo. "I'm looking for a room for a couple of weeks. How much?"

He heard a chair push back and soft, slow footsteps coming toward the door. A short, heavy set old lady came up to the front door, gray hair in a long braid. She gave him the once over through the glass. "What? For you? You're only a kid." She opened the door about halfway. "What do you want with a room. You run away from home?"

Gordo realized that this one had been around the block. He decided to be halfway straight with her. "I'm in from Tucumcari. I got into some trouble there and my folks kicked me out. I've got money. I need some time to figure things out."

She opened the door all the way. Looked him over again through the screen. "You're a big fellow, aren't you?"

"I get by. How much for the room?" He held back from sounding annoyed.

"Fifty dollars a week, in advance. No girls, no friends, no trouble. You come and go by the side door. No cooking. No smoking. No drugs. I've got family nearby and they check up on me every couple of days. I don't like you...you're out, comprendez?"

"Sure, sure Abuela" He smiled his best smile. "I just need some time and to be left alone." He reached into his back pocket. "Here's fifty. Where's the room?"

She opened the door, snatched the money, counted it. "Come around to the side of the house. I'll meet you by the door."

"Gracias" The door shut and Gordo headed around to the side. She met him by the back door and let him in.

The house was pretty beat. The floors were swept but worn. Most of the dirt was ground into the bare wood. She opened the first door on the left. "The bathroom is down the hall on the right. If you leave it dirty, you're out. You come and go by that door. No music. No noise. Today's Tuesday so next week's rent is due Monday. You go to the front door and hand it to me in person." She turned and went down the hall and disappeared into the front of the house.

Gordo went into the room. There was a bed, just a blanket on the worn mattress, no sheets. An old armchair in the corner and a little table with a lamp on it. An armoire. A rag carpet on the floor. He switched on the overhead light. One of the bare bulbs was burned out. There was a window looking out on the trashed out back yard. "Good." Gordo thought to himself. "I can slip out that way if I have to."

He tossed his gym bag on the chair and lay down on the bed. "This is perfect." He thought. He dozed off and had dreams of making a life for himself in his new home.

§

Gordo woke up at about eight that evening. The landlady must have gone to bed since the rest of the house was dark. Gordo went down the hall to the bathroom and washed his face to get the sleep out of his eyes. He went back to his room and put on his only clean shirt. He let himself out the back door and locked the door behind him. Walking out onto Coal Avenue he looked up and down the street, getting his bearings.

The neighborhood was rough. Some homes were abandoned. Pretty slim pickings. He headed west. As he came to the major intersections there were repair shops, convenience stores, nail salons and pawn shops. He knew the university wasn't too far and he still had the stuff he stole at Clines Corners. He figured he could find some students who might want to buy some of it. As he walked, he started to feel more confident. He knew that there was a good chance he could steal a bicycle or skateboard on campus and that would let him expand his territory.

When he got to the edge of the campus, he found a directory and located the Student Union. Because of his size and the large number of Chicanos on the campus he fit right in. The students he passed nodded to him. He looked over the girls although he never had any strong urges for girls. "Nothing but trouble." He thought. They were more like future marks, targets for his crimes.

When he got to the student union, he saw the bike racks full of bicycles. A closer look showed many without locks. He went up the stairs and entered the dining area. The tables were full of students. He looked them over and found one table with a group of Anglo guys who were laughing and cutting up. As he approached them, they quieted down.

"Howdy," he said. "I wonder if you guys could help me out? I've got some stuff I want to unload, cheap."

One of the guys stood up. "What'd you do, steal it? Is it hot?"

Gordo smiled. "Maybe a little warm. My Dad owns a store and he lets me sell some of the stuff for cash. You know what I mean." He shrugged his shoulders. "Just so I can have a little spending money while I'm at school."

The guy seemed convinced. He looked over at his friends at the table then at Gordo, "What you got?"

"Just some really cool bolo ties...and some sunglasses" He brought out his goods and put them on the table. "Fifteen bucks for the ties, twenty five bucks for the sunglasses." He didn't think these guys were disposable camera types.

The first student looked over the items and turned toward his friends. "Looks like a pretty good deal" He picked up a bolo tie and a pair of sunglasses. "Oakley's?"

"Yeah. The real thing," said Gordo. "That bolo is silver and turquoise."

"Okay. Sure. Will you take Thirty for both?"

"Depends. Any other buyers? I'll make you all a deal." These guys were too easy.

Another kid started fingering the goods. "Yeah, I'll take a pair of sunglasses." That seemed to spark a rush and they finally bought everything Gordo laid out. A quick couple of hundred.

"Thanks, you guys. Muchas Gracias. I'll look for you next time I have something good." Gordo walked away looking for a table of girls. Maybe some Chicano chicks who would go for the cameras. They liked taking pictures of themselves and each other.

He found a couple of tables and managed to sell all but one camera. Then, he headed back out and down toward the bike racks.

Gordo went down and sat on a step near the bikes. Looking them over he saw a couple that would do. More street bikes than road or mountain bikes. There was one that was unlocked. He walked over to it, trying not to attract any attention. Lifting it off the rack, he jumped on and pedaled away quickly.

§

It did not take long for Gordo to make good use of his newfound mobility. The bicycle allowed him to case out most of the city. Albuquerque is mostly flat with some hills and slopes all gravitating toward the Rio Grande River that ran right through the town. He was young and strong so he would spend the day going up to the north valley and down to the south valley. From Old town to the foothills of the Sandias.

He checked the doors of parked cars. He cruised through neighborhoods looking for open garage doors, unlocked gates and secluded back yards. He stole mostly stereos and computers when he could find them. Sometimes it was purses and with any luck credit cards. But working off a bicycle had it's limitations and he realized he would need a car or truck if he wanted to make bigger scores. The weeks passed and he managed to keep a low profile with the landlady, Senora Aragon. He hid the bicycle behind an old shed in the backyard and stashed his goods in an old freezer that was there.

The neighborhood where he lived wasn't very diverse. Older folks, some drunks, teens and young men hanging together in front yards. There were gangs and drug dealers. After a couple of months they started to take notice of the big kid on the bicycle. One afternoon, some of the gangster types saw him coming and sauntered out into the street, blocking his way.

"Hey Bato! You new around here?" The guy seemed to be the leader. Short, but very solid. He had some tats around his neck and on his arms. Signs that he had done time somewhere.

Gordo got off his bike and leaned against it. He looked the guy over and checked out the other two guys. "Yeah. Bato. I'm around."

The gangster hesitated. He didn't expect a kid like this to act so laid back, showing no fear. He took a step forward. "Nice bike. Let make take it for a spin."

Gordo smiled at him. "No. I don't think so."

"Do you know who I am? Do you know who owns this block?" He snarled.

Without warning, without any hesitation, Gordo sucker-punched him right between the eyes. He kicked one of the other guys in the groin and moved toward the third guy.

"Hey, hey. Cool down." The guy backed off. The two or three remaining boys in the yard stood up, stunned and not exactly sure what to do. The second boy was still down holding his balls. The Jefe, nose bleeding profusely, got to his feet.

"What'd you do that for? Cabron." He was clearly surprised that the kid was so quick to shut him down. He pulled himself together, looked back at his friends. "Okay, okay."

Gordo figured he made his point. "Sure, take the bike for a spin. Mind if I hang out here. You guys got any more beer?"

The Jefe, his name was Javier, but his crew called him Java. He sensed this kid was better as a friend. "Yeah, sure. Give this guy a beer. I'll be back." He wiped off his face with his shirt, hopped on the bike and with false confidence rode off down the block. Gordo went into the yard, sat down with the others and popped open a beer. The tension passed and by the time Java came back the boys were all hanging comfortably with their new friend.

"You know where I can sell the bike?" Gordo asked Java. "I can get more."

"Seguro! I know somebody in Old Town," Java said. "Come on by later. We'll take a ride."

Gordo finished his beer. He stood up to go and turned toward the boys. "Sorry about the nose. I've got a short fuse."

Javier realized this was an opening to save face and hang onto his position with the others. He took it. "Yeah, I probably would have done the same thing."

They shook hands. "Later."

Gordo got on the bike and headed back to his place thinking about the possibilities some good contacts would give him.

§

Gordo took advantage of the local boys. With Java's help, he made contacts in the neighborhood who were interested in handling some of the more expensive and bigger items that Gordo brought them. He eventually traded a very expensive bicycle he stole out of a fancy house in the heights for an old pick-up. The truck looked like Hell but ran pretty good.

Always a loner, and with a reputation for a short temper, Gordo remained a freelancer, never joining any gang or group. As the months passed, he became a welcome member of the Albuquerque underworld. His independence allowed him to keep a low profile with the police and the sheriff's department. The truck allowed him to expand his territory north to the upscale neighborhoods in Rio Rancho and Cerillos. He got himself a small dirt bike and graduated to stealing cars.

He would park his truck a mile or so away from his target, walk to the house or business where he would find a car he could sell to the gangs in Albuquerque, steal it and bring it back to town. Then he went home and got the dirt bike, ride it back to his pickup , load it into the back and drive home.

More time passed. He still lived in the back room of Abuela Aragon's house. He volunteered to pay a little more for the room, saying he got a good job, so she was perfectly happy to leave him alone, and ask no questions. Gordo wasn't interested in being flashy, in throwing his money around. He used it to cover costs and accumulate a stash in case he needed to make a quick getaway.

It was the act of stealing, the risk of capture, the sway he held over other petty criminals in his circle that was all the self-gratification he sought. He got into occasional fights, sometimes without a warning to the victim. It was something he had always liked to do. He was still a bully, still after the thrill of a violent encounter. The other gangsters and thieves put up with him because he provided them with a steady flow of profitable items.

He had grown bigger. Put on a little weight but he was naturally powerful. He started working out at a local boxing club. His brutality in the ring made it tougher and tougher to find sparring partners who could give him a good match. His need for greater thrills grew in him.

There were some pretty rough bars and hangouts around town so he had plenty of opportunities to get into brawls outside in the parking lots or alleys. He always won.

He started to mug folks in the wealthier parts of towns. He car jacked, robbed convenience stores, even supermarkets. Finally, the police started to take notice of this individual who showed up all over town, pulling off these crimes and disappearing into the underworld. It had taken the cops almost three years to realize they had a career criminal on their hands and maybe something had to be done.

The criminal grapevine started buzzing and Gordo knew it was time to move on. He had money, the dirt bike and a newer truck. He headed north to Santa Fe.

§

Santa Fe is a city that has two faces. One, known worldwide for artists, intellectuals and very rich folks who had second multi-million dollar homes and ranches. There were new suburbs outside of town and gated communities. Going north to Tesuque on Bishop's Lodge Road, the walled pseudo colonial estates were interspersed with large adobe style homes. Canyon Road was a mixture of wealthy artists and old timers still holding out and selling pinyon firewood from their back yards.

The plaza was a tourist mecca. People from all over the world came to buy silver and turquoise jewelry from the Native Americans who showed their craft on blankets spread out on the sidewalk in front of the governor's palace. The visitors stayed in the upscale La Posada de Santa Fe and ate at the many cafes and restaurants located on the plaza or on the side streets leading toward the state capital area. Many came to go to the museums. Others came for the Santa Fe Opera. St. John's University attracted intellectuals for conferences and lectures.

Yet, there was another face. Going down Cerillos Road to the southeast part of town the city transitioned into a barrio. Neighborhoods of little run-down houses with abandoned cars, trash strewn around the yards and in the streets. It was a gritty, sad part of town where most of the locals who worked in the tourist area lived. Blue tarps on roofs, crumbling adobe walls, broken fences.

Gordo cruised that neighborhood looking for another place to rent. No questions asked, cash for rent and the owners were grateful for the extra income. It wasn't hard to find something and he quickly gathered his few possessions and settled in. He had been in Albuquerque for around three and a half years, so now, at almost twenty-two, his commanding size and older look allowed him to go into the local bars, the ones with no windows, and fit in with the gritty crowd. He had plenty of cash and by buying a few of the rougher looking characters a beer or two, he started to gather the information he needed to continue what one might call his successful life of crime and violence in the underbelly of the city.

Santa Fe was perfect for him. Tourists, carelessly leaving their cameras and suitcases in their cars while on a stroll around the plaza. The small shops, where the women proprietors were often alone at opening or closing. By the plaza, the jewelry was laid out on the blankets and left occasionally unattended, barely watched over by the other vendors. The upscale jewelry shops had gold and semiprecious jewelry, often not kept in locked cases or displays.

For someone like Gordo, well-practiced in snatch and grab, he easily gathered up plenty of items he could fence to some of the locals he had met. The University had bicycles to steal. Unlocked cars were everywhere. The big houses were often empty for months at a time since the owners lived there only part time, having other residences in California or New York.

He once again got a reputation as someone not to mess with but who could be a lucrative source for upscale stolen goods. The fights continued. The close calls with the police.

Fortunately for Gordo, there was enough day-to-day crime in Santa Fe that the skills he had for avoiding attention and keeping to himself made his crimes a lower priority for the local authorities. They had their hands full with pickpockets on the plaza and the homeless in the railyard district. The break ins in the upscale neighborhoods ended up with primarily a cop showing up, making a report and telling the homeowners that "they'll be in touch."

The luxury second homes rarely had working security systems and the owners would only find out they had been robbed when they returned several months later.

More time passed. Some of the local gangs started to become jealous of Gordo's loner but obviously successful status. They knew he had a stash of goods hidden away and one group, led by an aggressive and envious lowlife named Heriberto or "Bertie" decided they needed to show Gordo that he had to share the wealth. Bertie couldn't allow Gordo to operate in his territory without some deference to him and his crew.

Gordo still had his truck and dirt bike. He kept his goods hidden in a storage locker at the south end of town. Bertie had a couple of his guys watching him, getting to know his routines and his methods. The problem was, Gordo picked up on what Bertie was up to. He spotted the guys watching him. He noticed that Bertie was acting differently, acting like his jefe when he brought him some of the items he stole.

Then, one day when Gordo came to Bertie with three high end bicycles to sell him, the inevitable occurred.

"I'll give you two hundred a piece," Bertie said.

Gordo smiled, "They're five hundred each." He took a step forward and got in close to Bertie's face, "Like always."

"Hey, I got expenses. The cops are watching me and my boys. You've got to make it worth my while."

"That's not my problem." Gordo noticed some of Bertie's flunkies stepping up behind him. "Five hundred. That's my price. You don't want them?"

Bertie was shorter than Gordo but solid, strong. His boys were tough but knew Gordo's reputation, so they showed some reluctance to confront him. "How about I just take the bikes. On credit," he said and glanced back at his guys.

In a split second, Gordo landed a hard blow to Bertie's chest. Then another between his eyes and a knee to his groin. Bertie was down. His guys were stunned, at a loss of what to do next. Gordo took down the next biggest guy and then went after the others. They scattered.

Turning his attention back to Bertie, he saw that he was getting back on his feet and was reaching for the gun he carried in the small of his back. Gordo knocked him back down and grabbed the gun. He shot Bertie in the chest, killing him instantly. The other guys were long gone. This was a neighborhood where shots were heard occasionally and did not attract much attention.

He looked down at Bertie. A strange expression came over his face. It was a mixture of peace and evil. Gordo had never outright killed anyone before. He had beaten some guys viciously, but they had always been able to recover, get up and limp off. Usually, it helped Gordo to gain respect amongst the gangs. He left them alone and vice versa. They could still do business and he maintained his autonomy.

This was different. Bertie was dead. This was final. Gordo walked back to his truck and got in. He still had the gun in his hand. He looked it over. Popped out the clip. Popped it back in. Pulled back on the slide and saw that another round was in the chamber, ready for use. It felt good, solid and powerful. Those few minutes changed Gordo's worldview forever.

§

Gordo went back to his storage locker. He gathered up all of his goods and threw them into the back of the truck. He went to his room and grabbed his cash stash and his clothes and drove over to a house across town, to another gang that had fenced items for him before.

A few of the guys were sitting around in the front yard. They nodded to Gordo when he pulled up. "Where's Flavio?"

One of the boys gestured to the front door and Gordo went in. Flavio was sitting on the couch watching television. "Hey Gordo. You got something for me?"

"Yeah, I'm moving on, leaving town. Tired of this place. Think I'll go to Texas or Arizona." It was pretty obvious that news of the killing of Bertie hadn't spread yet. "Got a load of stuff. I'll give you a good deal for all of it. Dirt bike too."

Flavio was a pretty big guy too. But he was sly and preferred to get a good deal rather than a fight. He figured Gordo had another reason for leaving so he knew he could lowball him.

They walked out to the truck. There were the bicycles, the dirt bike, cameras, a couple of computers and a bunch of other high-end items. Normally it would be easily worth a couple of grand. Flavio looked it over.

"Leaving town?" He rubbed his chin, then his neck. "What kind of a deal were you thinking?" he asked Gordo.

"Just don't screw me around. I might come back someday and business could be even better." He stood between Flavio and the truck. "Or I could go by Bertie's. See what he could give me."

"Okay! Okay! Calmate. Calm down." He knew Gordo had a temper and had been punished before. "How about a thousand dollars and some weed?"

"Keep your weed. Fifteen hundred dollars."

Flavio rubbed his chin and neck again. "Yeah, okay. Bueno." He walked into another room and came back out with the cash. "Here you go."

Gordo counted the cash, nodded to Flavio and headed for the door. The other guys were still in the yard. Flavio followed him and told the guys to unload the truck. When all the stuff was out, Gordo got in, gave them all a look and headed down the street. A car with some of Bertie's guys passed him going the other way. He gunned the truck and drove quickly out of the hood. He headed back across town, went down the Old Santa Fe Trail and toward the interstate. He was headed north, maybe Colorado. Pueblo or Trinidad. And then maybe Denver. After all, he had a gun.

§

Frank was down past the High School in the scrub and reeds by the Caballos River. The large cottonwood's leaves were starting to turn but the low hanging and broken branches provided cover. He walked carefully north along the river and under the bridge. The brush was denser on the other side and it was a place he knew well. The area was strewn with empty beer cans and liquor bottles. Broken glass. The usual food wrappers. Cigarette butts. It was still fairly early in the day so the usual matted down areas where other drunks went to pass the day were still empty.

He found himself a place that was well hidden and threw himself down on the ground, exhausted. He hadn't moved this fast or run this far in years. Frank was scared, he knew Gordo would probably never find him here, but he was still shaken by the experience. "What should I do?" he thought. He didn't have any place to go but home and for all he knew Gordo was still there. He had no real friends. Nobody who would risk helping him, fearing for their own safety. "I could sure use a drink." He felt the need rise in him.

Going back up to Duran's would be too risky. And Gordo had taken what little money he had. "Shit!" he thought, "What a mess."

He heard a noise further up the river. Someone was coming his way so he scrunched down and hid behind a rock. The footsteps came closer when he saw it was two of the other regulars along the river. Some guy called Ray and his buddy, Jose. They had brown bags in their hands and settled down in another well-used spot about twenty feet away from Frank.

Raising himself up from behind the rock Frank whistled "Ese. Ray. It's me Frank."

"Hey Frank." Ray saw that Frank looked a little rough. "You okay?"

"I got some trouble. Spare me a swig. I'm broke."

"Yeah, okay," Ray said reluctantly. "Just a swig."

Frank gratefully took the bottle and took a good-sized swallow. Ray grabbed the bottle back. "Cool it. Cabron! I said swig. Hijo de puta!" He looked at his bottle. "No mas for you. You owe me."

"Yeah, yeah. I'm sorry." He was feeling a little better. The booze cleared his brain a little. He felt a little stronger. "I've gotta go. Thanks."

The guys watched him go back toward the bridge. When he got underneath, he sat on a rock and put his head in his hands. "What the Hell am I going to do?" Gordo had said he liked this town. Maybe he was going to stick around. "Madre Dios! I'm screwed!"

He heard the traffic start to pick up overhead. The town was waking up. Time passed and Frank still had no idea what to do next. Then he heard a siren. It was either a fire engine or cop car. "Cop car? Joe! Sherriff Joe. He's always been good to me. Maybe he can help."

He got up and peered around the bottom of the bridge. Struggling, he managed to climb up the bank and got even with the street. Looking around, he didn't see any sign of Gordo. Besides, he probably figured that the cop shop would be the last place the big man would come. He went further down the river until he could cross the street to the alley that ran behind the Sherriff's office. Moving as quickly as he could, he made it to the back door of the building. He knocked on the door. No answer. He banged a little louder and heard the door unlock. It was Gabby, the cleaning lady.

"Gabby, please let me in. I've got to see Joe."

"He's not here," she said impatiently. "A little early for you. Isn't it?"

"No. No. I'm not drunk. I'm in trouble. I gotta talk to Joe."

Hearing the desperation in his voice, Gabby softened a bit. "Joe's up in Caballos Canyon. Some guy ran off the road into the river." She paused. "Okay. Come on in. You can wait for him in your cell. It's clean so don't mess it up."

"Thanks Gabby. Thanks a lot." Frank pushed past her and went into the cell. He lay down on the bunk and for the first time that day he felt safe. He dozed off, exhausted, waiting for Joe.

Gabby looked into the cell. "Drunks. They're always in trouble." She huffed off to continue her work.

§

Joe Lujan stood by the edge of the road. He looked down the embankment at the car lying wheels up in the river, wedged up against the rocks and boulders. "No way that guy is still alive." he thought. He got the call at around nine that morning and it took about forty minutes to wind his way up the canyon to the location.

Earlier, the guy who spotted the car was heading into town. He was an old man, one of the few who lived further up the canyon in preferred isolation. Unable to climb down the steep sides, and with little chance of anyone else coming along to help, he had little choice but to continue on and call it in once he got to a phone.

"Hello, Sheriff Joe?" he asked when Joe picked up the phone. "You better get up the canyon. Somebody is in the river about two miles from Baca's place. Looks pretty bad."

"Who's this?"

"Ralph. Ralph Vasquez. I live up by the old forest service place. I was coming into town for some stuff and I pulled over to take a leak. Saw this car on its back in the river. Couldn't get to it. Figured the guy was dead. Thought I better let you know."

Joe heaved a sigh. "How long ago was that?"

"About an hour. Can't drive too fast. Can't see too good with the sun in my eyes. I'm at my cousin's place. Over by the hospital." Ralph hesitated. "It was the first phone I could get too. Didn't know where else to go."

"Yeah. That's okay Ralph. I'll let you know if I need to talk to you later."

"Bueno Sheriff." He paused. "Pretty sure it had Texas plates. Luego."

Joe called the State Police. Let them know about the accident. They should have an officer in the area but Joe figured he'd get there first. He got his hat, strapped on his pistol and put on his Jacket. He headed for the door. "Gabby." He called back to the cell area. "I'm headed up the canyon. Got a Tejano in the river again. "

Gabby came into the front. "You want me to answer the phone?"

"Sure...and call Roberto. Let him know I'll be gone for a couple of hours. Use the radio if you have to." Roberto Castillo was his only deputy. Usually out cruising in the other car. He was a good cop, but he didn't mind patrolling the campus sometimes, trying to pick up some of the college girls at the local state university.

"Okay Joe. I'll let you know if there's anything going on."

Joe went out, got into his Ford Bronco and headed toward the canyon.

When he got to the crash site, Joe decided to ease his way down the bank to the car. The river was pretty low but the car had ended up on its roof with most of the windows submerged. Ralph was right, the car had Texas plates.

He worked his way toward the edge of the water and stepped into a shallow spot next to the car. When he bent over to peer through the window he saw that the driver was still at the wheel. His head was underwater and his hair was drifting with the current. He was an Anglo, dressed like a cowboy. "Another flatland asshole who thought he could handle the curves." Most of the Texans around had cabins up near the national forest. This one was most likely up in the hills to do some illegal hunting.

There was no one else in the car.

Joe, knowing there was nothing else he could do headed back up to the road. The water was freezing cold. He had dry socks in the truck. He got on the radio to check and see if the state cop was on his way.

"This is state dispatch. Go ahead, over."

"This is Sherrif Joe Lujan. Follow up on an eleven-eighty up here in Caballos Canyon, mile marker fifteen. No survivors that I could find. Better let the patrol know and send an accident investigation unit."

"Roger, Sheriff. Officer is in your vicinity. Should be there any minute. Out."

Joe reached into his kit and found a pair of dry socks. He pulled off his boots and dried his feet with a rag. By the time he had put on his socks, the trooper had arrived. It was Gil Armijo, the local state patrol officer for the area.

Joe got out of the car and met Gil by the side of the road overlooking the river.

"Hola Joe." Gil and Joe shook hands.

"Another Tejano driving too fast," Joe said. "Didn't make the turn and went over. Landed on the roof. No seat belt. The car filled up with water and he was probably unconscious when he drowned. No skid marks."

"Okay. Thanks Joe. I'll stick around until the accident team gets here." Gil shook his head. "These guys just don't get it. This is about the fifth one this year."

"I guess I'll head down the hill. Let me know if you need anything from me. Later." Joe headed back to the Bronco when he heard the radio crackling.

It was Gabby.

"Hola Gabby. What's up?"

"I got Frank in his cell," she said.

"Frank? Is he shitfaced already?"

"I don't think so. He hasn't been gone long enough." She paused. He's acting real scared Joe. Real scared. Something's going on."

Joe thought that was strange. Frank's been harassed before but he always kind of took it in his stride. Comes with the territory. "Can you get him to the radio?"

"No, he seemed really beat. Exhausted. He dozed off the minute he lay down." Gabby actually sounded worried about the pain in the ass drunk.

"Okay. I'm done here. Gil has things covered. See you in about thirty minutes. Out."

Joe Lujan was a patient person. Growing up there, he knew Las Puertas well. There was always trouble around town. Always conflict. Mostly between relatives and friends. On Saturday nights or holidays there were always brawls, sometimes shootings. But the participants almost always knew each other and showed up the next day at the hospital or the jail wanting to make up. If you couldn't get laid, you just picked a fight.

This felt different.

§

Gordo had been at the truck stop on the edge of town the night before. He was just coming out of the café when a beat up car full of Anglo punks pulled up too close to his truck and barely caught his back bumper.

He walked up to the boys who were getting out of the car, drunk and loud. They stopped, eyeing Gordo as he came over to them.

Gordo looked at his truck. It was barely scratched.

"Give me fifty bucks and I won't hurt you," he said to the group.

The boys, at first caught off guard, then figured they had nothing to fear. There were four of them and one of him.

"Go fuck yourself, Pancho!" One walked up to him and poked him in the chest. "That scratch ain't worth shit."

Gordo swung the boy around and got him in an armlock. "How

about a hundred? Is your arm worth a hundred?" He asked the boy.

"Hey, lemme go. Fuck you!"

The other boys gathered around. Gordo backed himself up against their car. He could have had them all on the ground in a minute but he liked the confrontation. He enjoyed the action and decided to provoke them some more. "Nice car..." He kicked backwards at the door, denting it. "Now it's custom."

"What the Hell is the matter with this guy?" they thought. They backed off.

"Now, how much do you putas have? I'm up to two hundred for your buddy's arm and the scratch."

"Why don't you just let the kid go, friend?" A voice said behind him.

Gordo turned around, still holding the boy. "Who the Hell are..."

Joe Lujan had been inside the café getting some coffee. He was working the night shift and always checked out the truck stop in the late evening. It was a place where trouble occurred all the time. Fights, some drug sales, the occasional stolen vehicle in the parking lot. He was inside getting a cup to go when he saw the situation escalating. The boys were no match for the big man who obviously could handle himself.

"Let him go, now!"

Gordo shoved the kid away. "No problem, sheriff. These guys hit my truck. I thought they could give me some cash to fix it and they seemed to be looking for trouble."

"I think you overreacted. Saw you grab the kid. Saw you kick the car. Maybe you need some time to cool off?" Joe turned to the kid Gordo had hold of, "You want to press charges? Assault? Property damage?" indicating the dent in car.

The boys looked at one another. "No. No sheriff. It's not worth it."

"Okay," Joe said. "Go on. Get out of here. Get yourselves some coffee and sober up." They sneered at Gordo and headed into the café.

"You got some ID? Registration? Driver's license?"

Gordo lived his life under the radar. He had a phony registration and license he had picked up back in Albuquerque. He handed them to Joe.

"Okay, Gaspar?" Joe said. "Why don't you come with me and you can spend the night with us and that should keep you out of trouble." He walked Gordo over to the Bronco. "You can pick up your truck in the morning. It'll be safe here."

Gordo thought about taking Joe on, but there were too many

witnesses, and he could use a place to stay for the night. "Yeah, all right Sheriff. Let's go."

§

Later the next morning at Frank's house, Gordo was pissed. "Piece of shit chair. I should have just hog tied him on the floor."

He went into Frank's bedroom and looked for a change of clothes. There wasn't much to choose from, but he found a shirt that fit. At least he would be wearing something different from what he had on when Joe busted him.

He made himself a cold bean burrito out of some pintos and tortillas Frank had in the fridge and headed out. He figured to walk back to the truck stop and pick up his truck, then try to find Frank. The guy crossed him and nobody does that to Gordo!

It was about a mile to the truck stop and by the time he got there, he had time to work up to a rage about Frank. "Little shit! I'll find him and give him something to remember me by."

His truck was still there. Somebody had keyed the driver's side door. Nice long scratch. "Bastardos!" He knew he'd never find those guys but by now, in his mind, everything was Frank's fault.

He got into the truck and headed back into town. He would cruise around. Looking for other local "culos" who might know places the bums drank or could lead him to where Frank may be hiding out. The town was small. It shouldn't be too hard.

He started to crisscross around West Las Puertas. Driving slowly, looking down the side streets, across the overgrown empty lots. He went around the plaza a couple of times, drove down Valencia Street and pulled over. Frank was maybe in his late fifties, maybe early sixties and in pretty bad shape. He couldn't have gotten too far.

Gordo got out of his truck and headed down to the river bank. When he got to the river, he saw that it was pretty low this time of year.

He walked out onto a sand bar and looked up and down the river. About a hundred feet upstream he saw areas where the brush and grass were beaten down. Downstream was the bridge. The bank was wide enough that you could walk underneath and head down toward the high school ball fields on the other side. He decided it was a better bet that the drunks were upstream, more cover and less people.

Slowly he moved upriver, quietly, so he wouldn't surprise anyone who might be hiding there. He came up on a couple of guys dozing, empty whiskey bottles at their sides. It was Ray and Jose.

Gordo stared down at them. He kicked Ray's boot. Nothing. He reached down and grabbed Ray by the collar, yanking him up so he could look him in the face.

"What the Hell?" Ray, startled, opened his eyes? He was face to face with el Diablo, a huge man who had him by the shirt and had hate in his eyes. He struggled to sober up. Jose was still out cold.

"Hello, amigo," Gordo said. "I think you might know a friend of mine, Francisco...Frank?"

Ray was scared. This guy was no friend of Frank's. Besides, it was an unwritten rule that when a stranger asks for someone in Las Puertas you don't' tell them anything. At least not until you know who they are and what they wanted.

"I don't know no Frank." He struggled to get loose, but Gordo backhanded him across the face.

"Sure you do...Frank. I think Ramirez. Has a little place up on Chavez Street. He's probably one of your drinking buddies."

He went to hit Ray again. Ray put his hands up to protect himself. Gordo punched him in the stomach. "What's your name puto?"

About that time Jose started stirring. He looked up and saw the two men and tried to scuttle away. Still holding onto Ray, Gordo grabbed Jose by the foot. "You're not going anywhere, Cabron! If I can't get an answer from this asshole, you're next."

Turning back to Ray, "I asked what's your name?"

"Salvatore" he lied. "I don't know any Frank."

Jose, kind of hazy and still drunk looked confused. "Hey Ray, what's going on. Frank was just here a couple of hours ago."

Gordo looked at Jose, then turned back to Ray. "Salvatore?" He laughed. "Lying son of a bitch." He punched Ray in the stomach, beat him hard around the head. He threw him aside, unconscious, breathing hard.

Turning to Jose, who by now was trembling with fear, knowing he was in trouble.

"Frank was here. He headed under the bridge. I don't know where he was going. Please don't hurt me."

Gordo stood up and looked down at the unconscious Ray and the quivering Jose. He kicked Jose in the ribs for good measure. "You guys have a nice day." He turned to go back to his truck, and stopped, turning back to look at the two wretches. "You never saw me, right?"

"Seguro!" Jose said. Tears in his eyes he turned to see if his friend was still alive.

§

Joe Lujan had known Frank for years. He knew the tough times he had, losing his wife, losing his job, getting older. He knew Frank's situation, like many in Las Puertas, scraping by on disability or welfare. Drinking to dull his senses and get through another day. But he had his home. He would be around until someday Joe would get the call from someone, maybe another old timer, telling him that they had found Frank dead.

But he had never known Frank to be scared. Miserable maybe…sick, unhappy, but not scared. "What the Hell is going on?" Joe thought.

The drive down the canyon took about half an hour. Joe pulled up behind the office and went in the back door. He went over to the cell where Frank was sleeping and looked in. Even for Frank, who was usually passed out cold, he looked exhausted. As Joe watched, Frank moved fitfully, rolled over and mumbled in his sleep. "He's gonna kill me. He's gonna kill…"

Joe frowned and went up to the office. Gabby was making some fresh coffee, figuring they would need it to get Frank to the point where he would answer some questions.

"Hello Sheriff. How did it go up in the canyon?"

"Another damn Texan who thought he knew how to drive in the mountains. He didn't. He's dead. Gil took over the scene." He took the cup of coffee she offered him. "Tell me what happened with Frank."

"I don't know. He just came up to the back door, banging on it" She paused. "I tell you Joe, he was exhausted, like he was running away from something, or somebody. He never comes to the back door."

Joe drank some coffee. "I'll go wake him up and see if he's in any shape to tell me what he's got to say."

The Sheriff went back to the cell. He stood over Frank for a minute then shook him by the shoulder.

Frank jerked awake and shrank back against the wall. "Leave me alone! Get out of here!" His voice was shaky, he turned toward the wall and covered the back of his head, as if to protect himself.

"Hey Frank. Tranquillo! It's me. It's Joe." He reached out to touch Frank's shoulder and ease him around so he could see his face. "Did you get some bad liquor?"

"Joe? Joe, you gotta help me. That guy, the one from the cell this morning. He's bad, really bad. He ripped me off, made me take him to my house, tied me up. I thought he was going to kill me." Frank was trembling.

"Okay! okay! You sure it was the same guy?

"Seguro. He came up behind me in the plaza. I was just sitting there and he took my booze, made me take him up to my house. Slapped me around and tied me up to a chair. I broke up the chair and ran. He was in my house, my house, acting like he owned the place. Took a shower." Frank took a breath, "He was still there when I left but I know he's going to come looking for me. He saw me as I was running away. He looked really pissed."

Joe recalled the incident at the truck stop the night before. He remembered how eager the big man was to take on the teenagers. How well he handled himself. Not someone who's used to not getting his way. Someone who wouldn't let anybody get the best of him.

"Okay Frank. You stay here. I'm going to lock you in in case the guy thinks you might have come here. You'll be safe." He got up and left the cell.

"Gabby, bring me the cell keys. Frank's going to stay awhile" Gabby had been listening at the hall door, she already had the keys in her hand.

Frank went back to the bunk and sat down, holding his head and still trembling a little. Telling the story, he scared himself all over again.

Joe and Gabby went back to the front office.

"Gabby...You stay here. Lock the back door. The front door too. If somebody comes make sure you know them. Tell them I'm out and will be back soon." He checked his weapon. "I'm going to look around town and see if this guy is still around."

He walked out onto Bridge Street. Looking East across the bridge, then west toward the plaza. He decided to head toward the bridge and check the riverbanks. He walked out to the middle of the bridge and looked south. Not noticing anything that caught his eye, he crossed the street and looked north. About a couple of hundred yards upstream, he saw two figures. One was prone, lying in the grass. The other was kneeling over him, looked like he was crying, wiping his eyes.

Joe walked off the bridge, climbed down the bank, and headed toward the two guys. When he got closer, he saw it was Ray and Jose, a couple of regulars down by the river.

"Jose!" he called out, "You guys okay?"

Jose stood up. He had been crying, streaks of dirt down his face. He was holding his side where Gordo had kicked him.

"Sheriff, I think Ray's dead. The guy killed him."

Joe rushed over. "Give me some room." Jose stepped away, wincing a little. Probably had a broken rib. Joe felt Ray's neck for a pulse...nothing. He rolled Ray over and saw the blood on his face. He wasn't breathing.

"Who did this?"

"No sé. Some big guy. Young. I never saw him before. He was looking for Frank." Jose was on the verge of tears. "He beat the shit out of Ray. I told him that we saw Frank." He swallowed. "I was scared. I told him we saw Frank and that he headed under the bridge." Jose looked over at Ray's body. "He was my friend. Why was this guy looking for Frank, Joe? Frank never hurt anybody. He couldn't."

Joe had his radio. He called the office.

Gabby answered, "Yeah Joe, nothing new here."

"Call Roberto. Tell him to get his ass to the station, now! We've got a problem." He paused, "And get in touch with Gil, see if he can come into town, we need some help."

"What's going on, Sheriff?" Gabby sounded worried.

"I'll fill you in when I get back. I'm just down by the river off Bridge Street. See you in five minutes. Oh, and Gabby, call Chief Flores. Ask him if he can come by." Joe looked down at Ray and Jose. "Better call an ambulance, too. Tell them we have an injured man and a body about two hundred yards north of the bridge on the west bank."

"Joe. Who is it? What happened?" Gabby was getting panicked. She was just the cleaning lady.

"Just do what I told you. Tell everyone no sirens when they get close. See you in five," Joe cut her off.

§

Joe told Jose to lay low, that help was on its way. He walked briskly back to Bridge Street and knocked on the office door. Gabby peeked through the drawn shades of the window and he saw the relief wash over her face when she saw it was him.

Opening the door, she couldn't help herself. "Dead body? Who? What happened?"

"Listen Gabby. There's a guy in town. Had a run in with him last night up at the truck stop. Mean son of a bitch. He was the guy I had locked up with Frank last night." Joe gazed out the window. "Didn't realize he was this dangerous." He looked back at Gabby. "You better go home. As soon as Roberto and the others get here things are going to get crazy."

"I can help, Joe. I can help with Frank and hold down the fort."

"Listen Gabby. I appreciate it but this guy just ruthlessly murdered a helpless barracho. I don't think he cares who gets in his way, man or woman. You could get hurt."

She just shrugged her shoulders. "I've been working here for twenty years. I know this place inside and out. I can work the phones, the radio. You and the boys have to be out looking for this guy. I'll keep the doors locked and Frank in his cell." She smiled, "I can help."

"Okay. But I'm going to have everybody keep their radios on. First sign of trouble you let us know. I'll make sure someone is close at all times."

Just then, Gil's state patrol car pulled up in front of the station. They heard the back door open and Roberto came into the office. "Hola Sheriff...Gabby. What's going on?"

Gil came in the front door. "What's up Joe?"

"Gabby, is the Chief on his way?" Joe asked.

"He said he'll be here as soon as he can. I told him it's an emergency."

"Okay. You guys grab a coffee. I'll fill you all in as soon as the Chief gets here. I'll tell you this. We got some kind of psycho in town. He's killed one person already, maybe more. And I think he's out to get Frank."

"But I just saw Frank in the cell back there," Roberto said. "Isn't he just drunk again?"

"No. He's in a panic. We're keeping him here for protection." Joe walked over to the window looking out on Bridge Street. "Where the Hell is Flores?"

He heard the sound of a siren getting closer. "Fucking idiot..." Joe muttered. Chief Flores wasn't the sharpest knife in the drawer. "Didn't you tell him no sirens?" He asked Gabby.

"What do you think?" she said. "You know Flores. Likes to think he's a big shot."

Chief Antonio Flores was the cousin of the state Senator, Carmine Flores. He was elected, but in Las Puertas whoever serves the most beer and burritos in the plaza usually wins the local elections. Backed by his cousin, the Chief cruised into the office no problem. He had a force of about three officers, two of them hard working cops, the third was his son, Raul. He was often found dozing in his squad car with marijuana smoke drifting out the windows.

The chief's car came speeding down Bridge Street, pulled a tire screeching u-turn and pulled up in front of the Sheriff's office.

Flores, a short, portly man, struggled out of his car, pulled down his shirt and walked in an unfamiliar hurried style into the office.

"What was the big rush. This better be good."

Joe heaved a sigh. "Tony, we got a murder. Maybe more than one." To the others, "This guy is bad. I had a run in with him last night and he's dangerous. A lot more dangerous than I thought."

He told them all the story about last night, about Frank showing up at the jail and about finding Ray and Jose by the river.

"The guy has a big, gray pickup. I need everybody out looking for it. I got the plates but I have a feeling it's either hot or it's got fake plates. Gabby, the plate numbers are on my desk, check them out. They might at least tell us where he's been." He walked over to the window. "Chief, get everybody out looking. He's a big Chicano guy, young. Maybe in his mid-twenties. About six three, two hundred sixty pounds. Tell them that if they see him to call me. Don't confront him. Just try to keep tabs on him without him noticing."

He went over to his desk, "I'm fairly sure he's still in town, looking for Frank. Something tells me he's a kind of sociopath and won't leave any unfinished business before he moves on. He might even go after the kids from the truck stop if he comes across them."

Chief Flores looked bothered. "Joe, this is city business. I should be heading this up. I'm the Chief of police."

Joe felt his neck turning red, "Tony, I met this guy. I know Frank and Ray and Jose. I found the body. You handle things over in East. But you report to me. This is something different for all of us. We've got to work together if we're going to catch him. Let's not worry about jurisdiction for now, okay?"

Flores was no hero. He realized this was out of his element and tried to sound like he was authorizing Joe to take the lead. "Sure. We do it your way. But if we bust him in the city, I get the collar."

"All right. But let's get him first." His impatience with Flores was tempered by his better judgement. "Let's get out there and start looking. Remember, he's doesn't care much about what happens to himself or anybody else."

§

Chief Flores squeezed himself into his squad car and headed back to police headquarters over in East Las Puertas. This time no siren. Joe figured he would just go back to his office and send out the two cops who did all the work. Odds are his son would come back to headquarters and man the radio. Tony wasn't about to put his boy in danger.

Gil called in the plan to state headquarters. They would most likely send another officer down from Raton. Not much goes on up there and his commander would not think it was important enough to pull anyone from Santa Fe or Albuquerque.

Roberto started cruising around town. He started up at Salazar Street and then worked his way back toward the plaza. Next, he would cross the railroad tracks to Commerce Street and cover the south end of town.

Joe would cover the plaza and everything north toward the canyon and St. Antonito, a small settlement on a back road north of town.

It would be a low-profile search, hoping to find this "Javier" and keep him in sight. If the opportunity to nail him occurred, Joe would want plenty of backup. Before he started his search, he went back to the river to see about Jose and arrange for the removal of Ray's body. When he got near the spot the ambulance was there and the EMT's were carrying Jose on a stretcher.

"Hola Pete. How's he doing?"

Pete, the head EMT in Las Puertas, helped his coworker load Jose into the ambulance. He walked over to Joe once Jose was inside. "I don't think he's hurt too bad. Busted rib maybe. But he's pretty shook up. We had to calm him down with a shot. We'll just take him to the hospital so they can look him over a little better." He shook his head. "The guy is harmless. Whoever did this just liked beating the shit out of people. Ray was worked over pretty well before he died." He paused. "These guys, they don't bother anybody. I know they're kind of useless, but they're harmless."

He got into the ambulance and called out to Joe, "I hope you find the guy who did this." He started the ambulance. "He's a real son of a bitch."

Pete pulled away just as the local mortician, Carlos Ce De Baca, pulled up. He got out of the hearse. "Where's the body, Joe?"

"I'll walk you over there. Bring your camera, we need to get some pictures before you take him away." He quickly filled him in about the morning's events. "Start with his body and work your way out in a circle so we can get an idea of his surroundings. There might be some clues."

Joe walked around the area, looking for some kind of clue. Carlos started taking photos. He didn't get to do murder scenes very often. Most folks just died of natural causes, old age or from drink or drugs. Brutal, senseless murder was something different and not a routine event in town.

Carlos took the photos. Jesus, Carlos' partner, came down with the stretcher. They loaded Ray up and took him back to the hearse. Since it was a nice day, they decided to kick back and have a smoke before heading back to the mortuary.

Joe looked around the scene one last time and headed back to his car. He radioed Gabby and told her to let the coroner know where Ray's body would be. Las Puertas didn't have much in the way of services but at least the coroner could examine the body for some evidence and maybe find something to tie the big man to the crime.

Then he radioed Gil. Nothing yet. Nothing from Roberto. Nothing from Flores or his men.

Joe got back into his truck and started to drive around the neighborhood. He hoped that the Big Man didn't notice the extra police presence in town. Although in a town like Las Puertas, cops were always cruising around. Not much else to do.

The search had begun.

§

Throughout Gordo's life of crime and violence, no one had ever gotten the best of him. Even as a kid in Santa Rosa, he always got the last punch, the best of a situation, the most money.

In Albuquerque he was the loner, feared and respected by the gangs who found it easier and more profitable to work with him. He did well and so did they. The same in Santa Fe. For Gordo, the incident with Bertie just reaffirmed to him that he could do whatever he wanted. Having the gun made him feel invincible, even though he never needed one before.

His natural street smarts and almost animal like wiliness enabled him to stay out of trouble with the police. Nobody knew much about him. He was a wraith, a ghost like criminal who until Santa Fe, had never been a target for either the police or the villains.

As he wandered around the town, he stayed around the river and Bridge Street. He circled out a ways, then came back to where he found Ray and Jose. As he came closer to the spot he saw the ambulance leaving and the hearse pulling up. He backed his truck into an alley and got out to get a better look. He watched as Joe talked to the coroner's men.

"So one of them made it." He thought. He knew from the night before that Joe would recognize his truck and that Jose, even though he was a drunk, had most likely described him to the Sheriff. Gordo went back to his truck, grabbed his bag and the gun and left the truck behind. He worked his way away from the scene and stayed in the alleys and back yards, looking for another vehicle. Behind the Post Office, he noticed that the mailmen were coming back from their routes. Several went to their cars and grabbed their lunch boxes and headed into the building, leaving most of the cars unlocked. These guys were some of the better paid people in Las Puertas and there were some pretty decent rides to choose from.

Gordo waited until they were gone, picked a good looking F-150 and slipped into the driver's seat. In about thirty seconds he had it hot wired and running. He drove slowly out of the parking lot and down the alley. The guy's hat was on the seat so Gordo put it on. To anyone in town, he just looked like another local.

He began his search again. This time knowing he was a lot less obvious.

He decided to drive by the scene and check it out. Joe and the ambulance had gone and he pulled up by the hearse. Carlos and Jesus were sitting in the hearse, smoking cigarettes and sipping on a bottle.

"Oye!" Gordo called out, "What's going on?"

Carlos got out and walked over to Gordo. "A couple of barrachos got the shit beat out of them. One's dead, the other is on his way to the hospital. He's in pretty bad shape." He took a drag on his cigarette. "Ray and Jose, you know them?"

Gordo smiled. "Yeah, I give them a buck or two from time to time." Shaking his head he said, "Too bad. They seemed harmless to me. Who do they think did it? I saw the Sheriff heading out."

"Some big guy. A stranger. Troublemaker from what I hear. Had a run in with the Sheriff last night, they locked him up overnight. Then he roughed up Francisco Ramirez at his house." Carlos took another drag. "Sheriff said he was in the same cell with Frank at the jail, then he followed him home. Probably would have killed him too, except Frank got away. They got him locked in a cell for his own safety." He chuckled, "Frank's probably feeling right at home."

"Yeah. I know Frank. Glad he's safe." Gordo started his truck, "I gotto go. You be careful. This guy sounds dangerous." He could barely hold back a grin as he headed back to Bridge Street.

He drove slowly down Bridge Street and peered into the sheriff's office. There didn't seem to be anyone around and there were no squad cars out front. He continued up to the plaza and then swung left at the corner so he could scope out the office from the alley behind. Once again there was little sign of activity and no cars parked near the back door. He pulled over and parked under a tree near the entrance to the high school.

After waiting a few minutes to make sure no one else was around, he got out and walked over to the back door of the office. He knocked loudly. After a few seconds, he knocked again.

From inside he heard a woman's voice. "Is that you Sheriff?"

Holding the hat over his mouth to muffle his voice, he said "Yeah. I'm going to need the shotgun."

He heard the door unlock and it swung open. Gabby was standing there, surprised to see it was big guy the sheriff had released that morning. She reacted quickly, trying to shut the door but Gordo pushed her and the door back, shoving Gabby to the floor.

"Thanks, Gabby isn't it?" She tried to scramble to her feet but Gordo grabbed her by the arm and held her down.

"Let me go you bastard. Get the Hell out of here. The Sheriff is coming back any minute." She struggled but could not break his hold. "Let me go. Leave me alone!"

"Seguro. But first I need to find my amigo Francisco." He glared down at her. "I hear he's waiting for me here." He pulled her to her feet. "Let's get the keys and then Frank and I will go."

He pushed her down the hall. From his cell, Frank called out, "Hey Gabby, what's going on. Who's there..." He froze as Gordo, holding Gabby, came up to the bars and smiled at Frank.

"Hello, Bato. I hear you've been waiting for me. Just take it easy, Gabby and I will be right back." His smile turned into a menacing grin, "We're going for a little trip."

Frank backed away from the bars and cowered back in the corner. He was shaking all over. Fear overcame him and he started looking for a way out.

Gordo dragged Gabby down the hall to the office. When they got out front he went over to the windows and closed the blinds. He made sure the front door was locked.

"Bueno, Gabby. Let's have those keys." He pushed her into Joe's desk chair and let her go.

"The sheriff's coming back. He just called in." Her voice trembled. Gordo knew she was lying.

"Sure, sure. That's great. I'm looking forward to seeing him again." He bent over her and put his face close to hers. "The keys. Now!"

Gabby was a strong woman, faithful to Joe. She was trying to think what to do next. "Joe took them with him. The cells, the guns, everything. I'm just the cleaning lady. He wouldn't let me have those keys. They're not in the office unless Joe or Roberto are here."

Gordo hit her hard across the face. Then again. He threw her out of the chair and onto the floor, kicking her in the ribs. "The keys, abuela, or their going to be cleaning you up."

Gabby spit at him. He just smiled. Then he started searching Joe's desk. The keys were easy to find, right in the center desk drawer with a set of hand cuffs. They were even labeled. Cell numbers, gun locker, utility room, spare keys for the vehicles. "Too easy," thought Gordo.

He went over to the gun locker, got out the shotgun, some extra shells, another pistol and more ammo. Then he gave Gabby another kick, she moaned but seemed out cold.

He walked back down the hall to Frank's cell and unlocked the door.

"Come on Frank, let's go for that ride."

He unlocked the cell and yanked Frank to his feet putting the cuffs on him. Frank was too scared to resist. Gordo dragged him out of the cell, down the hall to the back door. He looked out, once again making sure no one was around. Then he got Frank to walk over to the stolen pickup and shoved him into the passenger side. Gordo walked around to the driver's side and got in. He punched Frank on the side of his head and made sure he was unconscious.

"Shit. I'm thirsty." He thought to himself. He got back up and went back into the Sheriff's office. Stepping over Gabby, he went to the little office fridge and got out a couple of bottles of water and some cold burritos

Gabby had brought for Joe and Roberto. Gabby was motionless. He went back out and got into the truck. Frank was crumpled down, out of sight on the floor. Surprisingly calm, Gordo drank some water and ate a burrito. Then he started up the truck and headed back toward the plaza. He didn't notice Gabby peering out of the bottom of the open door.

§

She was dizzy, her ribs ached where Gordo had kicked her. But Gabby was shrewd and tough. She heard him rummage through the desk and from the sound, knew he had found the keys. After he kicked her the second time she pretended to be unconscious. She listened as opened the gun rack. She heard him walk down the hall toward Frank's cell and the scuffle as he manhandled Frank out the back door.

Not sure if the big man was really gone, she just lay quietly to ease the pain. She heard the back door open again and closed her eyes, pretending to be out cold. Gordo came back into the office and stepped right over her. She held her breath as he opened the little fridge and took the water and burritos. Then he stepped over her again and headed to the back door.

Painfully, Gabby sat up, glanced down the hall and saw Gordo walk out the door. She figured he was leaving this time and managed to get on her feet. Being very quiet, she went down the hall staying out of the sight line of the partially open door. Getting back on her hands and knees, she crawled toward the crack of daylight and looked out.

She could see Gordo sitting in the truck. Right away, she recognized the vehicle as belonging to Julio Aragon, the mailman. Gabby knew most of the postal workers in Las Puertas since she also cleaned the post office once a week. His F-150 was a two-tone white and blue older fleetside with extra large tires. Watching him eat the burritos she made for Joe and Roberto made her angry. "That cabron, that son of a bitch." Gordo finished eating, started the truck and drove off.

Gabby struggled to stand and hurried as best she could back to the office. She went to the radio and grabbed the microphone. "Joe, Sheriff, this is Gabby. The guy was just here. He took Frank!"

"Gabby? This is Joe, what's going on?"

"The big guy came here, he took Frank! You've got to find him, pronto!" she paused, wincing in pain. "He's one mean bastard. He's in Julio Aragon's blue and white Ford pickup. He's got Frank. Headed back up toward the plaza."

"Jesus Christ, Gabby, are you all right? Did he hurt you?"

"I'm okay, but you better send an ambulance over here. I think he broke a couple of my ribs."

"Hang on. I'll be right over."

"No, no. I'm okay. Just try to find him before he kills Frank too."

"I'll get the ambulance over there. You just rest. I'll track down everybody and update them."

"What a piece of shit" Joe thought to himself. He switched to the emergency channel and put out an APB. Then he called Gil.

"Gil, where are you?"

"Hey Joe, I'm up north by the Safeway. What's up?"

"That bastard came by the office. He beat up Gabby and took Frank. He's driving a blue and white Ford F-150. Might be heading your way. Maybe up toward the canyon. Call Roberto and let him know. I'll call Tony, see where his boys are?" Taking a breath, "Let's get this puto."

§

Gordo took one loop around the plaza. No cops in site. He headed up Montezuma Boulevard. toward the north end of town. He took what seemed to be a main road out of town and was glad to see La Puertas start to disappear in his rear-view mirror.

"I might as well get rid of this piece of shit," looking down at Frank. He continued north, past the state hospital. The houses started to be further and further apart. Soon there was only a house every couple of miles. He noticed he was getting closer to the foothills when the road narrowed down. The centerline disappeared and the walls of the canyon rose around him.

Gordo figured he was heading into the national forest, not a bad place to get rid of a body. He could always come back down and find his way to the interstate, and then...Denver.

Driving on the narrow canyon road was difficult for Gordo. He had always operated in more populated areas. Neighborhood streets and boulevards, four lane thoroughfares and wide main drags. Mountain driving was new to him and he tended to take the turns too fast or come out on the wrong side of the road. "Fuck this" he muttered, slowing down and being more cautious. He wanted to get several miles up into the forest before finishing off Frank, finding a good place to hide the body and then going back down the hill and beating it out of town.

After a few miles, he came to a logging road that went down into a glen and continued up the other side. There was a clearing at the bottom and he pulled the truck off the road.

Frank was coming around. Gordo lifted him up onto the seat.

"Well, Francisco. It was nice knowing you." He sneered. He got out and walked around to the passenger side. He opened the door and pulled Frank out of the truck. Frank seemed to collapse, his legs coming out from under him.

"Shit! I don't want to carry you into the woods." He held Frank's head up by the hair. "How about a little water. Then maybe we can get you to walk a ways." Turning his back on Frank, he reached into the truck to get a bottle. Suddenly he felt a hard blow to the back of his head. He reached behind his head and felt the warm blood oozing from under his hair. He was dizzy, disoriented...furious! "What the hell..." turning to see behind him, he fell to his knees. Another blow struck him above one eye, and another. Gordo, for the first time in his life, dropped to the ground. The last thing he saw was Frank, barely able to stand up himself and holding a large rock in his hand. Then, black.

Frank could hardly believe it. "Me, Francisco Ramirez, a weakling, a drunk, got the best of the big man." He was scared. He struggled around to the driver's side of the truck and got in. The ignition was a bunch of loose wires hanging below the steering column. Not knowing anything about stealing cars, he had no idea how to start the truck. He got out and started walking as best he could back to the main road. After about half an hour, he made it to the paved canyon road. Exhausted, he climbed down an embankment and lay down, hidden behind some boulders and under some scrub, catching his breath. There wasn't much traffic since there were only three or four houses before the road ended. Feeling weak, Frank passed out. He didn't hear Gil's state cruiser go by, heading further up the road.

§

Earlier, Joe was crisscrossing the north end of town. Tony's guys, except his son, were working East Las Puertas, the interstate and the roads heading east. Roberto was covering the south side of West.

Gil was up on Mills Avenue, near the Piggly Wiggly at the northwest part of town. They were all looking for Julio's blue and white Ford. Sitting at a light several blocks from the intersection of Mills and Montezuma Boulevard, he saw what could be Julio's truck go across the intersection, heading up Montezuma toward the canyon. He grabbed his radio and called Joe.

"I think I saw him. It looked like the Ford."

"Go ahead and follow him from a distance. Keep an eye on him. Try and get the plate number," Joe said.

"I got a better idea." Gil pulled a U-turn and made a left on 8th Street. "I'll work my way up to Antonito and come back down Motezuma. That way if he sees me he won't think I'm following him and I can get a good look."

"Sounds good. I'll head up your way and see if we can hook up. That road doesn't go anywhere but up the canyon. If it's him, we'll have him boxed in." Joe radioed Roberto, told him to follow his lead. He didn't call Tony. Maybe later.

Gil turned on his lights, no siren. He raced up the side roads to the little settlement at Antonito. He took the dirt bypass to Montezuma and headed south. He was pretty sure he got there ahead of Gordo.

Gordo was heading north on Montezuma. He was cruising, taking his time so he wouldn't attract any attention. Frank was still passed out on the floor next to him. Wearing Julio's hat, window open, arm resting casually on the door frame. Just another local heading up the canyon.

Ahead he saw the state trooper heading his way. Gordo knew they often went up these roads, part of their routine. As the trooper approached, Gordo waved at him, something he noticed folks did around here and it reinforced his cover. The trooper waved back and continued south. "Guess they hadn't gotten around to moving the search up here yet." he thought. "I wonder if the truck's been reported stolen yet. Maybe not. Those guys at the PO are probably still eating lunch." He continued on to the point where the road narrowed and headed up the canyon.

§

Joe's radio crackled to life. It was Gil. "Hey joe. It was him. He's in the Ford headed up the canyon. The son of a bitch even waved at me as we passed. I didn't see Frank but he could be in the bed of the truck. God...I hope he's still alive. I'm heading back up. I'll see if I can get eyes on him."

"Bueno! I'll let Roberto know. We'll be right behind you." Joe knew this was going to be rough. If Frank was dead there's no telling what the big man would do. A cornered rat is a dangerous animal.

Joe raced up toward the canyon. He radioed Roberto who was down toward the tracks and would catch up as soon as he could. "Use your sirens. Get through town as fast as you can, then cut the siren until we meet up in the canyon."

§

Gordo came to in the clearing after about thirty minutes. His head was bleeding and he felt dizzy. He managed to stand up. Looking around, he didn't see Frank.

"That little bastard puto son of a bitch." He saw the truck was still there and staggered over to it. "Little shit couldn't figure out to start the truck. Stupido!" He looked back up the forest road. "Must have headed back to the main road." Gordo's mind was clearing but he still had blurred vision and trouble focusing. He got into the truck, fired it up and spun out going back the way he came. He kept an eye on the sides of the road, looking for any sign of Frank.

"I'll kill that bastard and get the Hell out of this piece of shit town."

Working his way back he had some trouble staying on the track. He had received a severe blow to the head and likely had a concussion, something he was very unfamiliar with. When he got to the road, he hadn't seen any sign of Frank. "Probably headed back toward town." He floored the truck and started down the hill.

§

By now Joe had entered the narrow canyon road. Gil had reached the forest and saw no sign of the truck, so he turned around and cruised slowly back down, checking for tire tracks going into the woods or looking for the truck parked behind one of the few houses or cabins as he went by.

Joe was doing the same thing as he headed up. He saw Roberto coming up in his rear view.

"Hey Joe, I'm right behind you. What's the plan?"

"Let's just keep our eyes open. Look for the truck...Frank...any signs they turned off anywhere. Gil is coming back down so if the guy is still in the canyon we should be able to box him in."

They slowly worked their way up the canyon. Gil, coming down from the upper canyon, was getting close to the turn off Gordo had taken with Frank.

Down in the glen, Frank woke up, startled by the sound of Julio's truck coming out of the woods. He peeked over the rocks and saw Gordo turn back down the canyon. He waited until the engine sound faded in the distance and crawled out of his hiding place and scrambled up to the road.

"Maybe there's a house or cabin nearby." He thought trying to decide which direction would be safer. Which direction Gordo would be least likely to look. He figured he could head up toward the national forest. There were some houses up that way and Gordo would probably think he was heading toward town, toward safety.

He kept to the side of the road. If he heard a car coming he could duck into the underbrush and see if it was the big man, searching for him. Just then, he did hear a car coming from up the hill. He moved quickly into the brush where he could hide but still see the road. "God, I could sure use a drink." It hadn't occurred to him that since he hadn't had a drink for almost a day, he was thinking clearer. He was even feeling a little stronger physically. After all, he had beaten the big man, knocked him cold. He hadn't had the strength or the courage to do something like that in years.

The car got closer. As it came around the curve, he could see it was a state police cruiser. "Gracias Dios! Muchas gracias!." He crawled out from the bushes and onto the road, waving his arms frantically.

Gil saw Frank come out from the brush. He pulled over and got out of the car, his hand on his weapon. "Que pasa, amigo?" he looked over the wretched figure, blood on his face and shirt. "Are you Francisco Ramirez?

"Help me. The big man, he was going to kill me. I got away but he's still around. He headed down the hill." Frank sank to his knees. Completely drained from a combination of exhaustion and relief.

Gil helped him to his feet and walked him around to the car. He got Frank into the back seat and gave him a bottle of water. "Take it easy, amigo. Take it easy. When did this guy head down? How long ago?"

Frank drank the water, grateful for something to wet his parched throat. "He headed down, oh maybe ten or twenty minutes ago." He drank some more. "He was going slow. He was looking for me. I hit him with a rock, knocked him cold. He's pissed but I think I hurt him pretty good."

"Okay. You just take it easy, buddy" Gil got on the radio. "Hey Joe, he's heading your way. I got Frank, I think he's okay."

"Great Gil. Tell Frank we've got this covered. Roberto is here with me and we've got the cars blocking the road. Come on down but hang back if you see him. We don't want to spook him and there's no telling what he'll do if he knows he's cornered."

"What's going on Joe?" Roberto, overhearing the conversation, seemed a little nervous, tense.

"The guy is headed our way. We'll hold this roadblock and see what he does when he comes around that curve up ahead."

Joe knew this was a dangerous man. Someone who had never been trapped before. And he was wanted for murder, not a fight, not petty theft, but murder. And kidnapping. There was no telling what he would do.

Roberto asked "Do you think we should call for backup?

Joe thought about it. He could let Tony know about the situation, but Flores could do more harm than good and it would be at least a half hour or forty five minutes before he could get up the canyon. "Give Tony a call. Tell him to have his guys set up another roadblock at the mouth of the canyon. And find out if the other trooper from Raton is getting close." He knew that was a long shot and that the other trooper was probably a good hour out, if he was on his way at all.

It was down to him and Roberto and Gil. Three to one. Pretty good odds.

§

"Little pendejo bastard. Where the Hell is he?" Gordo was getting crazy. "Nobody does that to Gordo. Nobody. Little drunk son of a bitch."

He had shut off the engine and continued coasting almost noiselessly down the canyon, going about fifteen miles an hour. Scanning both sides of the road. Nothing. As he came around each curve of the winding road he figured he'd spot Frank, but no sign of him yet.

Concentrating on the shoulders, he didn't notice Gil's car behind him in the rear view. He thought he saw something but Gil, spotting the truck hit his brakes and let the truck disappear around the next bend. He called Joe.

"I'm at mile marker seventeen. He's about a quarter mile ahead of me, moving slow. You should see him in the next couple of minutes. Let me know and I'll hustle on down so we can trap him."

"Got it Gil. We're ready," Joe said. He turned to Roberto and said, "Showtime!"

They went around behind their vehicles. Joe opened the back of his truck and took out the spike strip. He had Roberto stretch it across the road about fifty yards down the canyon, in case Gordo broke through. Roberto had his 12 gauge. Joe had his .44.

They had set up at a narrow spot in the road, the embankment down to the river on their left, a high canyon wall that came within a few feet of the road on their right. If somehow Gordo broke through it would be almost impossible without causing some damage. Someone would get hurt.

§

Gordo was agitated, frustrated. He knew Frank couldn't have gotten far. "Where the Hell is he?" He muttered to himself.

He continued slowly down the canyon. As he came around a turn he saw Joe's and Roberto's cars in the road, blocking the way.

"Motherfucker!" He stopped, started the truck and put it in neutral. He reached for his gun, checked it to make sure it was loaded. The truck was idling, and he waited to see what the cops' next move would be.

Joe reached into his truck and got out his bullhorn.

"You there...in the truck. Step out with your hands where I can see them. Move slowly. Your vehicle has been reported stolen." He paused. "Let's try not to get anyone hurt, okay?"

Gordo sat silently in the truck. He knew they probably had found Ray and that he had kidnapped Frank. "I should have taken care of the old abuela at the jail." he thought. He had never been this close to capture, never been threatened by anyone or any situation where he could not control the outcome or escape from it. The night Joe put him in jail was his first time...and he had only allowed it because he figured he wouldn't be charged. Just had to spend the night and his fake ID had no previous charges. He pondered his next move. He could try to make a run for it back up the canyon. It might be a little tricky turning around on the narrow road but it still might give him time to get a head start on the cops, ditch the truck down some side road and work his way down the mountain through the woods along the stream and find another car to steal or jack. Maybe he could steal another car from one of the houses or cabins further up. The two cops were armed and ready for him.

He checked his rear view and spotted Gil's cruiser coming around the last bend. It stopped about a hundred feet away and angled to block the road. Gil stepped out of the car, his hand on his weapon. It was then that Gordo saw Frank, sitting in the back seat of the cruiser. Looking his way.

"That son of a bitch. Pendejo mother fucker." A sudden surge of madness, insane fury welled up in Gordo. "I should have killed him. I should have killed that bitch at the sheriff's office. That little piece of shit did this to me." Without a second thought, he rammed the truck into reverse and accelerated backwards toward Gil's car.

§

The truck roared toward Gil's car in reverse. Surprised, and caught off guard, Gil instinctively leaped to the shoulder. "Frank, get down! Get out of the car!"

Frank froze for a few seconds, then scrambled to get out the side door Gil had left open. He managed to fall out and started to crawl away a split second before the truck rammed into the cruiser. The cruiser flipped over with the force from the heavy truck, barely missing Frank as he made his way over to Gil.

Gil had pulled his weapon and fired several shots at the cab of the truck. Gordo ducked below the window and reached for his weapon. He tried to aim in Gil and Frank's direction but couldn't get a clear shot. He threw the truck into drive and headed toward Joe and Roberto, firing his gun out the window, headed for the narrow opening on the canyon side of the two cop cars.

Joe threw down the bull horn and pulled his weapon. Roberto had the shotgun on his shoulder and was pumping rounds at the oncoming truck. Joe fired at the cab.

Gordo noticed a pain in his right shoulder, warm blood was streaming down his arm. He had the gun in his left hand and continued to fire at Joe and Roberto. Swinging left of Roberto's car he rammed his way between the car and the canyon wall. Roberto's car spun around, knocking Roberto to the ground. The truck crashed its way through, the right front wheel wobbling.

Joe swung around and continued firing.

Gordo was excited, his adrenalin pumping, his heart racing. He couldn't feel the pain in his arm, or the pain in his back where Joe had managed to shoot him as he blew through the roadblock. He was dulled by the blow to the head from Frank, but that didn't bother him either.

"Fuck those bastard cops! Fuck Frank! Fuck them all. I'm Gordo, nobody can touch me. He thumped his chest, the way Ortega did when he met him leaving Santa Rosa.

"Me llamo Gordo." He boasted. "Nobody fucks with Gordo!"

At that moment, he hit the spike strip. All four tires blew. The truck swerved and flew out over the embankment, spinning over and landing on its roof in the river. Gordo was thrown first toward the roof, then crushed against the steering wheel, upside down with the ice cold water rushing in. Trapped, he watched as the water covered his eyes, then his nose, then his mouth. "Nobody fucks..."

Joe helped Roberto to his feet. Gil came running over, "You guys all right?"

"Yeah. We're okay. Roberto's a little shook up. Where's Frank.?

"He's up by the car. Seems okay."

As they went to the shoulder overlooking the river they saw Frank walking toward them. He looked worn out, still frightened but able to make it to the embankment.

"Is it over? Is he dead?" He asked.

The four of them looked over the edge, the truck upside down in the river. "I doubt he's alive," Joe said. He holstered his gun and started to look for a way down. "Gil, why don't you call this in. Let your boss know what happened. Get an incident team up here. Roberto, give Tony a call. Tell him it's over and they should send up a couple of tow trucks so when the state team is done we can clear the road. And give Julio a call. I think he'll be needing a new truck."

Joe started to work his way down the bank. When he got close to the truck he could see Gordo's legs twisted and contorted across the cab. His head and shoulders were completely submerged, blood in the water, the crushed steering column holding the body firmly in place.

"One loco son of a bitch," he thought. "Another flatlander dead in the river." He turned and climbed back up the road.

Reaching the top, he went to his truck and sat down in the driver's seat. He grabbed a bottle of water and took a long drink. He was parched.

Frank came over. "Thanks Joe. Thanks for saving my life. I don't think I'll be visiting the jail much anymore. Gonna try to sober up."

"That's good Frank." Joe paused. "Who was this guy?" Another pause. "I guess we may never know. Let's hope things just go back to normal in Las Puertas. We don't need anything like this to happen again."

Joe sat back and closed his eyes, knowing that may not be the case.

THE BOXING GAME

Fascinated by boxing, even when he was a child, Juan Carlos Abeyta Jr. couldn't wait for the time his father and mother would let him start the sport. His parents enjoyed watching boxing on television and did not think it inappropriate that their son expressed an interest in becoming a boxer.

Juan Carlos Sr. was a lifelong Las Puertas businessman. He had a hardware store on Mills Avenue at the north end of town and owned several properties around town. He managed to keep the store profitable even after the Walmart opened about two miles away. People liked him and he did his best to give them the best service and help them with their projects. He was knowledgeable about all his products and knew when they would do the job for his customer.

The Abeytas lived in a nice sixties ranch house close to the store on Montezuma Blvd. His wife, Rosa, took care of her two 'boys,' kept a tidy house and was active with the schools and church groups. Juan Carlos Jr. was smart, a good student and a promising athlete. He saw boxing as a competitive sport that took both strength and intelligence. His goal was the Olympics, not the fight circuit.

When he started high school, they asked the gym coach if he knew anywhere Juan could begin to train. The coach, Pete Moreno, was a boxer in college and still had some connections at the University of New Mexico, but that was all the way in Albuquerque. Juan's father asked Pete if he would consider some private lessons for Juan, and after a dinner at El Alto and a couple of beers, Pete agreed to give it a try.

Pete arranged with the school to install a punching bag and a heavy bag, (paid for by Juan Carlos Sr.) in the equipment room next to the gym. They already had a strength training room. Juan Carlos bought a pair of training gloves and some hand wraps. His mother paid for his shoes out of the housekeeping money.

Finally, a few weeks after his thirteenth birthday, Juan Carlos began a surprisingly disciplined two-year training regimen under Pete's supervision. Juan was on his way to becoming a skilled and promising young boxer.

§

"Watch your feet. Pick 'em up." Pete kept after 'Johnny' as he liked to call Juan Carlos. He figured Johnny Abeyta would look better on the posters. It had a nice ring to it. "Move around! Don't let him get you on the ropes." Johnny was sparring with another boy, a big kid named Felipe Reyes.

By the time Juan Carlos was a senior in high school, Pete Moreno had developed a real boxing program. At first, some of the other boys thought it a joke, but after watching Pete work with Johnny, some of the kids asked if they could join in. The school principal and even the school superintendent were fully supportive of Pete. They let him set up a regulation ring where the girls' volleyball court used to be. The girls could play volleyball anywhere.

Juan Carlos Sr. provided all the hardware for the ring. The school district managed to redirect some maintenance funds to build the ring itself. It was as close to the real thing that Las Puertas could come up with. But it was good enough to allow the boys to qualify for state competitions.

"He's a brawler. Keep moving." Felipe, or 'Flip,' was bigger than Johnny. He could take punches all day long and had a long reach.

"Come on Flip. Don't let him get away." Pete wanted to be fair, but Johnny was his favorite. He knew the kid was a natural. He was fast and strong. Had great footwork and knew how to avoid getting in a clinch or trapped against the ropes.

They went three rounds. "Good work out boys. Let's let the next two guys have a run. Go on and shower up."

Johnny and Flip bumped gloves and stepped out of the ring. They were good friends but, in the ring, both were eager to show Pete who was the better fighter.

In the locker room they cleaned up and were getting dressed.

"Do you think we can qualify for the next Golden Gloves?" Flip asked.

"I can," Johnny answered. "I don't know about a culo like you."

"Screw you! If you can, I can." They laughed and headed out. It was late in the day. "You want to go get a malt at Murphy's?"

"No. My Mom's picking me up in a few minutes. I've got a history test tomorrow. Got to study. Keep my grades up. I'm trying for a scholarship at NMU."

Flip shook his head. "Not me. I'm going for the circuit. Once I'm out of high school I'm heading for Albuquerque. See if I can get a job at a gym." He gazed off into the distance. "I think I can make it."

Johnny smiled at his friend. Just then, Rosa pulled up. "See you later, amigo."

§

Most of the towns and cities of New Mexico have a hard edge. There has always been a history of hard drinking, hard fighting pachucos, cabrons, cowboys or roughnecks not getting along, having huge brawls or car chases and even shootings. There was petty crime, conflict and thick heads keeping the police busy.

Trouble even happened within the close groups themselves. Drunk, almost closing time, the remaining hard core at a bar realized they weren't going to get laid that night so they would pick a fight with whoever was within range, sometimes their closest friend. Most of the time, the friend was more than willing to oblige.

But of all the towns and cities in the state, Albuquerque was the center for a more insidious level of crime. The city had youth gangs involved primarily in car theft, burglary, and drug dealing. Next up the ladder were the minor gangsters. They supplied the youth gangs with drugs and guns and staked out an area of the city where they collected protection money from the local businesses. Then there were the local bosses.

At the top level, the Denver crime syndicates and the Juarez drug syndicates shared the state. The syndicates handled prostitution, gambling and illegal sales of liquor and cigarettes. The cartels provided the drugs, heroin, cocaine, marijuana, speed and meth, and human cargo. The Denver group were branches of the major syndicates in New York, Los Angeles, and Chicago. The Juarez bunch were loosely associated with other Mexican cartels and the Columbians. Everybody accepted this arrangement, and they did not so much cooperate with each other but complemented each other, as long as it was profitable.

New Mexico is a unique state. Some people back East didn't even realize it was in the United States. If you told someone in Connecticut or Massachusetts that you came from New Mexico they would usually say, "Oh sure. I like Mazatlán or Puerto Vallarta. Great beaches!" So, you just let it go. No point in correcting someone that stupid or uninformed.

The state could be said to have four separate quadrants. The northeast, mainly Hispanics and Chicanos. The northwest, primarily the Native American reservations around Gallup and the Four Corners area. The southern half of the state was sort of mixed Hispanic and Anglo. Oil fields in the southeast and mountains and desert in the southwest. Even the local television stations separated the weather reports into four sections, specific to the four quadrants. The whole state was a thirsty, rugged landscape. But there were several smaller cities and towns that were well established and offered opportunities for the syndicates to squeeze more money out of even the poorest areas. Cities like Silver City, Roswell, Gallup, Carlsbad, and Farmington could be profitable.

Las Puertas, in the northeast, was one of those towns. I-25 connected Denver up in Colorado all the way to El Paso Texas and Ciudad Juarez across the border in Mexico. And it ran right through Las Puertas. The syndicates liked it because it was the kind of highway town where no one stopped, except for gas or to spend the night on their way to someplace else. It was a poor town and the owners of the various properties, warehouses and commercial, ranches and old run-down houses, were more than happy to rent to anyone who would give them a decent rate. Paid in cash and sometimes with as much as a year's rent in advance. No questions asked. Law enforcement was light. Besides, they had their hands full with the day-to-day crimes that can occur in a town whose residents were struggling to get by.

§

There was one rowdy bar on the edge of town that was a de facto meeting place for the syndicates. Appropriately named The Ringside. The owner, Cesar Reyes, was closely associated with both the drug cartels and the crime families. When a big powwow was scheduled, rather than meet in Albuquerque, the gangsters would meet at the Ringside. Locals were familiar with the occasional presence of black sedans and limos with Colorado plates and tricked out rides with Texas, Chihuahua or Sonora plates. It usually happened every two or three months. The bar would be closed to the public. But if it was Sunday, you could still buy beer at the back door.

For the locals, The Ringside was the only bar in town where they had off color entertainment. Other places, like the Faro's or The Meeting Place had bands playing on the weekends. The Ringside had bands as well. But it also had sad, minor circuit strippers and occasional boxing matches, both bare knuckle and gloved, as well as cage matches that got bloody and sometimes fatal. The fights were something Cesar had going from day one. That's why he called the place The Ringside.

For the city of Las Puertas, The Ringside was what it was. A semi legal, rough place that, if you were smart, you would avoid it. If you wanted to get a taste of the criminal underworld, you went there for the thrill of living dangerously. Or if you were just plain stupid.

§

Sheriff Joe Lujan was at his desk, catching up on some paperwork. It was Friday and things would soon start heating up around town. He had Roberto Castillo, his deputy, off for the day and was due to come back on duty about six. They would both be working or on call all weekend. That's just the way it was.

Gabby, the cleaning lady, office manager and dedicated unofficial deputy, was just finishing up. "You want me back here later, Joe? If things get busy, I could help cover."

"Seguro. I think we've got some action going on up at the Ringside."

Gabby cursed under her breath.

Joe wasn't looking forward to it. This was one of those weekends when the bosses would be in town. He knew there wasn't much he could do to stop it... but he could try to make sure the locals didn't get involved.

He had talked to Cesar earlier. "You're closed to the public for a couple of days? I just need to keep folks out of your way."

Cesar laughed. "Yeah. You better do that. Private parties this weekend."

Private parties. He didn't mean a wedding or Quinceañera. A private party at the Ringside meant the syndicates were meeting. They would arrive in the afternoon with their entourages. After dark, Cesar would have entertainment and the powwows would last from Saturday and on into Sunday. There would be some bare-knuckle fights between the different groups' champions, heavy betting, lots of food and drink. Big money would change hands, bodyguards and lieutenants would be armed. The bosses would have meetings about "arrangements." Forays would be made to inspect the various locations around town where goods were stashed.

Joe would like nothing better than to stop these meetings. He knew it went on, hated the fact that it was in his town. But without some action from the state, from the attorney's office or the governor, it was much too big for him. The sad thing was that there were some government officials who were susceptible to bribes. Big money brought power to politicians and other law enforcement agencies. The Feds would show up from time to time and the DEA would make a bust or two. Somehow, it was only the less important guys who got caught. Never a capo or jefe.

The state guys and the feds would display the drugs and guns captured in the bust, shake hands for the local news and say, "progress is being made." It was great for the media, while nothing really changed. Just a minor hiccup, chalked up by the syndicates as the cost of doing business.

So, Joe would just keep an eye on things. He kept records of the cars that showed up, some photos of who came and went. When he could, he would use his old Toyota sedan to follow some of the attendees and see where they went, tracking who was renting space to the gangsters. He had several thick files of information that he hoped, someday, would be useful to legitimate law enforcement who could help him cleanse the town.

In the meantime, he still had the day-to-day challenges of Las Puertas to deal with. On the weekends, he and Roberto would get the calls about drunks, fights, road wrecks and domestic incidents. When the syndicates were in town, Joe tried to have Chief Tony Flores of the police handle most of those calls, but they preferred cruising around town, rarely getting out of their squad cars.

§

Juarez, Mexico was a notorious border town. Rife with crime, it catered to gringos who would come for the cheap booze, drugs and the hookers. Locals saw the turistas as an opportunity to make extra cash. They hustled the gringos for whores, cheap bars, sex shows and of course, drugs. If a couple of cowboys got too drunk and were staggering around the streets or passed out on the sidewalk, they could be sure they would come to without their wallets and often without their boots. If you didn't stay vigilant, you'd be heading home without any ID and no money.

One cantina, the Kentucky Club, was home to the Juarez cartel. There, at the back table, Felix Carillo Fuentes or "El Mictlan," a nickname after the Aztec God of Death Mictlantecuhtli, could be found with several of his lieutenants nearby. He was on the phone.

"We will see you Sabado. Cesar knows and says he will be ready."

One the other end of the line, in Denver, Vincenzo Stefanelli, was silent for a moment. He turned to his brother, Carlito, who was listening on the extension. He nodded.

"Okay. We'll see you there. I got a new boy...he can beat the shit out of anybody you can put in the ring. Bring plenty of dough, you know, dinero. I plan to clean you out."

Felix laughed "Don't be so sure, my friend. I might have a surprise for you. Don't show up with empty pockets." He hung up.

Felix turned to his second in command, Ismael "El Martillo" Escoveda.

"That new boy, he better be good'"

Ismael smiled at his boss, "I've seen him fight. The wop bastards will be going home linguee. Many kilos lighter." He got up and gestured to Felix to follow him.

They walked out the back door of the cantina into the alley. Felix's lieutenants followed, hands on their weapons. A tall, heavy set rough looking man was leaning against Ismael's Cadillac. He was a brute. Six four, two hundred eighty pounds, all muscle.

Ismael scowled at him. "Tomas, if you scratched my car, I'll shoot you in the ass."

Tomas 'Tigre Negro' Mondragon casually stood up and looked over the car to make sure there were no scratches. He knew he was favored because of his ability to fight and his ruthlessness as an enforcer, but he wasn't going to take any chances. "Tranquillo, Jefe. See...No problem. No scratches." He knew El Martillo has killed men for less, but he was El Tigre Negro. He was a killer too.

Felix, 'El Mictlan,' walked up to Tomas. He looked him up and down.

He walked around him and felt his biceps. Suddenly he struck Tomas very hard in the stomach, then again in the chest. Tomas, the blood rising in his neck, almost raised his fist to return the blow. The bodyguards put their hands on their weapons. Tomas caught himself. This was Felix. The big boss. He relaxed, trying to hide his fury. He was not ready to die today.

"Looks like you can take a hit, Tomas. Save that anger. You'll need it this weekend." Felix patted him on the back. He turned to Ismael. "Let him know I'm betting big on him. I want to show those wops that even our lowest dogs are not to be fucked with." El Mictlan and his crew went back into the cantina. Tigre Negro burned. He was no dog.

Ismael, El Martillo, turned to Tomas. "Don't worry Tigre. You're moving up in the world. I've got you in the big fight. The only thing you need to see is red." He laughed, "The Italiano's boy won't last five minutes."

Tomas looked El Martillo in the eyes. "I'll kill that wop maricon."

"Good boy. Be here Saturday morning. It's a long ride to Las Puertas.

§

Back in Denver, Vincenzo and Carlito were looking forward to Saturday. They were bringing in plenty of cash from New Mexico. Chicago and New York were happy. The local punks were making their quotas in the outlying towns. One or two tried to skim but the Stefanelli's had eyes and ears everywhere. The small-town capos knew they were being watched but every once in a while one of them figured he deserved a larger share of the take. Thought he could get away with it. But the syndicate's head men in Albuquerque were blood, family. They had people planted everywhere and the greedy capos disappeared in the barren desert countryside, never to be seen again. Their replacements were always better behaved.

The Las Puertas meetings had a strict protocol. Everyone arrived by around 6:00PM. Each group had maybe ten or twelve people. The bosses, the lieutenants, the fighters and a few extra armed guards. Cesar would serve a big dinner, even the guards outside got a good meal. After an hour or so of "niceties," they would do their business.

The Cartels and the Syndicates would negotiate.

The Stefanellis got a percentage of the drug money in exchange for new outlets of product for the cartels. Often, the cartels brought product with them to be transported to Denver, and then around the country. This was balanced against the payments to the syndicate.

The syndicates offered weapons, territory and other assets that gave the Juarez group advantages over competitors. The cartel smuggled young girls and boys from the campo, illegally trafficked into the states. There was always demand for new, fresh inventory.

It was an ugly, depraved, big money business. The negotiations involved millions of dollars as well as clarification of territory and authority. Occasionally, if there was disagreement, tempers flared. Neither side could appear to back down.

When this happened, Cesar would bring over more booze and snacks. He would put on music and suggest that everyone take a break. The surprising thing is that both groups respected Cesar as the host. They got up from the main table and separated into small, mixed groups. The Stefanellis offered Cuban cigars and Felix brought boxes of Mexican Chocolate and sweets. When everyone calmed down, they returned to the big table and usually found common ground.

When negotiations were over, the Stefanellis and Felix and Ismael would get into one of the cars, either the Italian's or the Mexican's, and go for a tour of the various warehouses and safe houses around town. Checking on content, security. It was usually dark by then, so they were less conspicuous. The driver and one bodyguard, the capos and the bosses. They would cruise around for a while, making the rounds, and then return to the Ringside for the night's entertainment.

§

Johnny Abeyta was a star at the University of New Mexico. He graduated from West Las Puertas High School and started at the University the following Fall. Pete and his father went with him and made sure he got into the boxing club. Johnny was thrilled to be on the verge of a real boxing career. He trained hard. In the engineering school, he worked hard on his studies and kept his grades up. The coach, Bill Allen, arranged for the gym to open early. The other boys in the club looked forward to early training rounds with Johnny and became very competitive. Unfortunately, there was no athletic scholarship for boxing at the school, but that wasn't a problem. Juan Carlos Sr. could afford tuition and room and board. The potential of having a great athlete in the family was a matter of personal pride for him.

By Spring, the coach there figured Johnny was ready for Golden

Gloves competition in June down in Belen. Bill had set up several "box off" bouts and had Johnny in line to participate in the New Mexico-Colorado regional competition the coming weekend. This would be his first major fight and Johnny was eager to try out his skills against new opponents.

These bouts were highly regulated. Good, clean fights carefully refereed with the well-being of the fighters in mind.

Saturday came around and Bill Allen, Pete and Juan Carlos Sr. were all there at the FIT-NHB Fight Gym in Albuquerque. Johnny would face off against Matthew Torres, an older, up and coming fighter who had garnered a reputation in the state, undefeated in the amateur circuit. Even though Johnny had not competed on the state level, his reputation at the university had stirred up some interest in the boxing community. They were featured on the fight card as the premier bout of the day.

Johnny and his "entourage" waited nervously in the changing rooms. They were the last fight of the afternoon and when the time came Pete, Bill and Johnny went to their corner. Juan Carlos Sr. took his seat at ringside.

The bell rang and the fight began. The first round went slowly, each fighter testing the other, checking their reach, dodging blows, feeling each other out.

Round two was much more intense. Matthew was caught off guard by Johnny's speed. He had to adjust to the kid's footwork and found that he couldn't land the rights or uppercuts that had served him well in the past. Johnny was quicker. He easily landed blows on Matthew, body blows, head, jaw. He was holding back but realized that there were more openings than he expected and prepared to wrap things up in the next round. Just as the second round was almost over, Johnny briefly let his guard down trying to land a good solid blow to Matthew's head. Matt dodged him and landed a powerful right hook to Johnny's jaw. Johnny staggered back. He had never been hit that hard before. His vision blurred, black spots spun before his eyes, he lost his footing and fell backwards against the ropes. Matthew took advantage and began some body work on Johnny, keeping him on the ropes. The bell rang.

Johnny managed to get to his corner. Bill and Pete quickly jumped into the ring and started to work on Johnny.

"How you doing Johnny?" Pete asked. "Lean your head back, let me wipe you down."

"Drink this," Bill said, giving Johnny some water. "You're okay. No bleeding. Can you see all right?"

Johnny took a couple of deep breaths. He shook his head, trying to clear the cobwebs. "I guess I deserved that." He managed to smile.

Seeing he was pulling himself back together, Bill frowned. "You got greedy. You tried to show him up. You can beat this guy but only if you stay smart. If he shows you an opening, it's to sucker you, just like he did. Act like you're going for it then surprise him. You can do it kid. Stay smart."

"Okay, okay! I'll remember. I'm okay."

"Good" Pete looked him in the eye. "Go get this guy, he's all yours. Just don't be the sucker."

The bell rang and Bill and Pete climbed out of the ring.

Johnny jumped up. He was fired up. He never wanted to be tricked like that again.

The round started with the two men circling each other. Matthew felt he could fool Johnny again. He feinted a couple of blows and then moved in. Pretending again to show an opening for a blow to the head, he expected Johnny to go for it. Johnny faked a left to Matt's head then landed a powerful hit to the body. Matthew was on the wrong foot and staggered backwards, losing his balance. His gloves dropped down and Johnny surged forward, threw a corkscrew and then an uppercut. Matthew was bleeding. Johnny landed a solid blow to Matt's head. He tried to protect himself, but Johnny landed several body blows. Matthew went down. There was a count, and he was out.

Johnny Abeyta won his first major fight. The crowd went wild.

Juan Carlos Sr. jumped up and climbed into the ring with Pete and Bill. The referee held Johnny's arm up in the air. "The winner, Johnny Abeyta!" He was on his way to the Golden Gloves and, with any luck, the Olympics of his dreams.

§

Joe Lujan was parked by Perea's Auto repair just above Chavez Street so he could get a good view of The Ringside building. It was Saturday and Cesar had told him to keep everybody clear. The Jefe's were coming to town.

He was in his old Toyota and bareheaded, trying to be inconspicuous. It was almost four and the parking lot was empty. At a little after six, several dark colored cars coming from the north, turned in from Grand Avenue. There were two Lincoln sedans, a big Cadillac and two black

Chevy Suburbans. They lined up in front of the bar and shut off their engines. Nobody got out.

After about ten or fifteen minutes, six brightly colored vehicles came up from the south. Two Jeep Sahara's, a couple of big, brightly colored custom paint job Ford Pickups, a red Dodge Charger, and a sparkling Silver Corvette. There was nothing inconspicuous about these guys. They owned the road all the way to Mexico and knew that nobody would give them any trouble. They pulled into the Ringside's parking lot on the side of the building, where they had a good view of the syndicate's cars.

El Martillo and El Mictlan got out of the Corvette. Vincenzo and Carlito got out of the Cadillac. They walked over to each other and shook hands.

"I hope you had a pleasant journey," El Martillo asked. "As always, welcome to Nuevo Mexico." The tone of his voice seemed to indicate that this was his territory. More Mexican than United States.

Vincenzo Stefanelli glared at Ismael, then his face softened. "Welcome to our country. We have been looking forward to your visit."

"Shall we go inside, my friends. It is too hot today for you to be standing out here in the sun," Felix said sarcastically. "This is not the cool, high mountains of Colorado."

Carlito laughed. "This is the high desert, not like the valley of the Rio Grande. Don't let the altitude slow you down." Signaling to his men, they turned and walked to the door where Cesar was waiting to welcome them.

As the bosses headed toward the bar, the men from both sides started to get out of the cars.

The Italians were in suits, the bulges of their weapons visible.

The Mexicans carried their pistols in holsters. Several of each group followed their leaders into the bar. The rest stayed outside by the cars, keeping a close watch on one another.

Joe watched the formalities from his car. He had a camera with a telescopic lens and shot as many photos as possible, trying to get as many of the license numbers and faces he could. The men outside were milling around. Two of them were bigger, bulkier than the rest. One was squeezed into a suit, smoking cigarettes and joking with the Colorado group. The other was tall, broad shouldered and muscular. He wore a tight T-Shirt, blue jeans and cowboy boots. He was sitting on the hood of one of the Mexican's pick-up trucks. Sullen and alone.

Once the jefes went inside, he knew there wouldn't be anything to see for a couple of hours. He started his car and drove back to his office.

He got there at about six-thirty and Roberto was already there when he walked in. Gabby was making some fresh coffee. She knew that they had a long night ahead of them. She had also made up some fresh carnitas and bean burritos at home so they could keep their strength up.

"Our honored guests are in town," His voice was both angry and resigned. "I wish to hell we could just take them all down."

Roberto knew this was a particular frustration for his boss. "Maybe come election time we'll get a new Attorney General in this state with huevos." He paused. "Probably not."

"What about the Feds? Do they know they're here this weekend?" Gabby asked.

"Oh Gabby, unless there's some major merchandise moving through, they're just not interested." He took a cup of coffee. "If they were serious about busting these guys, they would have gotten them at the border. The Feds need to have something to put on the news. For now, customs just pretend to see them as some rich folks coming up for a visit. The boys from Denver are too smart to let anything leak about a meeting. The Feds may know about these meetings, but they're too busy glory hunting to bother with what goes on in a little town in New Mexico."

Joe walked over to the window and looked out onto Bridge Street. "We'll keep an eye on them. Keep gathering info. Maybe we'll catch a break." He turned and smiled at Roberto and Gabby. "In the meantime, we'll just take care of our own over the weekend."

§

August came on fast. The Golden Gloves National Championship was coming up later that year, and Johnny Abeyta was ready. Back in June he had the opportunity to demonstrate that he was going to be the smart boxer. He never wanted to experience anything like the hit Matt gave him back in March.

He kept a heavy schedule of training and competitive bouts. He was in the NMUSA Tournament in Hobbs and the Oso Boxeo tournament in Farmington. His reputation grew and when he entered the Colorado/New Mexico Regional Golden Gloves Open Division Tournament in Loveland, Colorado he felt he was on his way to the national championships.

He was undefeated. When in his bouts, which usually ran the full three rounds, he was closely watched by his trainers, Bill Allen and Pete Moreno. They gave him the insight and the value of their experience to make him a top-notch fighter. But in the ring, he followed his own instincts. He had an innate facility to work out his opponent's abilities in the first round. In the second round he allowed the other fighter to almost land a solid jab or uppercut. He even faked being affected by the blow, giving the other guy a sense of domination. But in the third round, Johnny could avoid punches, confuse with his footwork, and land a series of withering blows to the head and body where the judges could not but see that he dominated the fight, even if there was no knockdown.

Loveland was going to be his chance to show the Olympic Committee that he was ready for the next summer's event and would deserve a spot at the training facility in Colorado Springs.

Johnny's father, Juan Carlos Sr. was at every fight. He posted pictures and certificates from his son's victories on the wall behind the counter in the hardware store. His wife Rosa helped in the store to cover while Juan Carlos was away following Johnny's circuit all over New Mexico and Colorado. He even went with Johnny to a couple of extra league fights in Texas. For those who followed amateur boxing, Johnny Abeyta was a name that carried the hope of a champion from a little town in one of the poorest counties in the USA.

Word was out.

§

Juan Carlos Sr. knew going on the road with Johnny was a problem for the store. Rosa could carry it for a day or two, but his customers wanted to see him. She would call him when he was out of town, asking him "Paul Trujillo needs something to patch his concrete foundation. I told him I'd call him this evening so he could pick it up tomorrow." Or "Mrs. Castillo has red ants in her kitchen. The stuff you gave her last year wasn't stopping them. What should I tell her?"

Juan Carlos tried to help, but he felt the pressure to return. It was too much to ask of Rosa. But he could not give up being there for Johnny. Even though he saw the sales volume was slowing down. The extra costs of travel expenses, lodging and entry fees were another new expense. When they could, Rosa would go to watch her son fight, even if it meant closing the store for a couple of days.

In late June, with the big fights fast approaching, he was in the store. Business was slower than usual.

A dark grey Lincoln with Colorado plates pulled up in front. A big man in a dark grey suit got out of the back. The driver stayed in the car.

He entered the store and walked up to the counter and smiled at Juan Carlos.

"Are you Juan Carlos Abeyta?" he asked.

"Seguro, That's me. What can I do for you?"

"I understand you own that little warehouse on Commerce Street. The one by the lumber kiln and the old roundhouse. Is that right?"

Juan Carlos was intrigued. "Sure, that's mine. It's empty right now. Are you interested?"

"What kind of rent are you asking. My associates and I are interested." The man looked around the store. "I like your place. You've got a pretty extensive inventory for an independent shop."

There was something about the man that made Juan Carlos uncomfortable. He was acting like the deal was already done.

"Yeah, I try to have everything someone might need." He straightened up. Getting back to business he asked "What is your intended use of the warehouse? I like to know what's going on my properties."

"Imported good. Terracotta pots, decorative lawn ornaments...stuff like that." The man smiled, a kind of smile that hid his true intentions. "There's a real demand. Stuff that we could even give you a good deal on if you want to stock some of it here. Increase your margin. Most of it is from Mexico. Should appeal to the local clientele."

Juan Carlos wasn't a fool. "I'd like some references. Some from other landlords, if you have them."

"No problem. We have warehouses in Denver, the Springs. Even in Raton and Albuquerque. We do a very large volume throughout this region. Nationally too. Stuff moves from warehouse to warehouse, depending on demand. We like the I-25 corridor because there's access to the East West Interstates and the railroads. Las Puertas is in a sweet spot for us. So..." he paused, "What's the rent?"

The prospect of extra money was appealing. Juan Carlos was cagey. "Why don't you make me an offer?"

§

At the Ringside, the Syndicate and the Cartel finished their negotiations. There were no major changes in operations, so it was time for the Jefes to make their tour around town. It was dusk, about eight-thirty and the Stefanellis were taking Felix and Ismeal around town for the tour of the syndicate's stash warehouses and safe houses used for human trafficking.

Carlito was driving. "We're looking to get a couple more warehouses here soon. The crap we use for cover takes up a lot of room but keeps the inventory looking legal."

They pulled up to a warehouse at the north end of town. All four got out and Carlito unlocked the door. He turned on the lights and they could see the stacks of crates and open boxes of ceramic sun wall hangings, garden burros and statues of sleeping Mexican peasants with their sombreros pulled down over the eyes.

Working their way around some of the crates toward the back, Carlito grabbed a crowbar and pried open one of the boxes.

"We've got a gift for you, Felix."

He removed the top and inside were twenty or so shiny, oiled semi-automatic assault rifles. "Clean as a whistle. Brand new. No serial numbers. Modified to be fully automatic." He took one out and handed it to Felix. "This should help keep your competition under control."

Felix took the gun. Hefted it and checked the action. "Nice. Very nice, this is a wonderful gift." He handed the gun to Ismeal, who also looked it over. He smiled at the Stefanellis.

"It is a pleasure working with you, Vincenzo. A real pleasure." He put the rifle back in the crate. "I will have my men come and get them tomorrow morning."

Vincenzo laughed. "Tell them not to forget the other crates. Twenty more and plenty of ammo." Gesturing at the additional boxes.

"You are most kind." Felix shook their hands. Ismael did as well.

"Come. Now we have surprise for you," Ismael said. "Let's go to the safehouse on Valencia."

They walked out into the cool evening. Carlito locked the warehouse and they got into the car. Vincenzo and Felix in the back. Carlito driving with Ismeal in the passenger seat.

What they didn't know was that Joe Lujan was watching them from behind an abandoned house down the street. He was in the Toyota and he followed the Cadillac as they headed back into town, toward west Las

Puertas and around the plaza. They headed up toward the edge of town where Valencia Street ended. and stopped in front of an older house.

Joe watched as they all got out and knocked on the door. A woman answered and Joe could see that she was very deferential to the four men. They went inside.

"This is Maria. She takes care of this place" Felix gestured toward the woman. "Take us to them."

Obediently, the woman led them down the hall to a door. She took out her keys and unlocked it. Turning on the lights, they descended into the cellar. It was dug out of the clay and had been fitted with anterooms with dirt walls sealed with doors of steel bars.

Ismael turned on the string of bare lightbulbs that lit up the rows of cells, three on each side.

Inside the cells he gestured to the young girls and boys, most of them between their early teens or twenties. "Some fresh product for your 'burdeles.'"

Vincenzo and Carlito walked along the cells. Looking in at the frightened and sad children, shielding their eyes from the brightness of the lights. "This is just what we needed to brighten up our 'social clubs.'" Turning to Felix and Ismael, "You are very generous. I think we will have a very fair exchange. And you will have your regular shipment here by midnight?"

Felix smiled, "You will see we have anticipated your generosity. By an extra twenty kilos."

They headed back upstairs. Maria led them upstairs and turned off the lights, leaving the human cargo in total darkness. She locked the door behind her. "Senores, I could use some cash for food. We don't want to lose any of them."

Vincenzo patted Maria's arm. "Don't worry. We'll have them out of here by tomorrow."

Joe watched as they all came out and climbed back into the Cadillac. They headed back to the Ringside for the night's festivities and entertainment. He saw the Cadillac turn back toward town. His blood boiled at the thought of what went on in that house. Furious and frustrated, he drove carefully back to the office.

"I must do something about this." He turned over his options in his mind. "I will find a way. Así que ayúdame dios."

§

That night, at the Ringside, Cesar had the boxing ring in place on the dance floor. He had set up a side table as a buffet. Antipasto, pasta dishes, Osso Bucco, tiramisu and cannollis for the Denver crowd. Roast goat, pollo, mole, enchiladas, tortilla, flan, churros and sopapillas for the cartels.

He had hired a band with a singer out of Albuquerque that could play both Sinatra and Juan Gabriel.

He even had a couple of two-bit strippers to be ring girls who would parade naked between rounds.

And of course, plenty of red wine, sambuca, tequila and mescal.

Both groups made sure Cesar had plenty of cash to cover the costs, plus a generous gratuity for the host.

When the Jefe's returned the party started. All the men, including the drivers and the bodyguards were invited in. They would take shifts outside standing guard, but when the big fight started, everybody would be either inside or at the door, watching the action.

Tomas "Tigre Negro" Mondragon was ready. He had met his counterpart, the bulky Italian named Enzo "Gigante" Giordano.

The "Gigante" was also an enforcer, able to break a man's arm over his knee. He was the man the Stefanellis' used to make sure nobody skimmed from the takings or missed a protection payment, among other things. He had been working for them for ten years or so and had never gotten a scratch on him. He weighed about two-seventy but was only about six feet tall.

"Tigre Negro" weighed about the same but was about six inches taller. He was a vicious fighter, proven useful in brawls at the cartel's cantinas and battles with the police and the other gangs. Felix had chosen him to fight that night.

Ismeal knew the Italians wanted to show they were the big dogs, but he felt confident that nobody the Italians could bring would stand a chance against the black bull. When Tomas got mad, he was unstoppable, muy peligroso, like a Pacific hurricane.

By about midnight, everyone was ready for the fight. There was no referee. It was bare knuckles, anything goes. The winner was the last man able to stand. Death was a distinct possibility.

One of the strippers paraded around the ring announcing round one. The men cheered and threw money at her. She clumsily ran around picking up the cash.

Vincenzo and Felix rang the bell Cesar had placed where they were sitting and the fight started.

Tigre charged Enzo and met a brick wall. The man hardly moved. The Italian wrapped his arms around Tomas and started to squeeze. Tomas pummeled Gigante around the head and neck, but the Italian held on tightly. He would squeeze Tomas until he could hear the ribs crack.

But Tomas continued beating Enzo around the head and when he felt his grip lessen slightly, he threw himself backwards, dragging Enzo to the ground and rolling over so he was on top.

Enzo lost his grip. This was the opportunity Tigre was waiting for. He spun out of Enzo's grip and grabbed his arm twisting it behind the Italian's back. He put his knee in the middle of Enzo's back and grabbed him around the neck, both holding his arm and pulling back on his head.

Enzo managed to get to his knees and rose up like tsunami, lifting Tomas up off the ground and walking them both backwards to the corner post, ramming Tomas into the post that gave way under the weight of the two men. The spilled out of the ring, knocking over two tables, and causing the spectators to scramble.

The fall separated them, Tomas losing his hold, Enzo freeing his neck and arm.

Felix rang the bell. "Get back in the ring, we don't want to bust up Cesar's place. Get back in the ring."

The two men glared at each other. Tomas got up and started to climb back in the ring.

The other stripper started to walk around announcing round two but as soon as Tomas stepped in the ring, Enzo charged at him and ran a shoulder into the small of his back. Tomas stumbled forward and Enzo, leaped at him, hoping to pin him to ground with his weight and beat him on the back of his head until he was either unconscious or dead.

But Tomas didn't go down. He spun around and grabbed Enzo by the neck. "You wop bastard. I'll kill you." He lifted Enzo up off his feet. "Vete a la mierda, pedazo de mierda." He lifted Enzo higher off the ground, by the neck. Enzo struggled, landing blow after blow on Tomas' torso, trying to kick him in the balls, but Tomas, "Tigre Negro" was immovable, solid like the Árbol del Tule Santa María del Tule in Oaxaca. The biggest tree in Mexico. And like a tree, he held Enzo by the neck until he went limp.

The fight was over.

The Italians were furious. Vincenzo turned to Felix. "Carlito will give you your winnings." He got up from the table. "Next time, Felix... Next time..."

The Italians followed Vincenzo out the door. They picked up Enzo, who was barely conscious and carried him out. Carlito put a gym bag on the table in front of Felix. He looked at him and then at Ismael. "Next time."

Felix smiled. "My pleasure, Señores. My pleasure. Until next time."

§

The Colorado/New Mexico Regional Golden Gloves Open Division Tournament in Loveland, Colorado was a big deal. Pete and Bill entered Johnny in the open division for men eighteen to thirty years old. The matches were fair, classified by weight and amateurs only. Johnny was about one hundred seventy pounds, a light heavyweight. He would have to defeat five opponents to win the championship.

Juan Carlos and Rosa had decided to close the store for the weekend. The generous amount of extra money from the rent for the little warehouse made Juan Carlos feel that he could comfortably go to his son's fights and even bring Rosa with him to a few. The Loveland event was on a Saturday, so the store only had to close one day.

Since the fights lasted only three, three-minute rounds, the action was fast. The light weights started early. Then middle weights and finally the heavy weights. Johnny's first bout was at three in the afternoon. He was fighting an older guy from Greeley, Colorado. The man was slow and didn't have any real strategy. He managed to land a couple of light blows on Johnny, but he was no match for the younger man's speed and intelligence. The bout was decided with Johnny as the clear winner, dominating his opponent.

The next bracket was an anglo guy from Hobbs, New Mexico. He was a brawler and tried to lure Johnny into a roughhouse, kind of like a bar fight. But there was no way that was going to happen. The guy was so obvious that Johnny managed to sidestep his every move and finally knock him to his knees by the middle of the third.

Third in line was about the same age as Johnny. He had some good moves and was very quick on his feet. Not as quick as Johnny. The fight went for the full three rounds, but the referee could tell that Johnny out maneuvered the kid, keeping from being hit hard while landing some solid body blows, uppercuts and hooks. The kid took the punches but Johnny scored many more points than him.

The semi finals were exciting. By now Juan Carlos and Rosa were standing for the entire fight. Johnny was proving to be the extraordinary athlete they had hoped for. He took on his opponent with greater confidence than ever. Blocking his punches, dancing around him and landing blow after blow. This time his adversary was a short but solid Jicarilla Apache from Dulce. He had strong footwork and was hard to get off balance. Fortunately, he had a short reach so except for three or four times, his powerful right and equally dangerous left never really connected. The few that did connect only reminded Johnny of the fight with Matthew and the strong memory allowed Johnny to shake off the effects of the blows and come back with speed and fury. Johnny won by only a few points in a referee's decision. But it was still a win.

Juan Carlos and Rosa came up to ringside for the finals. They embraced Johnny and said a prayer with him. The championship could mean a real opportunity for a place on the Olympic team. Representatives of the US Olympic Committee were there.

His final opponent was a competent, capable fighter. Paulo Bianco was from the tight knit Italian community in Denver and there were many of his friends and neighbors there to cheer him on. His uncle, Carlito Stefanelli, was there. He was a great supporter of his nephew and was confident he could take any Mexican with ease.

§

The crowd was excited to watch the finals. Bill and Pete were giving Johnny their final tips.

"This guy is no pushover. He made it to the finals just like you. From what I hear, he's had some top-notch trainers. His family has money, so they brought in some out-of-town talent for him to spar." Pete warned.

Johnny shook his head. "I'll figure him out. Don't worry."

Bill looked concerned. "He had no trouble reaching the finals. Most of his opponents were on their heels by the end of the second round. Two bouts were decided before the third round ended. He's got real upper body strength. Keep those lefts away from your head. And watch the body blows. He'll knock the wind out of you if he can."

"Okay! I'll watch him." Johnny was no fool. He knew that as he went up in the rankings, his opponents would get tougher and tougher. "I'll figure him out. Tranquilo."

Pete smiled at his boy. "I know you will, Johnny. We're going to the Olympics. Nobody's going to stop us."

The announcer stepped into the ring.

"Welcome everybody to the final light heavy weight open match of the Colorado/New Mexico Regional Golden Gloves."

The crowd roared their enthusiasm. Juan Carlos and Rosa were on the edge of their seats.

The announcer settled the crowd. "In the red corner, from Denver, Colorado at one hundred seventy-five pounds, Paulo Bianco!" A rousing cheer came up from the home state crowd. Bianco came out of his corner and circled the ring. He was tall, had long arms and powerful shoulders. He seemed very confident. Carlito Stefanelli knew his nephew was going to go on to the nationals. No question about it. He had watched the previous bouts and considered Johnny Abeyta a contender, but no match for Paulo.

"And in the blue corner, New Mexico's undefeated champion from Las Puertas, New Mexico at one hundred seventy pounds, Johnny Abeyta!"

Rosa and Juan Carlos Jumped up, shouting and clapping their hands. Other families and fans of the other New Mexican fighters also stood up, whistling and clapping. Their boys did not make it to the finals, but Johnny was still a hometown boy from their home state.

Carlito Stefanelli thought, "Las Puertas. Some coincidence." He looked over the crowd and spotted Juan Carlos and Rosa. Out of habit, he filed them away in his memory. His devious mind realizing that this could be useful sometime in the future.

The referee came out. The boys bumped gloves. "All right fellows. Keep it clean. We're here as athletes. We're here for the sport. Let's have a fair fight. You're going for the Golden Gloves!" They bumped gloves again and went back to their corners.

Bill and Pete gave Johnny some water, patted him on the back and climbed out of the ring. "Go get him, Champ," Pete said.

The bell rang.

Paulo came charging out of his corner. Johnny watched him as he came toward him. It looked like Paulo wanted to make short work of this kid.

Paulo tried to land a strong jab with his long reach. Johnny countered with a check hook, stepping back and causing Paulo to momentarily lose his balance. He looked surprised.

With Paulo unsteady, Johnny threw a bolo, a hook and an uppercut. Paulo went down. Caught cold by this agile kid.

At ringside, Carlito couldn't believe it. He screamed at Paulo. "Get up you pansy. What the Hell are you doing. Get the Hell up and finish this guy!"

Paulo was shaken. Down in the first round. This had never happened to him before. The ref was counting. He got up. His face red with anger and embarrassment.

The ref checked him out and let the fight continue.

Johnny was cautious. Paulo was mad, so Johnny knew he could expect him to be careless, driven by emotion.

Paulo came at Johnny with a vengeance. But Johnny had brains, he allowed Paulo to get close. He rolled with the punches, played possum, letting Paulo think he was landing his blows, waiting for another opening. As Johnny seemed to be backing up to the ropes, Paulo started getting overconfident. "I'll show this spic bastard that Paulo Bianco doesn't go down easy."

Just as Paulo was about to lay a haymaker, Johnny quickly stepped aside. Paulo lost his balance again and ended up on the ropes. Johnny swooped in and landed several heavy body blows and as Paulo dropped his guard to protect his middle, Johnny landed a strong uppercut and a fast corkscrew and a powerful left hook.

Paulo was down again, a cut over his left eye, dizzy and shaken. The ref started counting. "..., nine, ten. You're out! The winner, Johnny Abeyta in the first round."

The New Mexico crowd went wild. Juan Carlos and Rosa climbed into the ring to hug their son. The reps from the Olympic committee could be seen conferring with each other. Johnny was on his way to the Olympics.

Carlito stood at the back of the crowd. Furious, with a look in his eyes that could kill. This was not over.

§

Word spread around Las Puertas. They had a Golden Gloves champion and a contender for the Olympics in town. People would come into the store to shake his hand. The town reveled in the fact that they had a world class athlete of their own.

Joe Lujan stopped at Juan Carlos' store to congratulate him. He knew the family well and this victory restored his faith in his town. He was even more inspired to make Las Puertas a safe place to live.

The last meeting of the syndicate and the cartels was over, and it would be a couple of months before the next one would take place. Joe knew he had to find a way to stop Las Puertas from being a safe haven for these criminals.

Over the past few years, he had gotten a good handle on the location of the various warehouses and safe houses the cartels and syndicates were using. The warehouses were all down by the tracks along commerce street. The safehouses were scattered around town but most were on the outskirts, in the less populated neighborhoods that drew less attention from the locals.

He compiled a thick file of the properties, dates they were rented and accessed, the landlords and which criminals used which buildings. He also had photos, records of dates of the meetings and the identities of the individuals who came to town.

One Monday morning he had all his information packed in two bulging bankers' boxes. He had asked Gabby to make copies of everything to take with him and stash the originals in a safe deposit box in the bank.

"I'm going to Denver. I've set up a meeting with the fed's organized crime unit to present my case to them and that we need their help." He told Gabby and Roberto. "Roberto, I should be back tomorrow. You and Gabby hold down the fort."

"No problem, chief. We can cover while you're gone." Roberto hesitated, "Any chance they'll take you seriously this time? Bypassing the State could make them reluctant to help."

"No sé." Joe looked resigned. "I've got to give it a shot. These Cabróns need to be stopped…or at least hurt. I want them out of Las Puertas. If they leave, it becomes somebody else's problem. And at least we tried."

He got up to go. Gabby had packed him a lunch. It was about six or seven hours to Denver. He'd stay the night, meet with the Feds the next day and head home that afternoon.

"Hasta mañana."

§

Carlito Stefanelli was furious. He lashed into his nephew. "How the Hell did that happen. What's the matter with you? You should have outclassed that stinking spic and had *him* out in the first round, not you." He paced back and forth in his sister's living room. Paulo was shrinking away from him. Looking very small in the big armchair.

"I'm sorry, Zio." He tried to make excuses. "The kid was fast. I don't know what happened." He was red-faced.

"I'm not going to let some lousy Mexican take your place. You're the better fighter." He paced back and forth. "I've checked the rules. You were runner-up. If something were to happen to this Abeyta guy, you're next in line for the nationals. Then those Olympic fags will have to give you a shot."

"You can do that? You can fix it?"

"Listen, nipote. You keep training. I'll get you into the nationals and make sure that chicano kid's career is over."

Carlito stormed out and got into his limo. "Vincenzo's. Let's go." Muttering under his breath, "I'm tired of losing to these wetbacks."

§

The same dark grey Lincoln with Colorado plates pulled up in front of Juan Carlos' store. The same big man in a dark grey suit got out of the back. The driver stayed in the car. His name was Giovanni Ricci and he was a lieutenant for the Stefanellis. Rosa was at the counter and Juan Carlos was in the back, taking inventory.

"Can I help you?" asked Rosa.

"You must be Rosa. Juan Carlos told me a lot about you, and your boy Juan Carlos Jr., Johnny the boxer."

Rosa had never seen the man before. She was surprised that he was talking like he knew them or knew a great deal about them. "Yes. I'm Rosa. How can I help you?"

Giovanni looked around the store. "You know, I am very impressed with the inventory you carry here. He walked over to the display of ceramic and metal lawn and garden displays by the door. "I noticed you have a lot of this stuff out front too. Is it selling well?"

Rosa started to feel uncomfortable. Giovanni noticed her reaction. "Don't worry Rosa. I'm the wholesaler for those things. I'm surprised Juan Carlos never mentioned me."

"He hasn't told me where he got the stuff. He said he had a new wholesaler. He never mentioned who." She paused, "I thought it was one of our regular suppliers." She felt a little better. "I'll go get him. Be right back."

"Sure, sure. No problem. I'll just take a look around. Might be able to give you a better deal on some of your other items." He walked casually into the aisles. Checking the merchandise.

Rosa found Juan Carlos in the back. He looked up when she came in, noticing the concerned look on her face.

"What's the matter, Rosa?"

"Some big guy is out front. Says he's one of your wholesalers. Were you expecting anybody today?"

"No, I don't think so." He wiped his hands on his apron. "I'll go see what he wants." Hesitating, "I'll cover the store. Can you get a count of the Rust-Oleum spray paint? We've got some colors we're getting low on."

"Of course, Juan. Let me know if you need me."

Juan Carlos went to the front of the store. The big man was behind the counter, looking over the sales receipts.

"Hello Giovanni. I didn't expect to see you until next year. What's going on?"

Giovanni leaned on the counter. "Are you making out all right on the product. Enjoying that nice profit margin?"

"Sure. It's been very helpful. The generous rent too." He was curious what this guy wanted. The deal had been they get free rein of the warehouse, no questions asked. The rent had been paid for the entire year. Juan Carlos could go and get product from the warehouse. He just had to log in what he took in the ledger in the little warehouse office. There were areas where he was told he could not enter. He stuck by deal and never questioned what was in the restricted area.

"I'm glad to hear that." Giovanni smiled that dominating, dangerous smile. "I'm sure you want to keep things running smoothly. Right?" He turned to Juan Carlos.

"Of course." Juan Carlos was confused. "Is there a problem?"

"No. No problem." Giovanni walked out from behind the counter and over to the window. He gestured toward his driver who got out of the car and came into the store. Thin, and smartly dressed, he stood by the door, arms crossed. "This is my associate, Luca."

"Hello." Juan Carlos was getting worried.

Rosa, who had been in the back, was now standing in the doorway. Listening.

Giovanni walked back to the counter, standing across from Juan Carlos.

"Some business associates of mine are coming to Las Puertas to look over the warehouse. We usually have a gathering after business is done. Dinner, some dancing, just a nice quiet social gathering." Looking Juan Carlos in the eye. "This time we were thinking of having an exhibition bout as the entertainment. Boxing. You know the place? The Ringside?"

"I know the place. It's not very nice. I think El Alto would be better. Music and dancing. I don't think they could accommodate a prize fight." Juan Carlos knew about the Ringside's reputation. He disliked Cesar. He was not exactly an upstanding member of the Las Puertas business community.

"Maybe not, but it's one place where we could have that boxing match." Giovanni paused. "I'd like your boy, Johnny, to be our featured attraction."

Rosa came running out of the back room. "Never! Never! Our boy is an amateur. He couldn't participate in a paid match. It would ruin his chance to be in the Golden Gloves championship. Maybe even get disqualified from the Olympics team. No! No! Never!" She turned to Juan Carlos. "Tell him, Juan. Never!"

Giovanni was very calm. "Señora Abeyta. I wouldn't think of interfering with Johnny's amateur status. Nobody's getting paid. His opponent would be an amateur as well. It would be strictly an exhibition. A pure sporting event." Turning to Juan Carlos, "Your participation would be a great benefit to your business. We would be happy to increase your discounts on a wider range of product. And you would become a regional attraction. You know how people are. They would want to patronize the store that was the origin of a great champion like Johnny." He gestured to Luca who opened the door for Giovanni. As he left, the big man turned back to Juan Carlos and Rosa. "The meeting is in two weeks. Shouldn't interfere with Johnny's training schedule. Think it over."

Giovanni walked out of the store. Luca winked at the Abeytas, standing together behind the counter. He left, the door closed behind him and opened the rear car door for Giovanni. He walked around to the driver's door, waved and winked again at the Abeytas, got in and they drove off.

Rosa and Juan Carlos remained standing behind the counter. Confused and worried.

§

As Joe Lujan headed for the interstate, he did not have high hopes for any help from the Feds. He knew they were more interested in operations at the border or in the big cities where a successful bust got more media coverage. He figured they had no idea or very little interest about the effects organized crime had on small towns.

But he figured he had to give it a try. Nothing to lose but the cost of gas, a motel room and some of his time. As he got to the on ramp past Pino's Truck Stop he took a sip of coffee and settled in for the long empty stretch of road between Las Puertas and Raton. About one hundred miles.

He was just getting to the Watrous exit when he saw a dark gray Lincoln sedan heading back to Las Puertas in the southbound lanes. Joe recognized it as one of the cars he would see at the Ringside gatherings. He hadn't heard any chatter about a meeting and thought the car could be heading down to Albuquerque.

He was only about twenty miles outside of town and figured he wouldn't lose much time by following the suspicious vehicle and see if it just passed through town, on its way elsewhere.

He pulled off at Watrous and got back on the highway, heading south. He sped up to about ninety-five until he could see the limo ahead. Slowing down, he held back hoping the driver hadn't seen him.

The Lincoln got off at the Grand Avenue exit and then turned right on Mills.

"Where are these guys going." Joe asked himself.

When they got to the corner of Hot Springs they pulled off, parking in front of the Abeyta's hardware store. Joe pulled around behind the NAPA Autoparts and shut off his engine. He had his camera and used the telephoto lens to get a close look. He watched as the Big Man, one of the Denver syndicates regulars at the meeting, got out and walked into the Abeyta's. After about ten minutes, the driver, another familiar face, got out of the car and went into the store.

A short time later, both men came out of the store. The Big Man got into the back. The driver paused, looking back into the store, then he got in the car and they drove off, heading back the way they came. Joe followed them until he saw them get back on the highway, north toward Denver.

Curious, Joe pulled into the parking lot of Pino's and shut off the engine. He took a sip of coffee and pondered why the gangsters' only business that day was to see the Abeytas.

"What the Hell. I'll go talk to Juan Carlos." He pulled out of the lot and headed back into town.

§

"Who are those men?" Rosa demanded. "What are they talking about? Why do they know about Johnny?" She paced around the store. "What are you not telling me?"

Juan Carlos was still stunned. "Rosa...Those men, I rented them the small warehouse on Commerce. They were very generous. It seemed like a great opportunity for some extra cash to help Johnny and let us travel with him to his fights."

"What about these discounts and inventory? Are they one of our suppliers too?" She crossed her arms. Juan Carlos knew he had to tell her the truth.

"All this new product, the lawn decorations, the ceramics...we get it for nothing. Selling it is pure profit." He shrugged. "I thought I wouldn't see them again for another year. They paid the full year's rent in advance. I just had to be discreet about their other stuff and their comings and goings."

"But they were just here. They acted like they owned the place." She walked to the window and started to sob, "And why do they want Johnny?"

"I don't know. I don't know." He walked up behind Rosa and put his hands on her shoulders.

Just then, Joe Lujan's truck pulled up to the store. He got out, seeing Juan and Rosa standing at the window. Rosa was crying.

Joe came in and Rosa and Juan looked at him, very upset. Worried looks on their faces.

"Hello Juan, Rosa. Is something wrong?"

Juan shook Joe's hand. "I don't know. I think you're just the person we need to talk to." He paused, "I think I've gotten us into some trouble."

Gabby was at the front desk, tidying up some paperwork when she heard the back door open. She got up just as Joe and Juan Carlos Abeyta came in from the back.

"Joe? What are you doing back so soon? What about Denver?" She looked at Juan. "Hello Juan. Is everything okay?"

Joe smiled at Gabby. "Everything is fine, Gabby. Juan is going to help us deal with those pendejo gangsters. I think we have an opportunity to get some solid evidence that we can use when we do go to the Feds. Call Roberto. Tell him to get back here so we can work out a plan."

Gabby gave Juan a cup of coffee. She called Roberto and luckily, he was just coming back and arrived after about five minutes.

They all gathered around Joe's desk. Juan Carlos had told Joe the whole situation about the warehouse, the inventory and about the proposal from Giovanni. He was concerned about involving Johnny and Rosa.

"You did the right thing, Juan," Joe said. "There's a reason they want Johnny involved and I'll try to find out why. Where do you stand with them?"

"The big guy, calls himself Giovanni, said I could think about it...But the meeting is in two weeks. I don't know what to tell Johnny. Or Bill and Pete." He was wringing his hands. "How do I know that they'll let Johnny do it? How do I know Johnny will even want to?"

Gabby poured him another cup of coffee.

Roberto had been listening carefully. "I think you need to get those guys up here. Be straight with them. They're good people. There's nothing Johnny wouldn't do to help you and Rosa." He stood up and put his hand on Juan's shoulder. "We'll figure this thing out, right Joe?"

"You're right, Roberto. Juan, call Johnny, Get him and Pete and Bill up here. I have a plan that could break you and Rosa free of these guys and help Las Puertas get rid of the gangsters for a while." He smiled at his team, at Juan. "This could get dangerous but at least we could give it a try and break loose of these bastards."

He filled in Juan about the activities of the Denver syndicate, about the relationship with the cartels, about the drugs, guns and human trafficking. He told him he wasn't alone in getting involved with the criminals. Many of the other Las Puertas landowners and businesses were caught in the same web.

This was the opportunity Joe had hoped for. His concern was that it was very risky. People could get hurt or killed. But if the plan that was formulating in his mind worked, Las Puertas could be cleaned up, at least from the outsiders whose tentacles were reaching all over town. Whose influence was growing like a cancer and had to be stopped.

§

Giovanni was in the Stefanelli's office of the penthouse apartment in downtown Denver. He had just returned from New Mexico and was waiting to report back to Carlito and Vincenzo.

Carlito came in and Giovanni got to his feet.

"Well, the spics are going to be there, right?" Carlito wasn't ready to hear anything else.

Giovanni hesitated. "I'm waiting to hear back. The old guy is going to talk to the kid. Shouldn't be a problem. They know they don't have any options, believe me."

"I want that kid out of the running. No matter what. I already made it clear to those chooches at the Golden Gloves that Paulo is the next in line for the nationals, should anything change with Abeyta. Had to make a donation to keep it on the up and up. It had better be worth it, capisce Giovanni?"

"Sure, sure Boss. It won't be a problem." Giovanni knew it had better happen. Carlito was on a real tear about this. "I'll stay on top of it."

The office phone rang. Giovanni answered it.

"Hello." He paused and nodded to Carlito. "Yeah? Still thinking? You talk to your kid yet?"

Carlito came over and stood over Giovanni.

"You don't have much time, Juan. Get the kid, get it settled." He slammed down the phone.

Carlito stared at Giovanni. "Well?"

"He's getting the kid to come home from Albuquerque. He wants to go over it with him and the coaches."

"Get ahold of Massimo in Albuquerque." He looked at Giovanni. "Let's put a fire under Juan...And I mean just that."

He stormed out of the office.

Giovanni called his head man in Albuquerque.

§

Johnny, Pete and Bill came up to Las Puertas that weekend. It was the soonest they could come without losing their jobs or interrupting the training schedule.

Joe Lujan joined them at the Abeyta home. It was late afternoon on Saturday and the mood was somber.

Juan explained to Johnny what was going on. The coaches seemed puzzled.

"Why do they want Johnny?" Pete asked. "They could get whoever they want out of Denver. And who's the other guy."

Joe leaned forward in his chair. "If these are the people who usually come to the Ringside, they've got a reason. And it can't be good for anyone, especially Johnny." He got up. "There's got to be a reason."

He turned to Pete and Bill. "Have you guys or Johnny had any run ins with the Italians in Denver? Any problems? Pete, I know you have a past in the fight scene. Anybody have it in for you?"

"Hey, Joe. Give me a break." Pete was taken aback, "I haven't had anything to do with the lowlife fight crowd in more than twenty years... And even back then, I stayed away from anything that had to do with the syndicates."

"Okay. Sorry." He turned to Bill. "Anything you can think of Bill?"

Bill looked thoughtful. "The only Italian connection I can think of recently is the regionals."

"What do you mean?"

"The kid Johnny beat for the finals. He was Italian. He had quite the crowd rooting for him. Most seemed like just plain folk. But there were one or two heavies there. A couple of big guys in expensive suits. I remember one of them real well. He came up to the Italian kid, Paulo, and laced into him. Gave him a real regaño. A real scolding. He was really pissed."

Joe grabbed his briefcase. He had some of the photos he had taken of the people at the meetings at the Ringside. He laid them out on the table. "Anyone of these look familiar?"

Bill looked them over. "This guy" he pushed Carlito's photo back toward Joe. "I think he was the kid's uncle. The kid called him 'Zio.'"

"That's Carlito Stefanelli. He and his brother Vincenzo are the Don's in Denver. If he's got a bug on it could mean real trouble." Joe rubbed his chin. His years of surveillance had finally paid off. He had a concrete connection to the extortionist policies of the syndicates. "Okay. This means we have to take this really seriously."

"I'm going to call Gil Armijo." He continued, "He's the one state cop we can depend on and probably the only member of law enforcement I can count on to work with us on this."

As the group of men discussed strategy, Rosa and Johnny looked on from the couch. Finally, unable to hold back, Johnny came over and banged his fist on the table. "I'm at the middle of this. I'm the guy they're after. You've got to give me a say in this." He looked at his father, at the coaches, at Joe. "Joe, tell me about these fights. Sounds like something you know about. Are they legit?"

Joe looked resigned. The kid was right. What they were planning put him at the most risk. He was smart. He had to be all in. He felt the Abeytas, especially Johnny, should know what they are dealing with.

"The fights are usually brutal and short. This social gathering wasn't dinner, dance and an exhibition fight. This is usually a meeting between the organized crime syndicates out of Denver and back East and one or more of the drug cartels out of Mexico. They cut deals, transfer contraband, and enjoy a no holds barred fight. Guys have gotten beaten to death, or close to it. The people with them are ruthless thugs. That guy, Giovanni...he's a top lieutenant for the mob. A killer from what I can gather. Luca, the driver, he's another one."

He walked over to the couch. "I'm sorry Rosa, but you are in a real mess." Turning back to Johnny. "You're right Johnny. You need to be in on this."

He went back to the table and went through a few more photos. He found the photos of Tomas "Tigre Negro" Mondragon and Enzo "Gigante" Giordano. He showed them to Johnny. "These are the kind of guys they'll put you in the ring with. Thugs. Dirty fighters. No rules, no holds barred."

Rosa started to cry. "Oh Juan. What can we do?"

Juan sat next to her on the couch. "We'll figure it out. We've got help. And Johnny will be all right."

"What have you done." She glared at Juan. "You are risking the life of our son."

Johnny came over to them. "Mama. It is my responsibility. I am the fighter. You and Papa have done so much to help me. But I am the fighter. Everything you've done, that Papa has done was to help me get to where I am now." He turned to Joe. "We can beat these guys. I can do it. I am not afraid."

Joe turned back to the others. Johnny joined them at the table. "Okay. Let's see how we can take these hijos de putas down."

§

That evening, Gabby was back at the sheriff's office. Joe had told her they would be at the Abeytas. He had told her to call him there if she needed him rather than use the radio.

She was watching the little television behind the counter when the radio crackled. "Romero Fire. Unit One, There is a structure fire at one twenty-one Railroad Avenue. Warehouse burning. Pumper and Engine Number Five on scene. Additional Type five required."

"Madre de Dios. That's all we need." She called the Abeyta's. Joe needs to know about this.

The phone rang at the Abeytas. Rosa answered while the men were huddled over the table.

"Hello?"

"Hola, Rosa. Gabby. Can I speak to Joe please? It's important."

"Hello, Gabby. I'll get him." Holding out the receiver, "Joe, it's for you. Gabby."

Joe took the phone. "Gabby? What's up?" The others looked his way. "Okay Gabby. I'll get down there. Roberto is here with me. We'll head on down."

Turning to the table, "There's a fire down on Railroad. Roberto and I have to go. We can pick this up tomorrow."

Juan looked incredulous. "Where on Railroad?"

"One twenty-one. It's a small warehouse."

"One twenty-one? That's my building." He was stunned. "I'm coming with you."

"I'm coming too," said Johnny. "Mama, stay here with Pete and Bill." We'll call when we find out what's going on."

They rushed out. Joe and Juan in Joe's truck. Johnny and Roberto in the squad car.

Rosa watched them go. Sadness and worry welling up in her breast.

§

When they arrived at the fire, the structure was already a shell. The fire department had managed to put out the major blaze and were hitting the hot spots.

Chief Diaz met Joe and the others on the perimeter.

"Hola Joe." The chief was looking tired. "Juan, this is your building. Any idea what happened?"

Juan looked at Joe. "No idea chief. Let me know what you find. Is it safe for me to take a look? I need to let my tenants know what kind of losses they had."

"Sure, Juan. Just be careful. We've still got some hot spots. Try not to go into the building."

"I'll just get a look." Juan had been in the building recently to get more of the items he sold at the store. The front wall of the warehouse had collapsed. Juan could see that the boxes and crates in the 'restricted' area were gone. The only things left were the ceramics, lawn ornaments and other things that were easily replaceable. He didn't mention the discrepancy to anyone.

He went back to where Chief Diaz and the others were talking.

"When can I come back and do a more thorough assessment. I'll let my insurance guy know and we'll come back when it's safe."

"We'll let you know. I'll have my inspector check it out. Try to find out the cause."

Joe told Roberto to stick around. The rest got into Joe's truck and headed back to the Abeytas. He radioed Gabby and let her know where he'd be.

Juan and Johnny were quiet on the ride back. When they got to the house, Johnny and Juan got out. "I'll go talk to Rosa, Joe. Give us some time to think about everything. I'll be in touch."

"Seguro, Juan. I understand. We'll get together later. But remember, time's running out."

Juan nodded and he and Johnny went into the house.

§

Later that day, Bill and Pete headed back to Albuquerque saying they would be back later in the week. Johnny stayed with his folks. He,

Rosa and Juan had to make some tough decisions and he wanted to stay with his parents.

Rosa was exhausted. She went to bed while Juan and Johnny went into the backyard with a couple of cold beers. They were quiet for a while.

"Papa. If anything is going to happen it's going to be up to us. If we don't agree to the fight, what's next? The store? The house? These people are evil. They've got to be stopped."

"We'll talk to Joe," Juan said. "See if he can drum up some help from the Feds."

"The Feds aren't going to help. Maybe they'll send someone down to investigate...but I think it's up to us. It's like being in the ring. You train, your coaches give you help, but in the end it's how you handle yourself during the fight. You either figure out your opponent and beat him, or you lose."

"What are you saying?"

"We call the bastards. This Giovanni guy. He's the one who probably ordered the warehouse burned down. Pushing us to accept." Johnny got up. He was working out his strategy, like it was the end of Round 1. "We tell them I'll fight. That's what they want."

Juan was surprised. Johnny wasn't a kid anymore. "Okay. Then what?"

"From what Joe tells us, those guys hate to lose. Their fighters are crazy. I know the type. If they lose they tend to go nuts."

"If they lose."

"Listen to me Papa. I've seen these street guys at the gyms. They have no skills. Just brute force. You can dance around them and they can't land a blow. Mostly just running at you and trying to wrestle or beat you to the ground. I've taken on a few of them and they have no moves. And when they lose, they blow up. Four or five guys have to hold them back. Usually, they get thrown out of the gym and told to never come back."

Juan thought about it. Was he getting soft? Had life been too easy for him? He liked his son's spirit. "So, you've fought guys like these." He gestured at the photos of Tomas and Enzo.

"Seguro. They never have a chance in the ring. Most of the guys with training can avoid their shots or catch them off guard and take them out." He smiled at his father, "I've taken a few out myself. Big guys like these. If I can take out their guys, maybe that will get them off your back. The warehouse is gone. They won't need you anymore."

"But this guy, Carlito, he's after you for beating his nephew." Juan Carlos warned. "He won't give up."

"Then we talk to Joe. Maybe he can get some of the Feds involved. Maybe they can raid the joint and catch the gangs with drugs or guns or something. From what Joe says, he's got plenty of evidence."

"Are you sure you want to do this. I don't think your mother will like it."

Johnny gave his father a hug. "I can do this. I know I can. Let's talk to Joe."

§

The next day, Juan opened the store as usual. He told Joe that he and Johnny, and Rosa, with great hesitation, had decided to let Giovanni know that Johnny was willing to fight. That it would buy some time and avert any other vengeful threats or actions from the mob until the big meeting. They insisted that the fight would meet standard regulations. Helmets, gloves, three rounds, just like any amateur fight. Of course, Giovanni agreed, but they knew that his cooperation was just a smokescreen.

It was the same for Juan and Johnny. They had accepted the invitation to fight but they knew the criminals couldn't be trusted. Time was short. Joe had already been in contact with the Feds in Denver. That could help the plan work. Less time to have doubts or second thoughts.

Johnny stayed home and helped Rosa. She was glad to have her son around. It calmed her and gave her comfort. Joe had called and he told Juan that he had made another appointment in Denver with the Feds and was going to be back the next day. With any luck, they would take an interest and send someone down before the fight.

§

Joe came back from Denver the next day. He went right to the store to update Juan and Johnny.

"The Feds are reviewing the material. They said it was very helpful and they would contact the Albuquerque office." Joe shook his head. "I don't think we can do anything about stopping the fight."

Johnny feigned resignation. "Don't worry Joe. Those guys are big. I'm fast. I can stay out of their way. We'll get through it and then let the Feds do what they can."

Joe was surprised by Johnny's courage. "Okay, Johnny. If the feds don't show, Roberto and I will be nearby. I'll get Gil to be there too." He turned to Juan, "You let me know if things get out of hand. I've got no problem going in there and breaking it up, understand?"

§

It was two weeks later. Saturday morning. Joe, Roberto and Gil, the state trooper, were in the sheriff's office. Gabby watched as they prepared their weapons, ready for the possibility that the guards outside the Ringside would give them trouble if they tried to crash the party.

The Feds had sent down four agents from Denver and some of the armed crews from Albuquerque were coming up to meet them. They let Joe brief them since he had the lay of the land.

"Okay. We station ourselves outside. We just use the local official vehicles, make sure they know we're watching." He turned to the Federal DEA officers. The man in charge, Frank Cameron, had met with Joe in Denver. He was impressed with the evidence and figured a bust involving drugs, guns and human trafficking was worth pursuing. And to grab the Big Shots from both the Juarez Cartel and the Denver Syndicates would be a real boost to his career. Maybe he'd get a gig in DC.

Joe paced back and forth. "Maybe they will be just a little intimidated less likely to do anything stupid seeing us out there. What do you think Frank?"

"Sounds like a plan. We'll set up out of site by the Ringside. We can deal with the other locations after we take them down." He turned to Joe. "You're sure they have no idea what's going on?"

"As sure as I can be. The Denver guys are really focused on having this fight. Both groups have a high comfort level here in Las Puertas. I don't think they have any idea that we are on to them." Joe turned to Gil. "To them, it will look like a local operation. Cesar, he owns the Ringside, just thinks I've got a bug up my ass to give his guests a hard time. He'll just tell them not to worry. What can a small-time sheriff do?"

Gil was hopeful. "I contacted Ron Castro. He's trying to get the okay from headquarters to come down from Raton. Headquarters said that one of the boys from Santa Fe may come by too."

"That would be a big help. The more the better." Roberto was glad to hear that local backup was a possibility.

Joe continued, "Gil and I will keep a lookout all day. They should stick to their usual routine and Roberto and the other state guys can join us at around eight. Before the fight starts. I updated Chief Flores about the action, but I told him we were just observing. I don't think he'll want anything to do with it."

They all shook hands. Gabby too. "I'll be here too, Joe. If you need me," she said.

§

The afternoon went as usual. The dark cars from Denver arrived and the flash cars and trucks from Mexico. The meetings took place. The bosses went on their tour.

Joe was observing from his Toyota behind the repair shop. For now, Gil was parked out of site down Grand Avenue. Frank Cameron and his men were stationed in various buildings nearby. The neighboring locals were more than happy to offer them cover.

It got colder as the sun set. At around eight Juan, Johnny and Pete pulled up to the Ringside. The guards outside frisked them. Johnny was wearing his fight garb under his clothes. Just then Joe, in his marked Bronco pulled up and parked by the side of the road, at the edge of the parking lot. Roberto, in the squad car, parked at the north end. Gil, in his state cruiser, at the south end.

The guards looked at the vehicles suspiciously. One of them went inside.

A few minutes later, Carlito came out with Ismael. They walked over to Joe's vehicle. He rolled down the window.

"Good evening sheriff." Carlito smiled. "What brings you here?"

Joe smiled back. "You've got one of our local boys in there. His dad told me you were having some kind of exhibition fight. I'm just here to make sure nothing happens to him."

"Don't worry, sheriff. We'll make sure it's a fair fight." He stopped, reached for his inside pocket. Joe straightened up. Carlito took a cigar out of his pocket. "Can I offer you a cigar?"

"Thanks. I don't smoke."

Carlito offered one to Ismael. They lit up.

Ismael looked at Joe. "Why don't you come in. Have a drink. The food is good. And you can watch the fight inside, where it's warm."

"No thanks, Ismael. I'm on duty." He gestured to Roberto and Gil. "They are too. Why don't you let Vincenzo and Felix know." He enjoyed the surprised look on their faces. He knew all their names. "Tell them that if there's any trouble, we'll be right outside."

Carlito bit off the end of his cigar. He spit it out on the ground. "I don't think we'll need your help. Why don't you and your friends just take the night off. We'll send you something in appreciation of your concern."

"Not necessary, Carlito. You and Ismael can go back inside. Enjoy your evening." He rolled up his window.

Annoyed, Carlito and Ismael turned and walked, a little too fast, back to the bar. Both called over their guards and had a short discussion. Then went inside.

§

Juan, Johnny and Pete had never been in the Ringside when it was all set up for a fight. Cesar came up to them. "Welcome, welcome. Johnny, I can't tell you how happy you have made my special guests. Let me introduce you." He brought them over to the main table, set on a platform so they had a good view of the ring. "These are my best customers. Our hosts, Vincenzo and his brother, Carlito. They are from Denver. And our guests of honor, Felix and Ismael. They are from Juarez."

Juan shook their hands, followed by Johnny and Pete.

"Thank you for honoring my son. He is looking forward to showing you what a young man, destined to be a champion, from a little town like Las Puertas, can accomplish in his sport." He nodded to Johnny.

"I am pleased to meet you. I hope your man proves to be a worthy opponent."

Carlito stood up, he gestured to the crowd to let a figure from the back come forward to the table.

"Let me introduce you. This is Tomás Mondragon. He has made quite a name for himself in northern Mexico. He has never lost a fight."

Johnny turned to meet Tomás, who stood a good head taller than him. Showing no emotion, he reached out a hand to Tomás. "Nice to meet you Tomás. I'm looking forward to a good fight."

Tomás' eyes flashed with anger. Why did he have to fight this kid? Where was a real fighter? Someone his equal. He was a fighter, an enforcer. If someone his equal died in a fight, that was the way things go. But to fight this kid, this puny kid, it was murder.

Reluctantly, he behaved himself. "Si. Buenas suerta, hijo. Buenas suerta." In fact, he was furious with Ismael and especially Felix.

Midnight approached and the fight was about to start.

Johnny and Pete went to their corner. Juan went over and stood where the guards stationed outside were gathering around, looking in, hoping to watch the fight through the open door. The chill air was blowing in, dropping the temperature inside from the heat of the day and the warmth generated by the crowd.

Pete looked around for the helmet and gloves. He called over to Carlito, "Where's the equipment. What's going on here."

Carlito signaled to Giovanni, standing near the table. Giovanni went over to Pete and took him by the arm. "I so sorry, my friend. But Cesar couldn't get the gloves. I'm afraid this is going to have to be bareknuckle."

"The Hell it is." Pete bristled. "Johnny's not going to fight your guy bareknuckle. That wasn't the deal."

"It is now." Giovanni called over a couple of men who grabbed Pete and dragged him over to where Juan was standing.

"What's happening?" Even though Juan looked surprised, he and Pete were expecting this. Juan tried to push his way toward the head table, but several men held him back.

Johnny kept a brave face. He expected something like this as well. But now, faced with the possibility of having to street fight a brawler like Tomás, even for one round, he was holding back a feeling of dread.

Carlito came over to Johnny. "Boxing. The rules. It is a nice sport. But this is how real men fight. This is the real world and people must expect the unexpected." He pointed to his father. "I heard you had some bad luck. A fire, wasn't it? I'm sure you don't want anything like that to happen again. Right?"

Johnny glared at him. He was a fighter, and he was ready to fight for his family. "Wasn't that your nephew I knocked out in the first round up in Loveland? I remember seeing you up there. Seemed like you were pretty disappointed."

Carlito was caught off guard. He was surprised that this kid had the balls to talk to him like that. Nobody talked to him like that. Some of the men nearby looked shocked. Saving face, Carlito poked Johnny in the chest. "Listen you little piece of shit. After tonight, you'll never fight again. I promise you."

Johnny shrugged. "You never know. You might be disappointed again."

Carlito was ready to waste the kid right then and there. He hadn't noticed Vincenzo coming up behind. "Calmati fratellino. Let them fight. Don't get your hands dirty on this punk." He pulled Carlito away from Johnny and back to the table. "Let Tomás do the dirty work."

Vincenzo turned to the crowd. The room quieted down.

"My friends, we have a special event for you tonight. You all know Tomás 'El Tigre Negro' Mondragon." The crowd cheered. He continued, "My amigos, Felix and Ismael have brought him here to challenge this young man from this small town, Johnny Abeyta" The crowd booed, laughing and yelling insults at Johnny.

"So, Let's see what a hometown boy can do."

He rang the bell.

§

'El Tigre Negro' came out of the corner. Johnny had kicked off his shoes. He let Tomas get close and then ducked and dodged out of the way. Tomas fell onto the ropes, missing his target. Johnny moved in behind him and landed two solid blows to Tomas' kidneys. Johnny knew that he had to disable Tomas, using everything he learned boxing plus everything he had been taught not to do. Tomas swung around and reached out to grab the boy. Johnny twisted around like a football running back and avoided the brawler's grip. He moved around behind him and landed two or three more blows on Tomas' kidneys. Tomas was quick, but he was used to grappling with an opponent his size or bigger. With Johnny's speed, there was nothing to grab onto. He had never had to fight anyone with such skill and speed. This wasn't 'mano a mano.' This was like trying to catch a hummingbird.

The blows to the kidneys were extremely painful. He was slowing down.

Carlito and Vincenzo could hardly believe their eyes. Vincenzo turned to Felix, "What's the matter with your boy. This should have been over. He's got to break this kid. Break his arm. Crack his skull. Cripple him."

Felix was as caught off guard as Tomas. This was an embarrassment. Hiding his surprise, he put on a relaxed face, "Just give him time. He'll get the punk. Don't worry."

Tomas was angry now. He was in pain. His confidence shaken. He also knew that he couldn't disappoint the Jefes. He knew he was a dead man if he lost. Desperately, he shook off the pain and made a lunge at Johnny. Johnny stepped aside and tripped him. Tomas went down. He was panicking. He jumped back up and grabbed Johnny's arm, pulling him closer and landing a glancing blow on the side of Johnny's head with his left. Thinking that slowed Johnny down, he released him and swung at the kid with his right. Johnny was used to taking a blow and managed to block Tomas. He sucker punched Tomas in the face, right on the bridge of the nose. He threw a left to Tomas solar plexus and while the big man was trying to breath again, he landed a sharp uppercut to his jaw. Tomas went down.

Vincenzo rang the bell. He told Carlito to get some men in there to revive Tomas. Johnny went back to his corner. One of the men in the crowd gave him a beer. He was winning them over.

Carlito and a couple of other guys were still working on Tomas. Johnny stepped out of the ring and went over to Juan and Pete. Pete assured him "He's big, but he doesn't have any skill. Good move with the kidneys. He's probably hurting. Might even need to take a piss."

"I don't think he's ever been hurt like that. These guys go for the face. I better not let him get a hold on me. I'd be finished." He looked back at the ring. Tomas was up, a couple of the men were oiling him down. He turned to Pete, "Pete...what are they doing?"

"He won't be swinging at you anymore. He's going to try to wrap you up. It's a wrestling trick..." Pete looked Johnny straight in the eye. "Get up against him. Pick up some oil off him. We'll make it work against him. If he grabs you, you can slip out easier. Keep punching the soft spots. Hurt him and stay out of the way..."

Carlito was staring at Johnny. He waved the boy back to the ring. "Fight's on, kid. Get over here."

§

Johnny went back to his corner. A few of the men kept Juan and Pete from following him. Tomas was back in the ring. He had a look of pain and madness in his eyes. Ismael came toward him. "You cabron. Get this kid. Get him now you son of a..." Tomas turned to Ismael. His face almost touching him.

"Vete a la mierda you piece of shit. I don't need you to tell me what to do. Fuck off!" Tomas turned back to the ring. Ismael was both astounded and enraged. Nobody talks to 'El Martillo' like that. Felix waved him back to the table.

"Easy. Tranquillo!" He gave Ismeal a shot of mezcal. "Let the fight end. He'll take the kid…then you can kill him, back in Juarez. Or maybe on the road."

Ismael sat down. Seething.

Felix rang the bell.

Tomas came charging out of his corner, eager to get the kid out of the way. In his mind Johnny was just a bump in the road. His real hatred was building toward Ismael and Felix. They put him in this position. They were the real bastards who put him in the ring with this nobody. It wasn't the kid's fault. Something was going on. Why would the Italians choose a local Chicano boy like Johnny for a fight for them like this.

Johnny came out to meet Tomas. He side stepped the 'Tigre.' Ducked under his grasp and slid his back against Tomas, picking up some of the oil off his body. Tomas swung around and tried to land a blow on the side of Johnny's head. Johnny pulled back, the blow narrowly missing him. He clinched Tomas chest to chest, picking up more oil on his own chest and arms. Tomas tried to bear hug Johnny, but the oil now let him slip down and out of the larger man's hold. He swung around behind Tomas and landed two or three fast blows again to the kidneys. Tomas felt pain unlike any he had ever experienced.

Fire in his eyes, El Tigre started flailing at the boy. He landed one powerful right to Johnny's neck, stunning him. Tomas went for another hit, but Johnny managed to dance away, backing up to the ropes. Juking to the left, he let Tomas fly by him and land on the ropes himself. Then Johnny landed another few blows to Toma's kidneys, and a haymaker to the back of Tomas head. El Tigre went down on one knee, in pain and dizzy. Knowing this was not a proper boxing match, and that there were no rules, Johnny came at Tomas while he was still on his knees. He landed two more blows to the back of Tomas' head and a hard left to the jaw. Tomas went down.

The place went quiet.

§

Joe was sitting in his truck. He could hear the bell ring and the crowd noise through the open door, so he knew the fight had begun. There was cheering. Roars for their champion, then the occasional outburst of surprise and cheers for the contender. The bell rang again. Then it was unusually quiet for a few minutes. Some muttering and chatter. The bell rang. There were more cheers, but muted. Not the usual rowdy laughing and yelling.

Maybe things were not going as planned, he thought. More crowd noise. Then dead quiet. He got out of the truck and walked up to the door. The guards hardly paid him any attention. Joe peered in and saw Johnny was on his feet. Cesar reluctantly holding up his arm. Johnny had won.

§

Carlito couldn't believe it. The plan had been for El Tigre to hurt Johnny. Hurt him bad enough to knock him out of the running for the Olympic Team. His nephew, Paulo Bianco, was next in line. Paulo's loss to Johnny in Loveland still enraged him and he was determined to get Johnny out of the way.

He had been in touch with Ismael, telling him to make sure they didn't kill the kid. Felix and Ismael cut a deal with Carlito on the side. Vincenzo had reluctantly agreed but it was Carlito's problem, and the payoff to the cartel was out of his pocket. And it wasn't cheap.

The Jefe's sat at their table. How did this happen? How could 'El Tigre' not take the boy out? Carlito tuned to Ismael. "What the Hell happened. Your guy is a piece of shit. A loser. You're not getting a dime from me."

Ismael remained calm. Felix gestured for his bodyguards to close in. "Listen, culo. You picked the kid. I can't help it if you underestimated him. Tomas was our best. The kid was better. That's your problem. Un trato es un trato. A deal is a deal. Pay up. Now!"

"Fuck you!" Carlito stood up. Ismael gestured to his guards. Vincenzo waved his enforcers closer to the table.

While the tension grew at the head table, Johnny had walked over to Tomas. "You okay?"

Tomas, shook his head, he glared up at Johnny. Then he looked over at the jefes. "Yeah, kid. I'm okay but you better beat it. Get out of here now." He got to his feet. "Beat it. Afuera!" Johnny saw that Tomas was pissed, but not at him. "It's those hijos de putas who fucked me. Nobody fucks with 'El Tigre.'" There was a momentary softening in his eyes. "Get out of here now. I'm already dead!" He gathered his strength and ran across the ring launching himself across the ropes and straight toward Ismael and Felix.

Johnny ducked out of the ring and pushed his way through the crowd toward the door. What had been a group from both factions watching a fight, suddenly became a gang fight with guns and knives. He got to the door where Juan and Pete were staring aghast at the sight of Tomas crashing onto the table and wrapping his arms around Ismael's and Felix's necks, dragging them to the floor. Carlito and Vincenzo had jumped up to get out of the way but in the confusion, their enforcers drew their weapons. The cartels guards saw this and drew their guns. Tomas was laying into Ismael, Felix was trying to crawl out of the way. In the crowd, men from both sides saw the weapons, and followed suit.

Joe, just outside the door called to Juan and Pete, "Get Johnny and get him out of there. Get behind me and head for my truck." Joe had drawn his pistol as well. He grabbed his mike and called out over all channels. "We're going to have trouble. Everyone close in. Take cover and be ready. There's going to be fireworks."

He covered Johnny, Pete and Juan working his way back to the truck, waiting for Roberto, Gil and Caldwell and his troops to form up outside the Ringside. The cartel and syndicate guards by the door had their AK's and shotguns ready and charged into the restaurant, joining the melee.

Just as Joe and the others reached the truck, shots rang out inside. It was a war zone. The sound of automatic weapons and shotgun blasts filled the air. Caldwell and his men swooped in with sirens screaming and spotlights blaring. But there was nothing for them to do. To enter the hot zone of gunfire would be suicide. Besides, they were not the targets. It was all going on inside.

The battle raged. Shots were fired, slugs thudded into the walls of the restaurant. There were screams of pain, curses and angry voices. The shooting went on for another ten or fifteen minutes. Men staggered out the door wounded, falling onto the dirt. Blood was everywhere. Finally, things quieted down. An occasional shot. Then everything went still.

§

Caldwell walked over to Joe. "What do you think?"

"I think maybe they did our jobs for us." He headed for the door. "let's take a look."

They moved closer to the entrance and took up positions on either side. Some of the Fed guys checked the men on the ground. Most were dead. The injured were tended to. Ambulances and Chief Flores' and his boys started to arrive.

Joe took a quick look through the doorway. He'd seen a lot of fights. Some with gunfire. But nothing like this. Nobody was left standing. Some were wounded, moaning. Others lay sprawled on the floor, across the tables, on top of one another.

Cautiously he entered. Caldwell and Roberto with him. It was nothing but devastation. They walked over to the head table. Felix lay dead. Ismael and Tomas were wrapped in a deadly embrace, Tomas' hand around Ismael's neck. A shotgun blast gaped in the middle of his back. Vincenzo had two or three bullet holes in his chest, barely breathing. Carlito was on his knees, leaning on the ropes, bleeding profusely from the neck. He died as Joe and the others were watching.

Cesar came out from behind the bar. "Look at this place. What am I going to do.' He turned to Joe. "This wasn't my fault. I'm just the tabernero."

Caldwell looked sternly at Cesar. "I suppose you had no idea who your patrons were. I understand they were regular customers."

"No, no, no! They were just good paying customers. It's not my job to ask questions. I'll serve anyone, as long as there's no trouble." Cesar feigned innocence.

Joe couldn't hold back a grim smile. "Well Cesar. I think you had some trouble. I think you're going to be shut down for a while. Could be permanently." He enjoyed Cesar's discomfort. "You could be facing charges. Now, this is an active crime scene. You better just go home. I'll be in touch if I have more questions."

Caldwell joined in, "I'll be talking to you too, Cesar. There may be Federal charges."

Cesar looked like he was going to object, thought better of it and just shrugged and slunk away.

"Frank, do me a favor," Joe said, turning to Caldwell. "I'll show you where all the warehouses and stash house are but do me a favor. I think lots of the owners were a lot like Juan Carlos. A little extra cash with no questions asked. That's just the nature of things around here. Let's try to go easy on them. You can have this bust. Sin problemo. But doing that will go a long way to making any future federal investigations a lot easier for you and your agency."

"I get you. I'm good with that." He headed for the door. "Might as well get to work. There's a lot to do and a mountain of paperwork in front of all of us."

Joe went over to his truck. He found Roberto and Gil talking to Juan Carlos, Pete and Johnny. "You guys all okay?"

Johnny and Juan Carlos shook hands with Joe. "Thanks Joe. I never thought something like this could happen in Las Puertas." Juan Carlos smiled. "What now?"

"Joe smiled back. "We'll need you to answer some questions. Make a statement. How about you Johnny? Are you good?"

Johnny nodded. "A little shaken up. I don't want to know what happened there. I just want to get back to training. Get ready for the Olympics. I don't ever want to be caught up in something like this again." He looked over at the restaurant. "Boxing is a sport. This kind of fighting, guys like Tomas, there's no place for anything like that in my life."

"Joe, can you keep Johnny's name out of all this," Pete asked, "He's just a kid. Has a great future. Something like this could prejudice the judges, the boxing commissions."

"I'll do what I can. As far as I can tell, you were just innocent bystanders. Stumbled into something you had no idea was going on." He looked at the restaurant, at the feds and police working to process the scene. "Why don't you guys just go home. Give Rosa a hug for me. Maybe you'll hear from me, maybe you won't." He turned to Roberto. "I think Las Puertas is going to be a lot better off. At least for a while."

THE STRANGERS

Spring in northeast New Mexico is the time of year when the reds, browns and earth tones of the high desert and mesas glow in the warmth of the sun. The mornings are bright, promising blue skies and longer days. It is magical.

Joe Lujan, Sherriff of San Miguel County, arrived at his office early. He had started a fresh pot of coffee and was drinking his first cup, standing at the window looking out onto Bridge Street. The kids were headed to the high school nearby, rough housing each other, harassing the girls and already planning to cut class that afternoon to go cruising around town or up into the mountains.

At about 8:30, his deputy, Roberto arrived in the squad car. He could see Gabby, his assistant, housekeeper and backbone of the station, coming down the street carrying her cooler that usually contained fresh homemade tamales or burritos that he and Roberto could take on patrol when they had no time for lunch.

"Hola, chief," Roberto said as he came in the door. "What a beautiful day."

Joe took a sip of his coffee. He smiled, "Another great day in Las Puertas. Let's hope it stays that way."

Just then Gabby came through the door. "Morning Joe, Roberto." She saw the coffee pot steaming on the hot plate. "You get here early? Anything going on?"

"No, Gabby. Just felt liking coming in and watching the town wake up." He gestured toward the back. "Nobody back there today. Seems like this time of year everybody gets mellow. Even the drunks and troublemakers."

"Just as well," she said. "I'll clean up number one. Maybe Fabio can get in here and give it a coat of paint. It could use it."

"Sure, just give him a call. Today would be fine."

Roberto had gone to his desk and was going through some faxes from yesterday. He frowned when he looked at one of them. "Chief, did you see this from State. There're some complaints coming in about the Tessier Ranch out by Tecolote. Something about fences being down. You know anything about this?"

"Let me take a look." Joe took the fax. He frowned. "Looks like this just started happening the last couple of months." Rubbing his chin. "Tessier, that's the big ranch north of Serafina. Texas folks. It's a big spread. I don't think they'd have anything to do with cutting wire. They like to keep the locals out."

"It said the fences were down all around. The neighbors found Tessier cattle on their side and some of their goats and horses on Tessier land. They had to go and patch the fences even though it's Tessier's fence. Doesn't make any sense." Roberto looked puzzled. "Maybe we should go take a look."

Joe nodded. "Why don't you head up there. Take my truck. It's all rough trails and dirt roads. You'll need it."

"Okay, Chief. And I've got a great aunt who lives in Tecolote. I'll stop in and see her. She knows everything that goes on out there." He turned to Gabby. "Guess I'll need a couple of burritos. I could be up there for a while."

"Seguro, Roberto. Fill up the thermos. I'll make some fresh coffee."

"Thanks" Roberto grabbed a couple of bottles of water, his thermos and some burritos and headed out the back. "I'll radio in if I find out anything interesting.."

§

Gabby went back to the cells to start work.

Joe went to his desk and picked up the phone. He dialed up the county clerk's office. "Hola, Francesca?"

"Hey Joe." Francesca was just the person Joe wanted to talk to. "Been awhile. What can I do for you?"

"Been too long. How's your mom?"

"Doing better."

Sensing the reluctance in her voice, he decided to keep it all business. "What's going on up at the Tessier place. Is the old man still running cattle?"

"No. Old man Tessier died. It's been about six months. He left it to his daughter, Rachel. The cattle have been left to roam the place. Alfonso Gutierrez is acting like a caretaker. Talked to him the other day. Hasn't gotten paid while the family sorts out the details."

"Got a number for him up there?"

"No phone. No electric. He's kind of on his own up there."

Joe felt some concern. "I'm sending Roberto up there to check things out. Got a report about downed fences, livestock straying around."

Francesca was quiet for a moment. "My sister in Tecolote mentioned that there are some strange goings on up there. I didn't think anything of it but it's good that you're checking it out. Let me know what you find out."

"Ciertemiente. Thanks Fran." Joe hung up and got on the radio.

"Roberto, come back."

The radio crackled, "Hey Joe. What's up?"

"Just got off the phone with Francesca up at county. She says there have been some odd things going on up at the Tessier. See if you can find Al, Alphonso Gutierrez. He's the caretaker. Turns out Tessier died and left the ranch to his daughter, Rachel. Things could be a little different. I'll fill you in more when you get back into town."

"Roger Chief. I'll keep an eye out."

§

Joe got up and walked back to the window. The sun was higher now, and Bridge Street was bright. He noticed a yellow school bus with California plates coming over the bridge from East Las Puertas. As it came down the street, he saw that it was decorated with flowers, stars, animals and other decorations reminiscent of the sixties. It also had the quotes:

"He who is cruel to animals becomes hard also in his dealings with men." —Emmanual Kant

"Only when we have become nonviolent toward all life will we have to live well with others." —Cesar Chavez

"I am in favor of animal rights as well as human rights. That is the way of a whole human being." —Abraham Lincoln.

Joe assumed there were more similar quotes on the other side of the bus. As it passed, he noticed that a young woman was driving. She smiled and waved. He saw other figures in the bus. All young men and women, long hair, beads and face paint.

"What century is this?" He thought.

§

Life in New Mexico for most is tough. For many it reflects the difficulty of eking out a living from the dry soil. It has been that way for centuries. First for the Indigenous peoples before the coming of the white man and then for the peasants under Spanish rule. Even after becoming part of the United States, the territory was poor. It was also rife with outlaws and cattle barons, taking advantage of the locals who were just trying to get by.

Modern New Mexico was still a tough place for the average citizen to do anything but make ends meet. Livestock, odd jobs or running a small business all presented a challenge. Even so, home, family and what little property they had were strictly defended. This culture of putting one's family and oneself first to survive made the locals have a very different outlook on the value of life. Cattle, horses and goats were highly prized and fair game if it meant a man could feed his children or get some cash for his basic needs. Animal life was always secondary. Folks from California or back East could find this hard to swallow. Even the family pet, though loved, would be denied food or care if the family's survival was at stake. If something were to complicate or exacerbate this delicate balance, it was not unknown for an individual to take drastic actions. Outsiders would encounter confrontations if they were ignorant of the reality of life in a land where necessity outweighed sensitivity.

§

Roberto carefully negotiated the rough dirt roads leading up to the Tessier Ranch. Most of the time it was just ruts and washouts that slowed progress. When it rained, which was rare, the roads became slick from the red clay, often causing a vehicle to slide off to the side or into an arroyo. Joe's truck had no problem, but the going was slow.

When he reached the ranch gate it was wide open, not closed the way it should be. The cattle guard was filled in with dirt, making it essentially useless to prevent stock from wandering through.

"What the Hell." Roberto drove through and headed to the main house. It was about a mile to the ranch. As he drove he saw some cattle wandering around. There was some cake and hay carelessly scattered around, not in the disciplined lines usually laid out when a rancher would go out on the range to feed the herd. When he was a kid, helping out on his uncle's ranch up by Mora, Roberto would lay out the cake on the ground in V's and S's and watch the heard line up on both sides of the food, following the pattern of the cake. He would go up on a rise nearby and enjoy his creation of a living design of bovines.

But things at the Tessier were not what they should be.

He approached the main house slowly, looking for Alphonso. No one was around so he stopped and got out. He walked around the house. It was a fine building. Casper Tessier was a wealthy man. He had the ranch house designed as a combination of a traditional Texas style with adobe accents since it was in New Mexico. It did look somewhat neglected. Dust had piled up on the big front porch. Debris had gathered all around and nothing had been done to clean it up. The big picture windows that looked out on the mesas were dirty. From what he could tell, the place went into complete disrepair since Tessier died.

As he came back around the house, he heard a vehicle coming from the direction of the outbuildings. It was an old pickup. "Must be Alphonso." He thought.

Sure enough, it was Al. "Howdy, Roberto." He got out of his truck and they shook hands. "What brings you out here."

"Good to see you, Al. I heard there were some fence problems. Livestock scattered onto other folks' places. Even some of your neighbors having to bring their animals back from wandering onto the ranch. You know anything about this?"

Alphonso seemed embarrassed. "Yeah, I know. Since the old man died, I haven't heard anything from the family. Some big shot Texas attorney has been my only contact. He never takes my calls. Occasionally I get a letter saying the family will be in touch. I haven't got any money for repairs. Sometimes I got some money for feed, but it was hit and miss.

The herd is getting thin. Lost one or two head already. I've been staying in the house but without any power or phone." He gestured at his truck. "I've been hauling water from the tank. Don't know how the cattle are getting by. Luckily, most of them have been able to find some water from the overflow but the windmill is on its last legs."

"So, this has been going on for how long?" Roberto asked.

"I think about three months. I haven't gotten paid a penny. Don't tell anyone but I sold off the two dead ones to JoJo Bustamante for hide and meat. Just a few bucks to get by. Otherwise, I haven't seen a dime." Alphonso was a proud man. He had always worked hard and accepted more responsibility than his job required. "I don't doubt that the fences are in bad shape. I can't cover all the ground alone."

"Okay, Al. I'll get all this back to Joe and see if we can find out what's going on." He got back into the truck. "Let us know if you need anything. Maybe we can scrape together some dinero for you. I'll tell Gabby. We'll get her to cook you up a good homemade meal. Joe or I will be back in a couple of days once we get some info."

"Thanks, Roberto. Tell Joe and Gabby thanks too. I got some cousins that might be able to help me out. You know Pablo and Heraldo. Let them know. I've just been reluctant to leave this place unguarded. There's still a lot of valuable stuff in the house."

"You're a good man, Al." Roberto started the truck and headed back into town. When he reached the main road, a yellow 'hippie' type school bus was headed his way. It turned into the side road and looked like it was heading toward the Tessier. The woman driving waved to him as did a couple of the passengers.

"Now what?" He watched the bus drive slowly up the rutted road through his rearview mirror.

§

Alphonso watched Roberto disappear down the road to town. His life had taken a real downturn since old man Tessier died. Up until then, things had been going well. The Tessiers only came to the ranch three or four times a year, usually over the holidays and for a couple of weeks during the Spring, Summer and Fall.

Tessier made sure Alphonso had the cash to hire some hands to deal with the cattle as needed. Moving the herd from one pasture to the other, during calving season and of course, at round up time. Other than that, he had the place to himself. He enjoyed being able to cruise around the ranch in Tessier's fancy Mercedes four-wheeler. Sometimes he would ride his own horse, Bermudo, that he kept in the barn. He usually lived in the little guest house. These days, because he felt it was his right, he was staying in the big house. He would start a nice fire in the big hearth and drink beer and watch television. At least he did until the power got cut off. Now he would just drink and sleep. No cash for taking care of the cattle, no money for food. But at least he had a roof over his head and could be his own man.

He decided to take the Mercedes for a turn around the north pasture when he heard what sounded like a heavy truck in the distance, coming up the road. The main house was on a rise, and you could see anyone coming from miles away. As he watched, he saw it was a school bus. Bright yellow with some kind of fancy designs and writing on the sides. It was going pretty slow, carefully negotiating the rough road.

He stood and watched. Finally, it pulled up to the main house.

Alphonso thought he should go in and get his shotgun, but the first person out of the bus was someone he recognized. It was Rachel Tessier. "What's she doing here." He thought. "She rarely came to the ranch as a child and hadn't been there at all since she moved to California.

Rachel was followed by the passengers. There were four young men, long hair, hippie style blue jeans and colorful tie-dyed shirts. Beads woven into their hair. Two young girls, younger than Rachel, followed wearing flowered dresses. None of them wore shoes.

"Hola, Alphonso! Do you remember me?" Rachel walked up to Al and shook his hand, then gave him a hug. "I'm so happy to see you. It's been such a long, long time."

"Señorita Tessier, it has been too long." He was somewhere between relieved to see her and apprehensive of what her arrival might mean. "I was very sorry to hear about your father. It must have been very difficult for you."

"No, not really. He and I have been estranged. Very distant for the past few years." She looked at the house, then turned around and surveyed the wide-open expanse of the ranch. It was as if she was absorbing the reds and yellows of the high desert, the mesas and the meadows, the distant pine forests and the scattered pinyons and the scrub oak. "I was surprised he left the ranch to me. But being his only child, and with my mother dead, I guess he didn't think he had any other choice." Her eyes became distant, as if another person was inside her. "I believe it was something bigger. Some power was making sure this beautiful place would be under proper guardianship."

"It is a wonderful place, Señorita. Your arrival is more than welcome." He agreed, though her words were strange and made him uncomfortable. Alphonso was also a little embarrassed, "Things have not been easy. I haven't gotten any money or help. The cattle are all over the ranch. Fences are down and no wire to fix them. I've barely been able to keep track of them and there has been very little money for feed. Some have died."

Rachel turned to him. "I understand." She smiled sympathetically. "Do not worry. I am the Mother Sun. I am here to shine upon this place and bring light to all who live here. All creatures here are now under my care, Alphonso. You included."

"Madre de Dios" Al thought to himself, then aloud, "I am very happy to hear you say that Señorita Tessier."

She picked up both his hands in hers and said, very seriously, "I am Mother Sun. And it is dawn."

Gesturing to the others, "Come with me, my spheres." They all headed into the house. She put her arms around the young girls, the men followed. "There is much to be done."

§

Roberto headed into Tecolote to see who else had issues with the ranch. The town was just off the Interstate, but many of the residents were families that had been landowners for centuries. They still owned most of the land further in the nearby hills and further north...except for the Tessier.

Tecolote was a place that had changed little in the past two or three hundred years. The twenty or so houses were adobe in the long house style. Most were still heated by wood stoves and the water was from a central well. Of course, they all had electricity and there were one or two satellite dishes that were shared with two or three other houses. Cars on blocks or just sitting in the long grass dotted the surrounding fields. Pickup trucks were parked by the houses.

As Roberto entered, he saw a few folks checking him out through the windows. A kid working on his cruiser, a '64 Impala, stopped and turned to watch him come into town. An old man sitting on a couch on his front porch eyed him as he pulled up and got out of the car.

"Buenos Dias, Amigo," Roberto said recognizing the old man. "Aren't you Diego De Luna?"

The old man said nothing.

"Soy Roberto Castillo. My Tia, Delfina Montejo lives just over there." He pointed to a house across the dirt street.

The old man's weathered, craggy face changed from stone to a warmer visage. His eyes, grayish from cataracts, looked more closely at Roberto.

"Little Bobby Castillo." He frowned, "You have not been to visit your aunt in a long time. She will be glad to see you."

"Yeah, I'm going over there now, but I wanted to say hello. You look well."

"Life has been good. My children come often. Grandchildren and great grandchildren too. They like to come and spend time with this old man."

"The town looks very peaceful." Roberto looked around. "No trouble?"

Diego shook his head. "En su mayoria. Seguro." Nodding at the Sheriff Department truck, "You're really here to talk about the Tessier, No?"

"Well, that and my Tia." He knew that this was one tight knit community. He or Joe had been expected.

The old man got up and went into the house. He came out with a couple of beers and he and Roberto sat on the couch. Roberto knew better than to refuse a beer. It was a test that one had to pass before there was the possibility of a candid conversation.

Diego began. "When we heard that old man Tessier had died, many of us were very concerned that things would be different. Tessier just liked having the land. It made him feel good, owning all that beautiful country." He paused. "He hardly ever came up here, and with Alphonso running the place, it kind of felt like it belonged to the gente. All of us. Local boys worked the cattle and Al always had odd jobs for them so they could earn extra cash.

When Tessier died, he stopped paying Al. Al couldn't pay the boys. The boys missed the extra cash and maybe a few decided that a cut fence was some kind of venganza, vengeance. They didn't have to bother because Al couldn't keep up with the work on his own. Fences break. The cattle started spreading around. Pero, it worked both ways. Lisandro Lisaro had some of his sheep go into the ranch and he couldn't find them. Javier

Martos lost three goats. Found them up by the pines, wolves must have got them. They went up and asked Al what was going on and that's how we found out that he'd been cut off. Your Tia and some of the others let the State Police know that there was a problem."

"Why didn't you call Joe?" Roberto asked. "Why didn't my Tia call me?"

"Tessier is big money. We figured it was something that needed state attention." Diego smiled "You know...big money to deal with big money. No offense."

"None taken. I guess the state decided to dump it on us. We got a fax from state police HQ in Santa Fe...So, it's our problem now." He got up to leave." Thanks for the beer. I'll let my aunt know what's going on. Luego, Señor De Luna."

"Nice seeing you, Bobby. Come around more often."

Roberto walked over toward his aunt's house. "I guess I'll be talking to Rachel again. Or Mother Sun... Or whoever the Hell she is." He thought. "Could be good. Could be bad."

§

Joe Lujan grew up in Las Puertas. He knew the people and how life had a consistency about it here in what they call Atzlan, their homeland. Change came but not to the heart and soul of the country. During the sixties, northeast New Mexico became a destination for hippies and others looking to live a different life than they had back East or on the west coast. There were communes, group homes and rugged individuals who came to make a new life. The people of Las Puertas welcomed most of them. The locals had been smoking marijuana for generations. Hitchhiking was a standard mode of transportation if you had an old, undependable car or no transportation at all. Everyone drank and there were always a few locals who were virtually homeless, either because of a disability or just from being too poor to afford a place of their own.

Some of the young Anglos were students at the university, others just settled in and got jobs, started businesses, contributed to the community. They had a respect for the citizens and became a part of the population, compatible and welcome.

But times change. By the mid seventies a cruder element of young people started to drift into town. They were on street corners panhandling.

Many were users of hard drugs and that created a tension between them and the townsfolk. Some of the local kids got caught up in the drug scene and petty crime increased. Joe tried to work with them. Occasionally he'd run a few junkies out of town. Drive them to the highway and give them a warning that if they came back, he'd lock them up or have them committed to the nearby state mental facility. Finally, some of the local men just started harassing some of the more offensive ones, beating them up or shooting up the houses where they were crashing. The town had a reputation for no nonsense. Either fit in or get out.

Joe had to accept the vigilantes, but he didn't have to like them. Cause trouble and, unless you were somebody's cousin, you'd be run out of town.

When Joe saw the hippie bus that morning, he wondered if this was going to be trouble.

It was, but in an entirely new way.

§

Alfonso followed Rachel and her entourage into the house. He found them in the main room of the house, sitting on the floor holding hands. They had their eyes closed and seemed to be praying or chanting quietly. Holding his hat in his hands he worked up the courage to interrupt.

"Lo siento mucho, Señorita Rachel. Forgive me but I have been staying in this house. There is no propane for the heater in the bunkhouse, so I was using the fireplace to stay warm."

Rachel opened her eyes and smiled up at him. "Don't worry, Al. We'll order up some soon. But for now, you can stay in the den. The fireplace will provide enough warmth for all of us until I get the power turned back on. I stopped by the co-op in town. They should be out tomorrow. The phone too. My spheres and I will take the bedrooms upstairs."

"Thank you, Señorita. I will gather up my things and get them out of your way." He quickly picked up his clothes where they were strewn around the room. Embarrassed, he also started to pick up the empty bottles and cans of food and beer that he had left carelessly around the room.

"Leave the tidying up to us, Alphonso." She seemed a little annoyed. "We are testing the house for balance. You may go now."

Al headed to the den. "Please close the door and stay there until morning," she said. "We will begin our work then." Al backed his way out of the room and went down the hall to Tessier's den, a room that had always been off limits to him. As he closed the door, he heard the whispering chanting begin again.

"Madre de dios, they are either crazy or dangerous." He put his blankets on the floor and lay down. "Maybe not. Maybe they mean well." Still hearing the murmur down the hall, he fell asleep.

§

The next morning, Al woke up to noises in the house. People were moving around, and something was going on in the kitchen. He got dressed, gathered up his things and went out into the foyer. It was shortly after sunrise.

One of the young women, one of the spheres, greeted him with a smile. "Good morning, Alphonse. Mother Sun would like you to move all your personal items into the guest house. Bring the Mercedes around front. It should fit all of us. You will take us all on a tour of the ranch. Go now. We'll be ready in ten minutes. We will bring refreshments. Plan on being out all day."

"Yes miss. I'll be right back." He walked quickly out and went over to the guesthouse. He tossed his clothes onto the bed. Grabbing a quick drink of water before he went to the barn to get the truck. Checking the gas gauge there was only half a tank, but that should be enough. "They wouldn't last all day out there." he thought. "Gets too hot, the trails are rough. They'll probably want to get back to the house after an hour or two."

When he came around to the front of the house they were all standing there, waiting. Rachel was dressed in a diaphanous long dress, her feet were bare. Her hair trussed up high on her head. The two young women were standing on either side of her. The four men were back a few paces, carrying picnic baskets, water and blankets.

Without a word, Rachel got into the passenger seat. The women behind her and the men in the back, one in the cargo area.

"Alphonso, we must explore the perimeter. See the fences. By noon,

I want to be at the highest point of the ranch. That's very important. We must be at the highpoint at noon."

"Seguro, Señorita. I know where that is. There is a spot on a small mesa where you can see the whole ranch, all four points." He paused. "I'm sure it is the highest place on the Tessier."

"Please, call it Rancho Madre del Sol. This is a cosmic place. A place for the coming of freedom and peace. A place where the Sun will make us all whole."

"Of course, Señorita." Al agreed.

"And I am Mother Sun, not Señorita. Madre del Sol, por favor mi hijo." She turned and looked out the window.

The big four wheel trundled over the countryside. They rode along some of the fence line. There were many gaps and breaks, broken posts and long sections where the fence lay on the ground. There was the occasional dead cow. Several dismembered sheep. In the distance a coyote would disappear into an arroyo. When they came over a rise there was a horse, trapped under the fence, unable to get up. Al went to stop the truck to see if he could help the distressed animal, but Rachel placed a hand on his arm. "No, Al. This is what a fence will do. Without the fence, that horse would be alive, able to run where he wished. Now, it must perish, from the hand of man."

Al was horrified. "But Señorita..., Madre del Sol. We could save that poor horse. I'm sure he belongs to someone close by. They would be very grateful."

"The horse belongs to no one. He has met his fate and we should not change that. He got himself caught in the trap of man. He will either find his own way or die and become one with the Sun." She looked toward the hills. "Noon approaches. Get me to the highpoint. There is no time to waste."

Al turned abruptly toward the higher elevations. He was heading toward Colina Alto, the name Rachels father, Casper Tessier, gave to a small tabletop plateau near the center of the ranch. He had a narrow road cut into the north side so he could have Alphonso drive him up there on occasion. There he could survey the beautiful expanse of his ranch. Al figured this would be the place Rachel would like to be at noon. It may not be the highest point, but she didn't need to know that. Besides, the truck was getting low on gas and he wanted to make sure they could make it back to the main house.

After a hair-raising ride up the rough path, they arrived at the top. Al stopped near the edge and Mother Sun and her spheres climbed down, out of the truck.

"This is perfect. Thank you, Alphonso. Please stay by the vehicle. You may observe us. Perhaps someday there will be a place for you."

They took their blankets and some water and walked over to a flat area, clear of rocks and pinyon trees. As Al watched, they started to undress. "Madre de dios. What now?"

They quickly removed their garments until they were completely nude. The four men laid out the blankets. One large circular one with a brightly colored image of the sun in the center. Two other circular ones east and west of the center. Four rectangular blankets at the four points of the compass. Once that was done, they took their places and sat down.

Rachel went to the center blanket and stood in the middle of the sun like image woven into it. She raised her arms and stared straight into the sun. "I am Mother Sun, your human presence on this mote, this tiny sphere. I know you have looked down on this place since the beginning of time. You have changed it a thousand times over. You made it barren, volcanic. Lush jungle. A great ocean. Now it is a place sculpted by your power into a breathtaking panorama of reds, browns, yellows and greens. A place of ancient life and present death. Your will has brought everlasting change. Like the rushing water or the blazing fire, it is never the same from one moment to the next." She held her arms out straight in front of herself. She pointed north, west, south and east. As she did, the men stood and raised their arms and stared at the Sun overhead. She turned east and reached out to hold both hands of the young woman sphere on the east blanket. "We shall greet you every dawn." She dropped the girls' hands and turned to the young woman on the west blanket. Repeating the contact, she said, "We shall be with you every dusk." Returning back to the center blanket, she again stared up at the Sun. By now, all of them had their arms outstretched, over their heads, reaching for the Sun. All were staring right into it. "This power, this peace, this understanding of your true purpose we will spread around this sphere to return it to your care, for you to do with it what you must."

They all bowed their heads. They knelt on their blankets and sat motionless for several minutes. Then they all rose up. The men gathered up the blankets, folding them with great care. They dressed and got back into the truck.

"Take us back to the ranch now, please, Alphonse."

Alphonso, who was at first stunned when they removed their clothing. He turned away but could not resist glancing over his shoulder every few minutes to see what was going on. Was this going to be some kind of weird orgy? When Rachel began talking, he heard every word. "Esta mujer está completamente loca." He thought. He got back into the truck. Mother Sun and the spheres were uncomfortably quiet.

They worked their way down off the mesa. Al decided to take a downhill route. Gas was low and he didn't want to run out halfway home. They made it, although just barely. The spheres and Rachel got out.

"Alphonso. We will meet this evening after sunset. I will give you your instructions." Her usual gesture of putting her hand on his arm was not comforting. In fact, it made Al cringe and somehow he resisted the desire to pull it away.

"Of course, Miss Rachel...Mother Sun. Seguro." Instructions? Al ran the Mercedes back to the barn. He'd gas it up from his truck in the morning. Apprehensive and worried, he went back to the guesthouse. He would meet with Rachel tonight, and tomorrow... "Quien sabe."

§

The people of Tecolote were surprised when Alphonso came into town in the big Mercedes G Wagon to let them know that the Tessier Ranch needed some hired hands.

Paulito Herrera had worked at the Tessier before. He was excited to get some work and jumped at the chance. "Bueno, Al. What's going on? What kind of work?" He was looking forward to riding herd. Maybe some branding since there had been several calves born the last couple of months.

"I'm not too sure." Al tried to sound positive. "It's good work. Lot's of catching up to do. Livestock needs tending. The buildings need some work. Fences...You know. Tessier's daughter wants to fix it all up. Pasable. "

"What's the pay?"

"She didn't say. Should be good money. She's kind of out there. Sounds like she's got mucho dinero to spend." This was true. Rachel had told Al that she had big plans for the ranch. And she had sold out of all her father's other ventures adding the proceeds to the huge inheritance and her own personal wealth. "She said she wants everybody to be happy, to share the wealth, the riqueza."

Paulito laughed. "Count me in. Seguro. I want a piece of that."

Al laughed along with him. "Si. Si. It could work out to better times around here." He got back into the Mercedes. "I'm heading into town. Got to start getting things organized. Spread the word. Looks like we might need about half a dozen guys to start with." He started the engine and waved. Paulito was already spending the money on his Impala.

Al got on the highway and headed into Las Puertas. "Mierda. I hope this goes well." He thought to himself. From what Rachel said, and where her head was at, Al wasn't too sure if money was enough to convince Paulito and the boys that what she had in mind was a good thing.

As he came into town he figured he'd stop in and see Joe Lujan. He needed to let someone know what Rachel was up to.

§

He parked on Bridge Street in front of the sheriff's office. When he walked in Joe was at his desk, going over some state police reports.

Gabby was just coming out of the back with a mop and bucket. "Oye, Alphonse. How are you?"

"Hey Gabby. It's been a while. La familia esta bien?"

"Oh, you know. Getting old." Gabby didn't like to share her private life with anyone. "How are you doing? Heard the ranch is back in business."

"I guess." Al took off his hat and was fiddling with the brim. Gabby could tell he was worried.

Just then Joe looked up from his work. "Hello, Al. Good to see you. Things picking up at the ranch?" He walked over and shook Al's hand.

"Yeah, well...That's what I wanted to talk to you about."

"Come on and have a seat. Gabby, could you get us some coffee? I think we might need it."

Gabby went to the pot and poured three cups. Joe and Al went over to Joe's desk and sat down. Gabby brought over the coffee and pulled up a chair.

"It's this woman, Rachel, Tessier's daughter." Al shook his head, "She's a little crazy, I think."

Gabby leaned closer. Joe asked, "How do you mean?"

"Well, they got this big school bus with all these animal rights sayings and pictures on it. And... they do these circles where they kind of chant, you know, like the monks up at the monastery in Montezuma. Except it's not about God or anything. From what I could hear, it's about the change, the rising of the Sun. Oh yeah, and she calls herself 'Mother Sun" and the others are her 'spheres'." Al shook his head, "I don't know what the Hell is going on."

Joe smiled and leaned back in his chair. "If they're not causing any trouble, there's not much I can do about that" Joe saw that Al looked puzzled, a little reluctant. "There's more, isn't there, Al?"

Al stood up and nervously took a few steps. Then turning, "About them not causing any trouble. Rachel has a plan to free all animals from what she calls 'human bondage.' She wants me to hire some of the boys to do crazy things."

Gabby seemed fascinated, "What sort of crazy things?"

"She wants to take down all the fences. She wants to put water tanks all over the place so the cattle and any other animals will always have water. She wants to use a lot of water to grow feed and other stuff to feed animals if we have a bad season. She wants to introduce more predators to keep the 'balance of the Solar System'."

"Does the Tessier have those kinds of water rights?"

"Seguro! He paid a fortune for the ranch and it included huge old, established ground water rights that was way more than a cattle ranch could ever use." Al paced again, rolling the brim of his hat. "That would suck up most of the water for miles, hardly leave any for the locals. There's not much around anyway, what with the dry last few years."

He looked at Joe, at Gabby, "I don't want to be a part of that. There will be resentimiento, la mala sangre...But, I need the money. I got nothing else."

Joe understood what Al meant. For a guy like him, there weren't many opportunities, His life for fifteen years was always with the ranch. If Rachel went ahead with her plans, there would be "la mala sangre," bad blood.

"You did the right thing, Al." Joe told him. Gabby nodded. "Someone like Rachel, coming from California, I think, has no idea how closely connected the folks around the ranch are to the land. Not to mention their pride and independence. If an outsider comes around doing things that effect the way they've been living for generations...well, there's going to be trouble."

He shook hands with Al. "I'll pay a visit to Rachel. You stay put on the ranch. If things get really crazy, you let me know."

"Gracias, Joe. Muchas Gracias. I better go now. I've got to buy a bunch of stuff she says she needs for her spheres. And to lay out plans for the 'Rising'." He smiled shyly. "That's what she calls her plan...Mother Sun's Rising."

§

Rachel Tessier always rose just before dawn. It was important that she was up to greet the sun every day. It was her source of spiritual energy. The only child, a daughter of a billionaire, her life was always one of privilege. Of great wealth. Tessier always gave her whatever she wanted, except his presence in her life. She went to private schools as a child and spent summers in various ecoles or programs in Europe. She attended Smith College and received a degree in philosophy, though her interests were mainly social. She had short lived affairs with other rich kids at university and later turned toward the more bohemian types, both men and women. She developed a more artistic and existential persona, becoming one of the leaders of the subculture at the affluent, Ivy League caliber university, if there really is such a thing. After graduation, she had her father buy her a small farm in Vermont, near Bennington. There she dabbled in the arts...painting, pottery, writing. She would go to her father's ranch in New Mexico when he called his rather small family together for holidays, putting up with her uncle and aunt and their spouses and children so as to keep her hand in with Tessier, and keep the gravy train on track.

Back in Vermont, word got out that she would occasionally offer shelter and patronage to other artists who could pursue their questionable muses at her expense. Others, as the simple minded often do, put her on a pedestal and looked to her for guidance in their shallow lives.

Rachel enjoyed the attention and developed an image of herself as the center of the group. The flattery and adulation, whether real or feigned, went right to her head. Soon she began to see herself as a prophet, a mystic. She made the farm a haven for animals, allowing her group to bring pets, farm animals, wild animals, all to be cared for but not to be abused or harmed. Only to live on the farm and suffer the fortunes or misfortunes of the "natural process." All beings were part of her "family."

After a couple of years, she began to feel restricted in Vermont. She did not like the cold weather and the long dark winter nights. She thrived in the warm Summers and felt she needed to feel the warmth of the sun all year long. On a whim, leaving the farm to those who wanted to stay, she decided to take a few of her more dedicated followers and move to California. To be in a place where the sun would nourish all year long. What better place to be for someone with her gift to develop her spiritual group into something of true substance.

She bought a small house on about fifty acres in Big Sur, overlooking the ocean and on top of a ridge where she could watch the sun both rise and set. Vermont had been beautiful, but here, with a clear view to the east and on the edge of the vast Pacific, she could absorb the energy of the sun from dawn to dusk.

Of course, the opportunity to enjoy the benefits of a wealthy, free spirited young woman...who had a seeming unlimited source of money, attracted many lost souls and opportunists looking to escape the mundane requirements of having to make a living. Rachel welcomed them all, but soon culled them for those that offered her the most praise and adoration until she had a small group of what she thought were dedicated followers. Once again, she felt the need to have animals around her. She welcomed rescue pets, spent farm animals and the abundant wildlife of the hills surrounding her. If there was conflict or even death amongst the animals, she would tell her followers that such is the way of nature. The sun will rise the next day and new life will come with it.

She lived this life of being the empress of her tiny empire for several years. When her father died, and she inherited his immense wealth, she realized that the ranch in New Mexico could become her true empire. Thousands of acres, open land, complete freedom. A place where her acceptance of life and death, conflict and killing, birth and renewal, could exist on a grand scale. She and the ranch could be the nucleus of her philosophic solar system, as the sun was for the planets...the spheres.

§

Paulito and the other men arrived at the ranch. Al had hired a group from Tecolote and Las Puertas. He told them to come up that Monday at exactly 9:00AM and gather in front of the main house.

He was there to meet them. "Hola, amigos. Welcome to the Tessier, now the Rancho del Madre del Sol." He paused. "I know some of you have worked here over the years and I am pleased to have you back here again." The night before Rachel had given Al a speech to use when he greeted the workers. He tried to sound casual but his discomfort in giving the speech was noticeable. "There is much work to be done, as you can see. The house and grounds need maintenance and repairs."

One of the men laughed, "What the Hell have you been doing up here Al? Having a long vacation?" The other men all got a kick out of that.

Al bristled. He went on, "The livestock will be tended to as needed and there is work to do all over the ranch."

"Shouldn't we get right to work on the fences" Paulito asked. "That's the biggest problem. We're losing livestock every day."

Trying to stick to his script, Al continued. "Seguro. We'll be dealing with that, but things are going to be different. Our priorities will be different and to introduce you our new mission, our new beliefs, let me present Rachel. Mother Sun."

The men laughed, "Mother what?" Landy Marquez called out. He was an outspoken, rough edged construction worker from town. "Mother Fucker?" The men started laughing.

Just then, the front door of the house swung open. The six spheres came out and lined up on either side of the entry. Two men and one woman on one side of the door, two men and one woman on the other side. Then Rachel walked out from the darkness inside. She was dressed in a long, colorful dress, a shawl over her shoulders, a gold hairband that caught the rays of the morning sun. She had a stern but benevolent expression on her face. The men were quiet.

Landy leaned over to Paulito. "What the Hell is this?"

Rachel walked over to Landy. "I am Rachel." She smiled. "But please, call me Mother Sun."

Landy was subdued by her forwardness. "Howdy ma'am. Landy Marquez."

They shook hands. "I am very pleased to meet you, Landy." Turning to the rest of the men, "I am very pleased to see all of you. You are all welcome." She shook hands with all of them, sometimes holding their hands with both of hers. She asked each one their names, warmly smiling at them and giving each one a gentle touch on their shoulders before returning to stand between her spheres.

"I was blessed with the gift of this ranch by my father. He bought it for the peace the land would provide him away from the brutal world that made him rich. When we spent time here at the ranch, although it was just for short visits, I also found the energy the land gave me was something that would help me when I was out there, in that heartless world. Now, it is up to me to make sure this land remains at peace. That its energy remains strong. And that is what I intend to do."

She walked back to her place between the spheres, in front of the house.

"I need your help to do this. I need strong backs and clear minds to understand my purpose and to get the work done." Smiling again. "I will be paying you well. But aside from the money, you must have faith in my goals and the real benefit to the land, both yours and mine."

Coming closer to the group of men, holding her arms up and looking straight into the sun, "Go now, go out onto the ranch. Learn the landmarks, the mesas, the arroyos, the lay of the land. Come back tomorrow and we can start our work."

She turned and headed for the front door, the two women opened the door for her and all the spheres went inside. The door closed.

§

As Joe Lujan eased his way up the long, rutted path to the Tessier, he wondered how to approach Rachel about her plans. "Probably need to know exactly what they are before I get into a debate with her." He mumbled to himself.

His truck had no problem with the road, but the years had taught Joe that dropping the truck into extra low gear and letting the engine run at idling speed caused less wear and tear on the vehicle. So, he traveled at five to ten miles per hour, rocking, sometimes not so gently, as the truck followed the terrain.

Finally, he came over the rise and saw the ranch house about a mile away. There was a crowd of men breaking loose and heading toward their vehicles. By the time Joe had about a quarter mile to go, some of the pickups were approaching him and were squeezing by him on narrow path leading back to Tecolote.

He knew most of them. Putting them to bed in the jail from time to time for getting way too drunk or running their cars into a ditch or punching out their cousin at La Casita.

He waved down the first truck. It was Landy. "Oye, Landy. Que paso?"

"Hey Joe. Just got to meet the new Ranchera Tessier. She told us to spread-out on the ranch and check it out. Guess she's got plans for the whole place."

"You know what they are?" Joe hoped he'd have a leg up on Rachel besides what Al had told him.

"No. Not yet. She said we'll find out tomorrow. What are you doing up here?" Landy liked to know what Joe was up to. He did have some friends who operated on the edge of what's legal.

"Just going up to meet the lady. Kind of a welcoming gesture." That seems reasonable, he thought. Don't want them to think he was going to spoil a good thing before it starts.

"Good idea." Landy agreed. "Just a heads up, she's kind of strange. Her and those, what did she call them...her spheres. Spheres? Ah, what the Hell. As long as the pay is good."

"Seguro." Joe agreed. "You heading home?"

"Todavia no. Going to get my horse and ride the fence line. Maybe go up on the mesa. Check things out." He smiled. "That's what she told us to do. Some are already headed out there in their four-by's. Trying to be ready for tomorrow morning." He put his truck in gear," Luego, Joe. Good luck."

Joe drove down to the main house. As he pulled up in front, Al came out of the barn and walked over to greet Joe.

"Hey Joe." They shook hands. "Guess you saw the boys headed out?"

"Yeah. Talked to Landy and he kind of filled me in what he could." He gestured toward the front door. "Any idea yet what she's planning to do?"

"No. I guess she's going to lay it all out tomorrow morning. She told the guys to come back then. I don't know much more than they do." He smiled weakly. "Nothing to tell."

Joe laughed. "No tengas cuidado." He turned and headed toward the door.

Al came up next to him, "Uh...Joe, I've got to let her know you're here and see if you can meet with her right now." He looked ashamed, "That's part of my job now."

"De verdad?" Joe wasn't surprised. "Okay. Rules are rules."

Al hurried to the front door, opened it, and went in.

While waiting, Joe walked around the house. He could see lights on inside and around the corner he could see by the truck tracks and levelled ground where a bigger, new propane tank had been recently installed. Looked like the ranch was back online. He figured phone service had been started as well.

Al came out and called Joe over. "She says she'll see you but in the future she will only be available to outsiders on Saturdays between 2:00 and 4:00 in the afternoon. I have to make a sign and post it way down by the gate. "

"It's her place. Lead the way."

Al opened the door for Joe. He stayed outside and Joe stood waiting in the entryway. One of the young women came from what Joe figured was the study or den. Without a word she took Joe's arm, smiled up at him and led him into the room. It had been decorated with those Indian tapestries, expensive ones, not the kind from Pier One, so it felt like he had entered some maharaja's tent. Soft lighting from behind the fabrics gave an even, peaceful appearance to the room. Fancy Middle Eastern carpets had been spread on the floor. Seated high on a pile of pillows by the fireplace was Rachel Tessier. A celling light had been modified to cast a light upon her face making her look very much like Mother Sun.

"Welcome Sheriff Joe. Welcome to Rancho Madre de Sol. The Ranch of the Mother Sun." She gestured for him to sit next to her, but on only one smaller pillow.

Joe eased himself onto the floor, sitting cross-legged. "Good morning, Ms. Tessier. Thank you for seeing me. I did mean to intrude."

"Not at all, Joe...If I can call you that."

"Seguro, Ms. Tessier"

"Please, call me Mother Sun. Since coming to this beautiful place, I am truly at an epicenter of nature. I feel the warmth growing in me."

Joe tried not to be amused and kept a straight face. "I am very happy to hear that. New Mexico is truly the Land of Enchantment." Trying to seem capable of being on the same level with Rachel...obviously she lived in another dimension.

"It is...it truly is." She agreed. "What can I do for you, Sheriff? What brings you out here today?"

"Oh, nothing really. I ran into Alphonso in town, and he told me you all had moved in. I just wanted to welcome you. I was sorry to hear about your father. He was a good neighbor."

"I'm sure he was. And be assured, Sheriff," she put a hand on his arm, "I shall be a better one. I have made it my life's work to be a positive presence, wherever I have lived. I feel this ranch will be my final home and I want nothing more than to bring the light of goodness, the power of the sun, to this beautiful place."

Joe placed his hand over hers, but she pulled it away. "I am sure you will, Mother Sun." He stood up. Rachel seemed surprised.

"Please Sheriff. I would be honored if you would join me in a cup of tea." She had not dismissed him yet.

"Thank you, but no. I have business down in Tecolote. Maybe another time."

"Life is short, Joe. Another time may not come." She called over one of the young women, trying to regain control. "Our guest is leaving now. You may show him out."

"It was a great pleasure to meet you. If there is anything you need, please call me. You do have phone service, don't you?"

"Of course. Of course. I will have Alphonso give you the number. May the Sun give you the strength you need in your difficult job."

The sphere escorted Joe to the door. She knocked on it twice and went back into the study.

The door opened. Al was the doorman. "How'd it go?" He walked with Joe back the truck.

"I guess we'll have to wait and see." Joe got in and sat behind the wheel. "Keep me posted, Al. I think I need to know what she's up to." He started the truck, closed the door, and rolled down the window. Al had a worried look on his face. "Don't risk your job, Al. I know you need the money...but if things get too weird, let me know."

"Sure thing, Joe. She's kind of out there. It's like the sixties all over again."

Joe waved and drove off. "The sixties all over again. Just what I needed."

§

Back in the sixties New Mexico had become a destination for the youth subculture. Joe was a young deputy and had had his share of encounters with communes and co-housing and hippie hangouts. Conflict was inevitable. The sheriff at that time was Carmelo Herrera, a rough old bird who didn't like change. He was hard on the new folks, making sure they knew he didn't like them or the way they lived. But he was getting old. The mayor of Las Puertas, Joe Robert Delgado, never got along with Carmelo and thought with the changing times, the county needed a new regime in the sheriff's office. He partnered up with the local state senator, Rosario Montejo, and they decided to push Carmelo out and bring in the young deputy, Lujan, as the sheriff.

When election time came around, for some reason, Carmelo decided not to run for another term. Joe was the heir apparent and with the support of the powers that be, was elected sheriff, the youngest ever for San Miguel County.

Joe took on the job with a goal of being independent of the local politics. He was fair in his dealings with everyone, locals and newcomers alike. In the seventies, the hippie scene started to become less an exception and most of the remaining newcomers succumbed to the unique lifestyle of northeast New Mexico. Keeping a low profile, they were absorbed and accepted into the community.

Over the years, Joe's levelheaded approach to the job kept the local politicos happy. They saw no reason to interfere and were happy that things were being handled in a competent manner. Joe liked the fact that he was free to run things the way he wanted. He and Roberto were respected by the community and generally given a wide berth by any of the local troublemakers. Joe was someone who could be counted on to deal with domestic disputes, major crimes and emergencies.

The changes at the Tessier were different. The presence of a new religious seeming "cult" was not that unusual. In the Sangre de Cristo mountains and the Pecos Wilderness there were many groups who lived a non-conforming lifestyle. There were ranches owned by celebrities and the wealthy, like old man Tessier. There were religious retreats spanning multiple denominations. Baptists, Buddhists, Catholics. But they all kept to themselves and caused little or no trouble as long as they were left alone.

Joe sensed that Rachel might be intending something more intrusive. The Tessier was one of the largest ranches in the area. Thousands of acres. It bordered on many other properties, several ranches and the town of Tecolote. If her actions started to impose on the locals, some whose families have been living there for hundreds of years, there would definitely be trouble.

§

The morning after Rachel's introduction to the job seekers, most of them came back to go to work. Some rode their horses or came in 4x4's. Ready to take on the rough terrain of the ranch. Al was in front of the house, waiting until it seemed like anyone who was coming was there.

The men had gathered around and were talking amongst themselves. Al mingled with them shaking hands and thanking them for coming.

He walked back to his place by the front door.

"Oye, amigos. Good morning." He went up to the door and knocked three times.

He walked off to the side of the path and gestured to the door, "Mother Sun," he announced.

The door opened and Rachel walked out arm in arm with the two young women. They were dressed in long dresses in bright pastel colors, Rachel had a wreath of flowers on her head. The four men came out and inconspicuously stood by the door, two on each side.

"Good morning my friends." She went over to the crowd of roughly dressed men, greeting each one by the names she had only learned yesterday. When she came to Landy she held his hands in hers and said, "Thank you, Landy, for coming back. We will all do great things here."

Going back to her place between the two spheres she turned to the men.

"The Tessier Ranch, Rancho Madre del Sol, is now a refuge for all living things. It will be energized by the Sun. It will be a place of pure nature. But to bring it up to its full potential, it must spread that energy outwards, across the high desert, across the wooded mesas and deep into the valleys and arroyos.

I need your help to allow this energy to reach out and bring new life to our home here in New Mexico. To reach out to all the points of the compass. To Colorado, to Arizona, to Texas. To reach out and cover the earth, as the light from the sun covers the earth."

Al was watching the men. Some had confused looks on their faces, Others seemed entranced. Most were looking at Rachel like she was completely loco, demente.

She went on... "I will make the Rancho Madre del Sol a place where men and beasts can visit, find a place to spend time and absorb the power of this land. To do this, all the fences must be removed." A surprised and loud muttering came from the crowd. "I also want to dig wells throughout the ranch, install tanks and windmills, have water available for all creatures." More muttering, this time in a lower, disapproving tone. "Your livestock, your friends and your neighbors will be welcome to graze and roam throughout the ranch."

An older man, Guillermo Blanco pushed his way to the front of the group. "Lo siento, Señorita Tessier. How do we keep track of our flocks? We have sheep and goats that must be cared for. They must be kept safe. The ranch is too big to have no fences. And water is precious, where will it all come from? Even now, some of our wells go dry during the summer. Our herds will scatter. Coyotes and wolves take enough of our animals already. This is a crazy idea." He glared at her. "You can't change the way things have been for centuries. You can't change the nature of the land. It is our lives."

"You are Guillermo, Si? It is us who have changed the land. It is us who have denied all creatures of a natural life...or death." She turned back to the crowd. "What has this life given you? Poverty? Subsistence? A life of hardship? Let yourselves be free in a life within the power of the sun. To be born. To live without the shackles of society. To die free and part of something bigger than you. This is the life we all must lead."

"My life is a good life. I have worked hard for the little I have." Guillermo turned to the rest of the men. "This woman is mal de la cabeza. She is a stranger to us. She thinks she knows better. She has all the money in the world. How can she know what is good for us." To Rachel he fumed. "Your nuts, lady. I want nothing, nada from you. Not your job, not your money. Not any of your crazy ideas."

Most of the men nodded in agreement. Others seemed surprised.

"You're right, Gil." Landy agreed. "Let's get out of here. Nobody's taking down my fence."

"Crazy. Loco, loco. Mujer muy loca." Paulito joined in. "I'm out of here. Screw her and her money."

Most of the men headed back to their trucks. A few construction guys from town hesitated.

As Rachel watched, stone-faced, they all started to leave, laughing at Rachel. Patting Guillermo on the back. The crowd of thirty or more dwindled down to three. Two of the men remaining were Anglos from East Las Puertas. One guy named Cedro from Mora. "Thank you for staying, my friends. Al will show you where to start. Don't worry...others will be joining us." Unfazed, she turned and went back to the house. Followed by the two girls and then by the four men." The door closed.

Al watched her go in. He turned to the three remaining workers, "Follow me. I'll show you where the tools and supplies are. Then we can go out and start taking down the fences."

Tom Robertson, one of the Anglos grabbed Al by the shoulder. "I guess you're the foreman, right Al? How much are we getting paid?

Al shook his hand. "Five Hundred a week. Includes breakfast and lunch. You work six days a week, dawn to dusk. You can board in the long house by the barn if you want."

With the average wage at around $3.00 an hour, this was very good money. Tom, the other Anglo named Mike and Cedro looked at one another.

"Sounds good to me." Cedro took the gloves out of his back pocket. As he put them on, he asked Al. "You need more guys? I can get some others down here from Mora and Raton."

Tom agreed. "I know some guys in Santa Rosa looking for work. What about you, Mike?"

"At that pay, are you kidding. We'll find some guys."

Al nodded. "Okay. You can have them come up ready to work." There was apprehension Is his voice. He knew the kind of men they were talking about...and he wasn't that sure that he wanted to try to run a crew of tough, itinerant workers who were only in it for the money. But then, that was why he was there too. He had nowhere else to go.

§

Old Diego De La Luna had taken his truck down to the end of the road leading up to the Tessier. After hearing the talk of the men who were up at the ranch the other day, he had decided to keep an eye on things himself.

He pulled over into the scrub taking his lunch box and thermos, he got a lawn chair out of the bed and set himself up under the shade of a large pinyon pine. An early riser, he had arrived at about 6:30AM and was ready to spend most of the day there. He figured there'd be enough action to keep him interested. Probably more than he'd see from his front porch in Tecolote.

He was right.

Around seven, a group of five pickups came down the main road and turned up to the Tessier. Two had out of state plates, Texas. He watched as they disappeared over the rise toward the main house. About ten minutes later, four more drab trucks and two tricked out pickups followed suit. The arrivals continued for another half hour. About thirty vehicles in total.

Diego poured himself another cup of coffee. He took out one of the tamales Roberto's aunt made for him and ate it slowly.

At about 8:30, a big Flatbed from BTU Builders Supply out of Albuquerque, loaded with four stock tanks and what looked like four standard 27' Windmill Kits. The driver stopped the truck at the intersection and got out to survey the condition of the road to the ranch. Shaking his head, he got back in and drove back toward town.

An hour or so passed with nothing going on. A few cars passed coming down from the foothills or up from the highway. By noon, Diego had dozed off in his chair. The loud roar of the big, wide load semi flatbed woke him up. It carried a massive Caterpillar 150 Grader. Pulling over, the driver and another man got out and prepared the flatbed to off load the grader. Seeing Diego up on the hill, the driver waved. He waved back.

Once off the flatbed, the second man got up into the graders cab and started it up. Lowering the blade, he slowly started up the road to the ranch, smoothing the surface.

The driver of the semi grabbed a thermos and a jacket out of the cab and headed up the hill toward Diego.

"Mind if a join you? My buddy's going to be awhile, and I got to wait here so we can haul the rig back to Albuquerque today."

Diego gave him a slight smile. He knew this guy might know more about what's going on at the ranch. "Sure, my friend. I could use the company."

"I'm Ruben."

"Diego." He paused, "So, you're up from Albuquerque."

"Yeah." He laughed. "Hell of a thing. The boss had us ready to go to a new subdivision in Cerillos and then he got this call. Came back out of the office with a map and told us to get up here right away. Like it was muy importante. I can't believe he blew off the big contract for this shit job."

"Sounds strange" Diego agreed. "Guess he goes where the money is."

Ruben looked surprised. "Yeah. The boss said if we got up and back in time to make a few runs in Cerillos, he'd give us a couple of hundred a piece." Looking up the road, "Whoever this is, they must have paid him a bundle."

Diego nodded. "Big money, amigo. Big money."

§

When Gabby arrived at the Sherriff's Office at about seven, she had to let herself in. She put on a pot of coffee and put the burritos in the fridge. With nobody in the office, she assumed the two cells were empty and decided to give them a good cleaning. She was gathering her brooms and mops together when the phone rang.

"Good morning...Buenas dias. Sherriff's office."

"Hola Gabby. It's Delfina, Delfina Montejo...Roberto's Aunt."

Gabby knew Delfina well. She was kind of the de facto mayor of Tecolote, keeping track of everything going on. The one you came to for advice if it concerned the town. "Hello Delfina. How are you? Are you calling for Roberto? He's not here now."

"Shouldn't he be there by now. What about Joe?" Delfina not happy that neither of the men were there.

"Joe should be here any minute. He's probably taking a quick run around town before he comes in. Roberto too. They usually do that on Monday mornings. Just checking things out after the weekend. Can I help?"

"Just have them call me as soon as they get in. I'll be waiting."

"What is it..." Gabby asked but Delfina had already hung up. "Que demonios. What on earth..." She sensed there was something more going on than a reprimand to Roberto for not visiting often enough. Anxiously she went to the front window and looked to see if she could catch Joe or Roberto heading down Bridge St.

When she heard the back door open, she rushed back to meet Joe as he came down the hall.

"You better call Delfina up in Tecolote. She called and sounded furioso. She wanted to talk to you or Roberto as soon as you got here." Gabby was holding Joe's arm.

"Buenas Dias to you. What's got you so worked up."

"It was Delfina. It was all business. No gossip, nothing. Just where were you or Roberto and to call her right away. She's waiting by her phone."

Joe nodded and went to his desk. "Let's find out what she wanted." He knew her number by heart and dialed the phone.

"Hola! Is that you Roberto?" She did sound angry.

"Hello Delfina. This is Joe. Can I help you with something?"

"I hope so. I'm worried that things could get bad around here."

If Delfina thought things could get bad, then things were probably already not good. It takes more than a local dispute or argument to prompt Delfina to call Joe. She liked to have Tecolote folks settle things amongst themselves.

"What do you mean? Why are things going to get bad?"

"That woman up at the Tessier. She's got a bunch of obreros from all over up there. They're tearing down all the fences. They're scattering their livestock and some of ours are going onto the ranchlands and disappearing. Paul Rojas lost his whole flock. She's digging wells all over the place. There're trucks coming and going. The workers come and go at all hours. They wander into town drunk, looking for booze, and trouble too, I expect. They're tearing up the roads, except hers. She graded and graveled it. Whatever she's doing, it must be illegal. Water rights? Fences? Folks are complaining from Rowe up into the Pecos."

"Thanks for letting me know. I knew she had plans but I didn't think she'd be moving ahead so quickly. I'll get up there today and see what's going on."

"You'd better. Like I said, things could get bad. Paulito, Landy and some of the other boys want to shut them down. It's going to cost a lot of money to put up new fences. Paul and the others can't afford that." She paused. "Stop and see me on your way back. You need to talk to those boys. I'll tell everyone you'll be here late this afternoon." She hung up.

Joe, holding the receiver, shook his head. He turned to Gabby. "It's the Tessier. Things are happening fast up there. Sounds like Rachel is spending some of her dad's money."

"You were right. I hope Al is okay." She was worried that rough times were coming. She knew how folks felt about the land. Whether ranching, farming or just living in and around Las Puertas, they did not like strangers rocking the boat. They burned down a McDonald's being built in town twice before the company gave up the idea of a store in Las Puertas.

"I think I know what I have to do today. I'll head up there now. Let

Roberto know where I'm going. He needs to cover things down here. I'll be in touch as soon as I have something to tell you."

Joe grabbed his hat and headed out the back to his truck.

§

Paulito, Landy and the other men from Tecolote had gathered together around Paulito's Chevy. They were drinking beer and getting worked up about things at the Tessier.

"Those putos from Albuquerque, Texas too. They're making good money." Landy was seething. Pacing back and forth. "What the Hell does that woman think? She can't run a ranch. It's not a ranch anymore. She's spending all this money. We get nothing." He threw his beer bottle against some concrete blocks. The glass shattered. "Why can't she just raise cattle? Then we could all have jobs."

"Jobs...Bullshit." Paulito stood up and went over to Landy. "Jobs? You're worried about a job? This is bigger. We've gotten by without work before. That's nothing." Now he was getting angry. "She's fucking up the everything. The land, the water. Money...everybody has lost livestock. Lost our horses, dogs...I saw Al the other day. He said all the fencing she's torn down is coiled up by the barn. Posts too. I was thinking, let's go get it. We can use it to put up our own fences. She can't touch them if they're on our side of the boundary."

Guillermo was sitting on a couple of spare tires. "Buena idea. What's she going to do with all that wire? Nothing. We could let Al know. He's a good guy. I don't want him to get in trouble."

"Seguro." Paulito turned to the rest of the men. "What do you say. Vamos a hacerlo?"

"Sure. Why not?" They all agreed.

"Landy, get your cousin's flat bed. Rojas has one too, right Pablo?"

"It's a stake bed, good for wire," Paul said.

"Okay...tonight." Paulito was excited.

§

It was mid-morning when Joe found himself at the base of the Tessier Road. It was graded and graveled. He pulled over. Once he left the highway the roads to Tecolote and then on toward the ranch were bad. Worse than ever. "Looks like Mother Sun is only shining on her turf." He muttered to himself. It took him over an hour to get there. He just wanted to stretch his legs and think about the situation before meeting with Rachel.

He got out of the truck and got out a bottle of water from his ready bag in the back seat. Leaning on the fender he gazed up the road to the ranch. The place was over 300,000 acres. Almost five hundred square miles. Only Ted Turner or Henry Singleton owned more land in the state. The impact of Rachel's actions would be felt in Mora and Harding Counties as well. As he was watching, a tall truck came over the rise and down to the end of the drive. Joe waved the driver down.

"Morning." Joe greeted the driver. The truck was from Baker's Farm and Ranch Supply out of Albuquerque. "Long way down to the city. What brings you up here?"

The driver was a pleasant looking guy, Had a cheroot in his teeth. "Howdy Sheriff. Been coming up here every day or so for the past two weeks. Hauling Water Tanks, windmill kits, prefab buildings. They're doing work all over the ranch. She pays us extra to drive up here. Pays for any repairs to the vehicles. The boss, my brother-in-law, has been up here once to meet the lady but she don't see nobody. Kind of bothered him. But she put a wad down on account and just adds more when she needs it. We don't ask no questions."

"Two weeks. How many tanks and mills have you brought in?"

"Lemme think...I guess about two dozen so far. She's got the boys up there working hard. By the time I bring up another load, the one before is gone. Must be putting up tanks all over the ranch."

"Guess I'll go on up and see for myself. You all right going back down to the highway?"

"Sure. I just take my time. With her empty it's not so bad. Coming up with the load. That's another thing." He shook hands with Joe. "Nice talking, Sheriff." He put the truck in gear. "Hey Sheriff, you think you could get a road crew out here. It's bad now, but if we get any rain, it'll be slick as snot. See ya."

Joe nodded. "I'll see what I can do. Don't get your hopes up." The truck drove off, in extra low gear, at about ten miles an hour.

Joe got back into his truck. He drove up the drive to the ranch. He knew that Rachel most likely had some sort of permits to sink most of those wells. Maybe not. The bureaucrats at the state water utility would have been no match for Rachel's legal team and all too eager to suck up to her money. There were rules about fencing and property rights, livestock and open range as well. Of course, if someone had the resources, they could do what they want and tie up any rulings by the agencies in court for years. Rachel certainly had the resources.

It was a wide range of issues to cover. But there was also the human factor. The people in San Miquel and the surrounding counties had little tolerance for an outsider disrupting their lives. And Rachel needs to know this and to understand that unless she respects the rights and feelings of her neighbors, she should expect some push back. Over the years there had been 'incidents.' Texas folks with summer homes, developers interested in a commercial park or subdivision and generally anyone from out of the area who tried to put in a project that the locals found too imposing often experienced 'setbacks' that would put them off enough to abandon their projects. This done by the same people who Joe knew to be welcoming, friendly and helpful to newcomers who just wanted to live in peace.

Mother Sun might say she wants peace and happiness for all creatures but certainly had a strange way of achieving this.

Joe came over the rise and saw things were certainly different than on his last visit. Men loading trucks, a well drilling rig parked next to one of two or three new prefab sheds. Several pickups parked here and there. Piles of fencing and fence posts. Materials and stock tanks loaded on flatbeds being strapped down. On the hills surrounding the ranch house were newly worn tire tracks leading in all directions.

As he pulled up near the main house, Al Gutierrez rode up on Bermudo, looking much better than the day he visited Joe in town. He was dressed like some jefe on some big Argentine estancia.

"Hola, Joe. Good to see you." He slid out of the saddle and walked over to Joe's truck. "Can I help you with something?"

"Just here to talk to Rachel. I have a few things she and I need to talk about."

Al shook his head. "Sorry Joe. You need to make an appointment. No way she can see you without one."

Joe got out of his truck. "Al... you go and tell Rachel I'm here to see her on official business. I don't need an appointment. We've got some things going on that she needs to be aware of. It could be she's in danger. You know what I mean."

"But Joe. It doesn't work like that with her. I can't..."

"Al. I'm here on official business." He repeated. "Go and let her know. Now!"

"Sure. Sure, Joe." Al led Bermudo to the hitching post and went to the front door." He knocked tentatively. A few minutes passed. Nothing.

Joe went up to the door. Banged his fist on the door. "Sheriff's department. Official business. Please answer the door."

Al backed away. More worried than afraid.

After about a minute, the door opened.

§

One of the female spheres smiled at Joe. "Hello Sheriff. How can I help you?"

"Please let Rachel know I'm here and that I must speak with her."

The young woman continued to smile. "I'm sorry, Sheriff. Mother Sun is not available. Would you like to make an appointment for some time next week. I believe she will be available Wednesday or Thursday. Sometime between three and five."

"As I said... please let Rachel know I am here, and I must speak with her now. This is, as I said, official business. It would be wise for her to make the time for me immediately." Joe was reaching his limit. Rachel needed to know everything could not always be on her terms. In fact, she was due for a lesson in the hard reality of life in Atzlan. If not from Joe, then from her neighbors.

"Sheriff. Mother Sun is meditating. It is approaching the noon hour, and the sun will be at its apex. This is not a time when she can be disturbed. It is her time to absorb the sun's energy to give her the wisdom and power to deal with earthly things."

"Listen young lady," Joe was done with this. "It is about the earthly things that Rachel must be made aware of. Otherwise, I will have to depose her to give testimony and answer my questions at my office in town. It's possible that she has violated several regulations. I would like to avoid issuing an arrest warrant if she refuses."

The sphere was clearly out of her depth. She looked like a deer in the headlights. She bowed her head briefly. "Please come in and wait here." Closing the door on Al, she turned away and left Joe in the foyer.

Calming down, he looked around. Things had changed inside the house. There were paintings and photos of sunsets and sunrises everywhere.

There were images of eclipses. Candles burned in every nook and cranny. The place felt like some Tibetan monastery. A place on another plane from the world outside.

From the direction of the den, he heard whispering. The four men came into the foyer and stood two on either side of the hall entrance. The two young women came out and stood, one on each side with the men. Then Rachel came out.

"Sheriff. Welcome to Rancho Madre del Sol. I have a little time before I must be with the sun. Please tell me what I can do for you." It was obvious that he was not being invited into the study or to have tea.

"Rachel..." he began. She winced slightly that he had not addressed her formally. "There are people around here who are very unhappy with the way things are going. Your efforts are affecting everyone for miles around. And not in a good way."

"I can't imagine that my 'efforts' can be seen as anything but good. The ranch will soon be a place where all are welcome. Where man and beast can live in harmony and participate in the natural way." She seemed genuinely surprised. "How can open land, water and spiritual peace be seen as not good."

"Your neighbors don't see it that way. They are losing livestock and worried that much of the water will be denied them. They have crops that need the water. Your cattle are on their land, eating the meager grass they have for their own animals. Many have died. Both yours and theirs."

She shook her head. "But that is the way of the sun. Better for all men and beasts to be free and die as the sun dies everyday than live in service to man. For we will all be reborn as the sun is reborn every day."

"Rachel. You're a woman of great privilege. The people around here have to struggle to just get by. The beasts they keep are a lifeline for them. Without their livestock, their pets, their horses and the safety of their own land they have nothing. Without crops they can't eat. There is a certain freedom and peace of mind in having what little they do have without someone coming along and denying them that. You must respect that and realize that what you are doing threatens their way of life."

"No Sheriff. You don't understand. What I am doing is to allow everyone to see that true freedom that comes only when you accept the way of the sun." She placed a hand lightly on Joe's arm. "If a man or beast has no boundaries, nothing limiting his movements, access to life giving water and the warmth of the sun. That is all he needs. Living or dying, it is pure freedom."

Joe had his limit. "I am the law around here. I am concerned for everyone's wellbeing. If you pursue this activity, I can't guarantee your safety or what actions these good people around you will take. I am here to protect everyone, you included." He turned and headed toward the door, brushed past the spheres and opened it himself. "I'll be investigating the legality of your actions. Checking permits. I will talk to the folks and ask them to be patient." He glared at Rachel. "But I'm warning you. People are angry and they will not hesitate to take action if they feel they are threatened. Your sun may set and your morning may never come. Comprendez?" He closed the door behind him.

Al was hovering around out by the truck. "What's going on, Joe?" He could see the sheriff was barely holding his temper.

"You better keep on your toes, Al. Things could get messy." He got into his truck. "Maybe you should go talk to the folks in Tecolote. Something's going to go down and you're going to be in the middle of it." He started the engine and roared off.

§

It took a lot to get Joe Lujan angry. As the Sheriff of San Miguel County and the most responsible law enforcement officer in the area, he had always controlled his emotions in response to difficult and disturbing situations. But this woman, Rachel Tessier, or Mother Sun or whatever the Hell she called herself, was beyond reason. Having inherited what might be called a small kingdom, she felt she could do whatever she wanted in her part of the world. Even worse, she had the financial resources to do it. Throw in the demagogue factor and there was no way to reason with her... to get her to see what kind of reactions her actions could cause...to get her to understand the way people would respond to their way of life being disturbed.

He cruised rapidly down the drive and almost lost control when he hit the ruts and potholes of the public road. "Son of a bitch!" he cursed out loud as he slowed down and brought the truck back under control.

He negotiated his way toward Tecolote and had to pull over twice to allow the big flatbeds from Albuquerque to get by heading toward the ranch.

It was a little after noon when he got to the town. He noticed some of the men gathered around a couple of flatbed trucks. They saw him coming and not too obviously dispersed into smaller groups.

Joe pulled up by the trucks. "Morning Landy. Que paso? You guys got a job somewhere?"

"Hola Joe. Yeah. Paulito has a cousin in Pecos who found some junkers he could use for parts. An old pickup too. We're going to go up there and haul them back." Landy was a consummate liar, but he figured this would work as a cover story.

Paulito came over and picked up on the story. "Hey Joe. Looks like I'll finally get what I need to get my ride back on the road." He leaned on the truck. "What are you doing around here? Checking up on us or on the crazy woman at the ranch?"

"Both, actually." He got out of the truck and shook hands. "How are things going here? Anything I should know about?"

"No. Nothing new."

Guillermo walked over to join them. "You been up to the ranch? You going to get her to stop her bullshit?"

"I'm working on it, Gil. I got some ideas that should work but that's my business. I'll let you all know how things are going." He looked at the three men. "Don't do anything stupid. You know I have my limits. For you and for her."

He shook their hands again. "I'm going to drop in on Delfina. Hasta luego." As he turned away and headed toward Delfina's house, he glanced back at them. He knew something was up.

When he got to Delfina's house she was already at the door. "Hello Joe. Venir."

They went into the kitchen and she gestured for Joe to sit. "It's lunchtime. I've got some fresh pozole on the stove. Fresh tortillas too."

Before Joe could say anything she spooned some of the pork and hominy stew into a bowl and brought it over to Joe with some tortillas rolled up in a paper towel.

"Thanks Delfina. Smells great."

"You want a beer? Maybe a Jarritos? You are on duty, aren't you?" There was no fooling Delfina.

"Sure. Orange if you got it. Anything will do." Joe smelled the bowl. "Best pozole in San Miquel County. Gracias Senora."

"So, you went up there? Saw your truck go by earlier." She sat down across from Joe.

Joe ate a couple of spoonfuls of the stew. Then he dipped a tortilla in it and took a bite. "This is delicious, Tia." He wiped his mouth and put down the spoon. "I had a talk with Rachel. I made it clear to her that what she was doing was a situación inaceptable." He paused, "I'll be honest with you, Delfina, I don't think she gets it. She lives in another world."

The old woman nodded. "That's what I hear."

"Understand, I am the law. I have to approach this in a way that will work for all of us. I'll be in touch with Santa Fe and see if she's got any violations. If she doesn't have the right permit, or if her actions are in violation of any trespassing laws, I should be able to get her to stop. Get her fined. Some of the fences she took down might not have been hers to remove. The number of wells she's drilling probably exceed even her water rights. If you all can give me some time, I should be able to get this resolved." Joe couldn't help but feel he was only paying lip service. Between the pandering of state officials to the wealthy, let alone the possibility of graft, he could only hope that Delfina would convince the locals to hold off on doing anything crazy.

From her expression, he knew that wasn't what she wanted to hear.

"Joe, things are happening pretty fast up there. By the time you get the state involved, it will be too late."

Joe put down the spoon. "What do you mean, too late?"

"Just that. You go back to town. Tell Roberto to be ready. Tell that bum, Chief Flores, to keep his distance." She picked up Joe's plate. "There has been too much loss. Too much anger about the mess she's made of the land. And too much conflict between those cowboys up at the ranch and our boys. Those anglos come and go all hours. They ride through town looking for trouble and our men are happy to give it to them."

She put Joe's dish in the sink. "I'll do what I can for you, Joe, but I don't like what's going on at the Tessier and I think the rest of us don't like it either." She walked over to the door.

Joe got up to leave. "Okay, Tia. But if anybody gets hurt...anybody, I'll be back."

He walked out the door and over to his truck. The men had gathered again around the flatbeds. Delfina watched him as he got in and drove out of town. He could feel the eyes on the back of his head.

§

Paulito, Landy, Guillermo and the rest of the men from Tecolote spent that afternoon drinking and working themselves up to raid the

Tessier. After Joe left, a few went home and brought back their rifles, shotguns, and handguns. No one intended to use them, but their past experiences with the rough crowd of workers and cowboys up at the ranch made them figure it was prudent to show they were armed in case someone tried to stop them.

Guillermo took charge of the operation since he had past military experience and was one of the oldest in the group. Paulito was his right-hand man and was the de facto jefe of the younger men and boys. Landy hung with Paulito and Guillermo. Although contributing little, he was always around when the others were doing any planning.

"Those guys up at the ranch usually stop work around 5:30 or 6:00. Then most of them head into town or back to the longhouse. I think Al gets to live in the guest house now. It's on the other side of the main house so we can probably get to him before anybody else spots us."

The other men nodded. Guillermo continued. "We've got to get Al in on this. Either that or just keep him out of it. He's been suckered by the witch and will probably come around to our thinking once things get rolling."

Paulito gestured to his friends, "We'll go up on foot and make sure the cowboys stay put. I'll go over to Al's and let him know what's going on. Then I'll either keep him there or see how he wants to handle it."

"We could tie him up and gag him. Even if he's with us, that will get him off the hook," Landy said.

"Al's no tonto. Maybe he'll come up with something. We'll let Paulito deal with him." Gil went on. "So that's about it. Paulito and his boys go up there and handle the workers and Al. Don't forget to bleed the tires on all the vehicles. We give them about a half hour. Then we bring up the trucks. We load up all the fence stuff and anything else that will help us put up those fences."

"We'll be making some noise so the 'spheres' will wonder what's going on. Paulito, you better cut the phone lines and the power. If they come out, I don't think they'll be much of a threat. If she comes out, a couple of you just quietly, with respect, get her back into the house. Shut the door. We don't want to hear any of her fancy talk, and we don't want her riling up the cowboys.

Then we load up the trucks, everybody pile on and we get out of there. Good thing they fixed the drive. Without vehicles, they won't be able to catch us even after we hit the main road."

He looked around. "How does that sound hombres? Everybody okay with the plan?"

Paulito held up his beer. "Eeee, wow! I like the plan" Everyone toasted to the sky. "Hey, here's to Mother Sun." The crowd started cheering and laughing. They brought out more beer and lit up some mota. Later the families joined them with food. It became kind of a celebration. A fiesta. The Tessier will be beaten. Life will be like it was.

§

Around five-thirty the men at the Tessier were coming in from the day's work. Al was there to greet them, get the reports and give them tomorrow's assignments. Cedro, Tom and Mike were still there. About twenty-five other men had joined at the beginning. Some worked a week or two and then took their pay and moved on. But at these wages, the grapevine for workers always led to newcomers looking for either permanent or part-time work. The problem for Al was that these men had no allegiance to Mother Sun other than the money. He could line out the work, but he was the only one who would ride out and check to see if the work was getting done. Often, he'd find some crews assigned to a distant site sound asleep in the shade of the stock tanks. From the base at the ranch, it looked like a lot of work was happening. In reality, other than pulling the fences, very little had actually gotten done.

Besides that, the work was grunt work. Pulling fence posts, stripping wire and setting up water tanks took little or no skill. Assembling the windmills took some talent but it was like playing with an erector set. Instructions were clear and after the first one or two they could put one up in half a day. The drillers were from Dylan Well Drilling in Albuquerque and only came up when they had 3 or 4 Wells to drill in a day. Once drilled, the ranch hands took it from there. But it was frequent enough for the drilling company so they could afford to leave one rig on site all the time.

The men were a rough bunch. They would come into Tecolote and hit the convenience store near the highway for beer and liquor. After a few hours behind the 7/11 they'd either head into Las Puertas to do some more drinking and maybe get lucky...or in a fight. Others would drive through Tecolote, looking for any action they could find. Usually finding nothing but pissed off residents. The ones bunking in the long house would go back to the ranch and others to the few nearby motels by I-25. Things usually quieted down by 11:30 or Midnight.

§

Landy, Gil, Paulito and the rest of the men rode out of town on the two flatbeds and a couple of pickups at about 12:30AM the next morning. Headlights off. They took their time along the rutted road, sometimes at a snail's pace. Men could jump on and off the trucks, take a piss and easily catch up. Some just walked beside the trucks, gun and beer in hand.

When they reached the end of the drive they stopped.

"Okay, Paulito," Guillermo said. "You and your guys go on up there. Stay in the arroyos whenever you can. Stay quiet. If cosas van mal...fire that 12 Gauge of yours three times, then three times again. We'll come up ready for trouble. By then it won't matter if you wake anybody up."

The group of boys and young men headed out and disappeared into the high desert darkness.

Gil went over and sat on the running board of the old truck. He lit up a cigarette and leaned against the truck door.

One of the men came over. It was Paul Rojas. "Got another one of those?"

Gil reached into his pocket.

Paul took the pack, slid out a cigarette, lit it and handed back the pack to Gil. "I hope nobody gets hurt. Whatever happens, this has got to change." Taking a deep puff. "She's got to know that she can't just do what she wants. She doesn't feel the land beneath her feet. It sends out the espíritu, the alma, the corazon but she doesn't feel it. She looks to the Sun, but it's in her eyes. She forgets that she's standing on the ground."

"Seguro, my friend. Seguro." Gil looked at his watch.

§

Alphonso was in bed in the guest house. He usually stayed up until the workers settled down. He would often go for days without seeing or talking to Rachel or any of her spheres. Sometimes he'd find notes or roughly drawn maps giving him vague instructions about the buildings and some arbitrary locations for new wells. Evidently, Rachel took orders from the sun. Often the places she would pick for wells made no sense and they would come in dry. She had a large area behind the house built with ironically high walls around it so she could be outside receiving her "energy" without being disturbed. Besides limiting access to the Mesa, the Colina Alto, she had several similar enclosed retreats built around the ranch. She would have one of her spheres drive her there in a new Land Rover she bought for her own personal use. Either that or she would drive herself, spending late morning to midafternoon at one of her special places. She insisted that the private structures were only needed to concentrate the sun's ability to communicate with her.

It was obvious to Al that since establishing herself in New Mexico, she had become fanatic about her mission and completely devoid of any common sense or awareness of the outside world. He had thought about leaving. He could go to Española, to his uncle's place. You could usually find work up there and rent was cheap. But the Tessier had become his home. He had lived and worked there for years and found it hard to think about living anywhere else.

As he lay there, going over things in his mind he heard footsteps outside his door. He reached for his shotgun that was near his bed and went to the door. Opening it he found Paulito and another boy just about to knock, holding their weapons.

"Paulito. What are you doing here? What's going on?"

The boys were surprised to find him at the ready, gun in hand. Paulito raised his shotgun over his head. "Hola Al. We don't want any trouble. We just need to talk."

"Get in here. Cállate!" He let them in and looked over to the big house before shutting the door. It was still dark. "Why are you up here? You can't be here. Rachel doesn't want anyone up here unless she knows about it. Especially at night."

"We're here for the fences. For the wire and posts. Everyone around the ranch is going to put up their own fences. We need all that stuff so we don't have to buy new. Nobody can afford new." Paulito looked Al straight in the eyes. "That woman has caused all of us a lot of grief. You know that."

Al put down his gun. "Sure, I know that." He walked over to the kitchen table. "But why in the middle of the night? Why didn't you just come and ask me?"

"She's got to know that we've had enough. She wouldn't give us anything to build fences. She's crazy that way."

Paulito and the other boy sat down at the table. Al nodded. "You're probably right, but this is just as loco. The cowboys like the money she pays. They'll try to stop you."

"I don't think so. We've got some our batos holding them up in the bunkhouse." The two boys smiled. "They won't give us any trouble."

"How are you going to haul all that stuff out of here. There's a shitload."

"Gil, Landy and more guys are coming up with trucks. They'll be here any minute. Just let us load up and leave. Nobody needs to get hurt."

Al paced around the room. "I can't let you do that. Let me talk to Rachel tomorrow. Maybe I can just tell her that I hired you to haul it out for us."

"No, Al." Paulito stood up. "We've got to let her know that she's not wanted around here. That she isn't safe. We hope she'll take a hint...We've got plans for the wells too."

"What the Hell are you talking about."

"We're going to run free on the ranch. That's what she wants, right? We're going to trash the wells." Paulito was on a roll. He was improvising but it did seem like a good idea. "If it's open land then we can do what we want."

"Es no bueno! No good. It means trouble."

"Look Al. We'll tie you up. Gag you. That way you're off the hook." Paulito was adamant. "This is happening Al, but we don't want you to get hurt."

"You're crazy. I can't let you do this." He headed for the phone. "I'm going to call Joe, he needs to know what you're up to."

As al headed to the phone, Paulito and the other boy grabbed him by the arms. "Sorry Al, phone lines are cut.'" They wrestled him to the ground and tied his hands behind his back. Then they gagged him and lifted him onto his bed. "You lay low. I'm sure Mother Sun or someone will find you in the morning. Then you can tell them what you want. She's got to know that we won't put up with her anymore. She's got to go."

They turned out the lights and left.

Al lay on the bed. Dreading the morning.

§

The two flatbeds trundled up the graded drive leading up to the main house. When they came over the rise, only the lights by the barn were on. Paulito and the boys were standing outside the bunkhouse, holding their weapons. All seemed quiet. They followed the signals of a few of the boys leading to the huge pile of wire and posts piled up behind the barn. Others had opened the barn door and were dragging out power post hole diggers and other tools.

The men jumped off the flatbeds and started loading the materials. The two pickups went over to the barn and the boys started loading the tools into the truck. Of course, the noise of the trucks and the men shouting as they began the haul, caused lights to come on at the big house.

The front light came on and the spheres came out and took their usual positions. Two men and a girl on the left. Two men and a girl on the right. Rachel walked out and stood in the pool of light.

"I am Mother Sun. You must stop. You must not be here. You will destroy the opportunity for peace and freedom of all things." She started toward the barn. Paulito and two other boys came over and stood in her way.

"Get back in the house. Take your friends. All this is ours too, isn't it Mother Sun?" He took her roughly by the arm.

Suddenly all four of the male spheres charged Paulito and his friends, knocking them to the ground. The two sphere girls rushed over to Rachel and spirited her back into the house.

The sphere men were thin but wiry and surprisingly strong. Outnumbering Paulito and his guys, they soon had them on the run. After getting some way ahead of them, Paulito turned and pointed the shotgun at them. "Alto, pendejos. I'll drop you where you stand." The other two boys pulled their handguns."

The spheres never left the lighted area. Without a word, they stopped, turned, and went back into the house. The door closed.

Gil came over. "Que paso?"

Paulito was confused. "No idea. But I don't think we'll get any more trouble from them."

"Okay. Let's get this done and get out of here." They both headed back to the barn.

The rest of the raiding party had gotten most of the wire and posts on the flatbeds. So far there was no activity coming from the bunkhouse. Landy had begun to drag more items, power tools, anything that might be worth a few bucks, out of the barn.

"What the hell are you doing, Landy. We got what we came for." Gil sounded pissed.

"Why not make it harder for them to do any work around here." He threw an armload of drills into a pickup. "She's got the money. She'll just buy more."

"Doesn't make it right." Gil shrugged. "Oh Hell...we're breaking the law anyways." He looked things over. "I think we got what we wanted. Let's go."

They piled onto the trucks and started back down the drive.

As they approached the rise, some of the workers burst out of the bunkhouse. Two or three of them had weapons and fired into the air. The Tecolote men thought they were being fired on. They returned fire and the cowboys fired back. As they reached the rise, Paul Rojas saw some headlights coming up the drive heading toward the house.

He stopped and leaned out the window calling to Gil in the truck behind him. "We've got company!"

They stopped at the top of the hill. Paulito and the rest of the men jumped out of the trucks and lined up across the road, holding their weapons. They could see it was just one pickup, but it had about four or five of the cowboys coming back from town. They stopped about a hundred feet from the flatbeds. Meanwhile, the guys from the bunkhouse were cautiously approaching from behind.

Gil realized that they were in a bad spot. He called out to the workers. "We've got you outnumbered. Just back off. We don't want trouble. Back off."

One of the cowboys down the drive hollered back. "What the Hell are you guys doing. We heard gunshots!"

Landy yelled back, "Damn right! We've had enough of you putos fucking things up around here. Get out of the way. We're going to make things right."

"Go to Hell." The cowboy yelled back. "We've got a good thing going here. Don't mess it up."

Landy fired two shots into the air. "Get the Hell out of the way."

Meanwhile, the men from the longhouse had closed in on them from behind. One of them joined in. "Why don't you drop your weapons. You're not going anywhere."

Gil spoke softly to his crew, "Just get back in the trucks. Paulito, hold them off from behind and we'll run that pickup off the road. Landy, fire a few shots over their heads. We'll ram them. Try not to kill anybody. Go. Now!"

They all jumped back into the trucks. Paulito and one or two others took position in the back of the last truck and fired at the men by the house, aiming high. Landy stood on the running board of the first flatbed and fired over the heads of the guys by the pickup. The cowboys took cover, the flatbed roared off down the hill sideswiping the pickup and shoving it off the road. Some of the cowboys took some shots at them but they managed to break through and were followed by the rest of the raiders in the other trucks. They sped down the drive. Nobody followed them.

By the time they got back to Tecolote, the sun was coming up. Paul Rojas had an old metal building near the 7/11 by the highway. They pulled the flatbeds inside and unloaded the pickups. Then they headed back into town to celebrate.

Next, the wells.

§

Al was waiting by the door when Joe arrived at his office. He was disheveled and exhausted, holding a cup of coffee with both hands.

"Joe...It's bad...The ranch is...I don't know."

Putting his hand on Al's shoulder. "Easy, Alphonso. Easy. Come on in and sit down."

They entered the office and they sat down at Joe's desk. "Que hasta pasando? Dime."

"I had to walk down to the highway. They flattened all the tires. There were shots." Just then Gabby came in.

"Morning Gabby. Could you put on a pot of coffee right away. I think Al could use another cup."

"Good morning to you too..." Seeing Al's condition she realized he was in bad shape. "You bet, Joe. Hey Al... just give me a minute."

"Hola Gabby. Thanks." He turned back to Joe. "They cleared out the barn. Some of the cowboys tried to stop them. Nobody got hurt, I don't think. But all the vehicles were disabled. One pickup got pretty smashed up."

"Who did this Joe? Did you recognize anybody?" Joe had an idea who it was, but he wanted to hear it from Al.

"I didn't see anything. Anybody. It was pretty dark. Someone jumped me and hogtied and gagged me...Couldn't see their faces." His voice wavered a bit. He went on, "They cut the power to the house, my place and the bunkhouse. Cut the phone lines. One of the cowboys came looking for me after they had gone. Cut me loose. That was about dawn."

" What exactly did they take?"

"Mainly tools and hardware." Al paused. "They took all the fencing stuff. Posts, wire..."

Gabby brought over the coffee. "Here you go Al. Want a burrito? I made them this morning."

"Please, I could really use something to eat." She went to her cooler, brought him one and sat down nearby. Al went on. "Joe, they left the power on in the barn. Really knew what they were doing. Slashed the tires on the Mercedes and Rachel's Land Rover. They just bled the tires on the cowboys' trucks. The spheres told me to get into town and tell you what happened. Took me a couple of hours to get here."

"And you have no idea who they were?" Joe was suspicious. Al wasn't telling him everything, but that was to be expected. Whoever was behind this were his people, locals. No way was Al going to rat them out.

"Sorry Joe. I didn't see a thing. When I went to the barn the cowboys were mighty pissed. Furioso!" Al looked a little relieved. "Most of them told me they would be gone by the time you and I got back there. Said they didn't sign up to get shot at. Rachel is going to be in for un rudo despertar, a rude awakening. She'll never get anybody to work there now. The money's good, but not good enough to get shot. Word travels fast."

"Okay Al. Let's go. See what we can find out." He paused, "You up for it?"

"Creo que si." He got up to go.

Gabby stopped him. "Go in the back and wash your face. Clean up. Then you can go."

Joe smiled at Gabby. "Call Roberto. Tell him to meet us up there. I've got a hunch about this, and he'll be helpful when we go into Tecolote asking questions."

§

Later that morning Gil and the men from Tecolote had rested enough to regroup for the next step. They got together and jerry-rigged some of the fence posts onto the front bumpers of their 4x4's. Paulito, Landy and Gil led two or three other trucks out of town and headed up some of the old trails that led to the property line of the Tessier.

"Bueno. Let's split up and start finding some of the wells." Gil was once again the organizer. "We'll just shove the stock tanks off the bases and knock down the windmills. It's kind of a shame. I know some of us could use a new windmill or stock tank, but I figure once we chase the sun witch out of here we can always go back and salvage some of the stuff if we need it. Right now, we just want to sabotage this woman. Get her to leave. That's the goal." He paused. "Everybody comprendez?"

They all agreed, and the trucks took off in different directions, looking for targets.

§

Joe and Al arrived back at the Tessier around Noon. The place seemed deserted. The one truck that got run off the drive the night before was still there, but all the others, except for the Mercedes and the Land Rover, were gone.

Over by the barn, someone had dragged out a compressor.

"They must have found some way to turn the power back on," Al said. "Looks like they pumped up the tires and lit on out of here."

Joe and Al got out of the truck and looked around.

"I'm going over to the main house. You better wait here, Al." Joe walked over to the front door and knocked. "County Sheriff. Anybody home?"

A minute passed. Joe knocked again. "Rachel, it's Joe Lujan. Open up!"

He heard footsteps through the door. When it opened the six spheres were there in the foyer. They were looking uneasy. From down the hall Joe heard a voice chanting, actually more like wailing. He headed down the hall, the spheres making no effort to hinder him.

When he came to the den, Rachel was on her knees in the middle of the room, chanting. He stood in the doorway for a moment, then... "Hello, Rachel. Are you all right?"

She stopped murmuring her chants. Straightened up and turned toward Joe.

"I only wanted to bring freedom to this land. Freedom of nature. A life without the imperfections of man. How can these people find that wrong? How can they reject what the power of the Sun offers them?" She stood up. "You know them, Joe. How could they be so wrong?"

"Well, Rachel. It's not a question of right or wrong. I tried to tell you. This is a place that is unique, with people who are very much in touch with their land and their way of life." He tried to be diplomatic. "You have to embrace them and then they may be ready to listen to your ideas. You basically steamrolled over them and that was no way to gain either their trust or understanding, let alone their cooperation."

"I am Mother Sun. I bring only light." She stiffened. "I am the only way for them to really be free. To be one with the Sun. In Vermont, in California, all the people listened to me. They came to me and I gave them light."

"Maybe so. But they came to you. You can't make people believe. The traditions are too strong. You might want to give that some thought before you decide your next move." He gave her moment. "In any case, I understand that some laws have been broken. I'm here to take a report. I will do what I can to find out who did this and see if we can hold someone accountable."

Rachel looked at Joe, her eyes both angry and sad. She tried to regain her composure. "Come with me." And she walked out of the den to the front door. The spheres parted and one of the young women opened the door.

She walked out into the bright, New Mexico sun. To the top of the rise, followed by the spheres, the two girls behind her and the four men behind them. Joe followed at a distance, joined by Al. Stopping at that high point she could see the ranch spread out before her in all directions. The sun seemed to give her strength. Turning toward her spheres she once again looked like the prophet she thought herself to be. Calmly, she spoke to her followers.

"My children, I am going to Tecolote. I will go with the sheriff and talk to the people. You must remain here." The four male spheres looked at her in disbelief. The two young women threw themselves down at Rachel's feet.

"Please, let us go with you. They have guns. They are angry." They begged her, "Please do not go alone."

"I am Mother Sun. Look up at the sky. The sun shines on us all. I do not fear them. The sun will guide me or take me into its heart. If I do not return, you may stay or go. I will still be here, shining down upon this land."

She turned to Joe. "Sheriff, take me to Tecolote."

Joe shrugged, "If you wish. But I'm asking you to listen to the people. You could learn a great deal from them."

§

They rode in silence down the drive past the damaged pickup truck and out onto the rough road leading to Tecolote. Rachel stared straight ahead. Joe didn't try to make conversation. Looking up toward the ranch he noticed a dust cloud from a vehicle high up on a hillside north of the main house. He pulled over and took out his binoculars. He could see it was a pickup with some kind of big bumper on the front. He couldn't see who was driving but he knew the truck. He panned away to the east and saw a similar truck off toward a nearby mesa. "Estupendo!" he just shook his head.

"Looks like they're not finished with you yet, Rachel."

She said nothing.

When they arrived in Tecolote, except for Diego sitting in front of his house and a woman hanging out her wash, the town seemed deserted. Most of the vehicles were not around, Joe pulled right up to Delfina's house. She had heard him coming and was at the door to greet him.

"Hola Joe." She saw Rachel in the truck. "You must be Rachel. Please, come in and have a cup of coffee." Without waiting, she turned back into the house and Joe started to follow.

Rachel stepped out of the truck. She gazed around the small village, took a deep breath. "I would prefer to stay outside. I must be in the light of the sun."

"Delfina is kind of the matriarch of this village. It would show her great respect if you entered her house and accepted her hospitality." Joe looked at Rachel. "This is important."

Rachel ignored him and went over to one of the battered kitchen chairs by the front door and sat down. "Please tell her I am happy to meet with her...out here. I will have tea."

Knowing things were off to a bad start, Joe went into the house, leaving Rachel outside.

He sat down at the kitchen table and Delfina poured him and herself a cup. She sat down across from Joe. "Where is the woman?"

"She will only meet with you outside, in the sun." Joe knew Delfina would find this an insult. "Something went down at the Tessier last night. Do you know anything about that?"

She smiled at him. "Everything was quiet here. Same as any night... Although I might have heard a gunshot way up in the hills near there." Looking Joe in the eye, "I got up and looked outside. Seemed normal. Everybody's vehicles were here. No lights on. Probably just some kids shooting coyotes or rabbits."

"Seguro." Joe smiled back, "Well, someone raided the Tessier. Must have had a bunch of guys, several trucks...Hard to miss at that hour."

"Why don't you ask around. Maybe I was asleep. Somebody else may have heard something." She stood with her arms folded. "Why is that woman here?"

Joe got up and faced Delfina. "She wants to talk to the people here. But since everyone seems to be gone, perhaps you can speak with her." Tentatively he asked, "Would you consider offering her a cup of tea."

"Seguro!" She went to the cupboards and took down a ceramic jar. "I have prickly pear and Mormon tea. It will do her some good and perhaps get her talking."

"That would be fine." Joe went back outside.

Rachel was not sitting by the door.

§

While Joe was inside Delfina's, Rachel sat in the sun with her eyes closed, feeling it's warmth. Trying to absorb the strength she believed it gave her. She sat like that for five minutes and when she opened her eyes, she saw an old man across the dirt street, sitting on a couch on his front porch. He was smiling at her, as if he just got a joke. Without thinking, and for some unknown reason, Rachel got up and walked over to the old man.

"Who are you?" She asked.

"Hello Señorita. Please come and sit next to me." He gestured for her to sit on the worn and weathered couch. Rachel sat, strangely drawn to the man. "I am Diego de Luna." He reached down to his cooler and offered her a beer.

"Thank you, no." She refused.

Diego popped the top and offered it to her again. "Por favor. I have nothing else."

To her surprise, Rachel found herself holding the cold beer, even taking a sip or two. "I am Mother Sun. I have come here to make this beautiful land the origin, the source of the ultimate freedom for all creatures."

Diego smiled at her. "Do you know what my name means. Diego de Luna can mean 'Teacher of the Moon.' As Mother Sun, you should know that there is much to learn from your reflection on the face of the moon." He paused. "Do you know what the moon wants you to learn?"

Rachel looked confused. Who is this old man? Why has the sun sent me to him? "I only know that we would not see the moon were it not for the sun."

"As I said, it is the reflection from the moon that gives the message of the sun a greater meaning." He leaned toward Rachel. "You see the sun's light only during the daylight hours. Pero, a noche, at night, the moon gives the sun its reflection, like a mirror. You want to give all creatures the freedom of the sun's light, true freedom to live and die as the world intended before the coming of humanity. Do you not?"

"Yes, yes. Of course. You have heard my beliefs?"

"No, but I understand. To know how to complete your mission, you must look to the sun's light both direct and reflected. I am of the moon. I know what you must do. What you did not learn from only daylight."

Rachel was captivated by this old man. How did he know this? "What is it I must do?" she asked.

"The unrest you have caused here is irreparable, perdido. Do you understand?"

She looked down at her hands. "But I cannot give up. My mission..."

"Your mission is bigger than here. Bigger than your ranch." He took a sip of his beer. Rachel drank as well. "You must find a place where you can gather all the energy. A place away from others. Such a place will allow you to become like the sun, anchored at the center, never moving. Radiating your message around the world without ever leaving your sanctuary. No distractions. Only your mission."

"I understand. There is no need to be amongst people who do not understand. It is too much for them. Too great for them to realize it for their wellbeing." She stood, putting down the beer. Gently placing her hand on Diego's arm. "You are truly a teacher. I will be watching the moon, as well as the sun. They will work together to bring the peace and freedom of natural life to all. Thank you, Deigo de Luna." She turned and walked back to Delfina's house where Joe and Delifina, holding a mug, were standing, watching.

"Delfina, thank you for your hospitality. Please let me take this tea from you. I am honored." She drank a few sips, then turned to Joe, "Please take me back to the ranch. And thank you for bringing me here. It was truly meant to be."

She climbed into Joe's truck.

Joe, a little baffled, handed Delfina her cup. "Thank you for your hospitality, Tia. I'll be in touch." He shrugged his shoulders and got in the truck. They drove off.

Delfina watched them leave and looked over at Diego. He smiled and waved, taking another sip of his beer. She smiled back. "Que zorro astuto. That old trapacero could charm the rattle off a sidewinder." She laughed to herself as she went back into the house.

§

Once again, they drove in silence back to the ranch. When they arrived, Rachel got out and walked into the house without a word. Joe sat at the wheel for a few minutes. "I wonder what old Diego said to her. Must have been something good. Diego was no fool, and he had a reputation for being able to figure things out."

He noticed Al coming from over by the barn.

"How did it go? Is everybody okay?" Al looked desperate. "I've got to get this place back together."

Joe was about to answer when the front door opened. Rachel led the spheres who took their places by the entry. Rachel turned to them.

"We will leave this place. In time, it will once again bask in the true light of the sun. Now we will find a place where we can spread the power of the sun around the world, aided by the shining power of the moon. We will find a new place, perhaps an island... where we can gather and prosper and radiate the glory of the sun... and the moon... to all humanity. Gather what you need, my spheres. We leave today."

Joe and Al couldn't believe what they were hearing. She came over to them placing a hand on their arms. "Al, you must remain here. I will be making the ranch a sanctuary. Let them put their fences up but also let them feel free to wander the ranch. I am done here. My attorneys will be in touch with you. You and Tecolote will be blessed" She smiled at them both. "Please go now, Sheriff. I will not be pressing any charges. Goodbye. Perhaps the sun will find a way to reach you and the sad people of this place." She turned and walked back to the house. The spheres followed. The door closed.

§

They walked back to Joe's truck. Al was in some sort of state of shock. He stood with his hands in his pockets, not knowing what to do next.

Joe climbed into his truck. "Listen Al. I'll let Roberto know you're up here. We'll contact the power company and the phone company. Get you hooked up." He closed the door. "I'm going back to Tecolote. I still want to know what those tontos did. The gente down there blindsided me. I don't like to be blindsided." He started the engine. "I'll get Max at Santino's garage up here to fix the tires on the Merc and the Land Rover. Just hang tight and keep on eye on..." He nodded toward the main house and drove off. He could see Al standing there, looking lost.

As he passed the damaged pickup, it reminded him to have Max bring the tow truck and haul that into town as evidence. Best get it out of sight. He continued down the drive and reached the main road, heading toward Tecolote,

When he arrived in Tecolote he pulled right up to Delifina's house again. Roberto had arrived and he and Delfina were standing by the cruiser, talking.

"Hey, Joe." He leaned on the car door. "I had Gabby call the power and phone companies. Got Max to go the Tessier right away." He furrowed his brow, "Is Al okay?"

"He'll be all right." He turned to Delfina. "Rachel said she's leaving the ranch...Not sure what she has planned but Al will still be up there. I'm pretty sure she's going to be gone soon, very soon."

"She did not understand that she has her world and we have ours. To her there was only freedom in her world." Delfina shook her head. "She is a fool."

Joe nodded, "That doesn't make it right for her to be trespassed against. To be robbed and frightened. Things could have been much worse.

Someone could have gotten hurt or killed. I can't accept that." He turned to Roberto. "You stick around here. I want everyone to come clean about what they did. Rachel's not going to press charges. She just wants out. You tell Gil, and Paulito...and especially Landy, that if things were different, I'd come up with something to lock them up in Santa Fe for a few months. They know I can do it.'

He got into his truck, "I understand that things had reached their limits, but that doesn't mean they can pull a stunt like that on me. Not if they want my help in the future. It might have taken me a little longer... but I'd have figured something out. Adios Tia." He drove off.

When he got to the highway, he stopped at the 7/11 for gas. He noticed a new lock on Rojas' storage building out back. He filled up and pulled his truck over to the building and got out. Through one of the rust holes in the wall he could make out the two flatbeds loaded with wire and posts. There were tools and other supplies pitched carelessly along the walls. "Cabron! I can't wait to hear the stories about this one." He got back into the truck and went to pull out onto the road.

Back up toward the Tessier, he saw a dust cloud from a vehicle approaching. As it got closer, he could see that it was the school bus...the time machine from the sixties.

It came around the turn and he saw it was Rachel driving. She saw him and waved. The bus got on the Interstate and headed west, away from Las Puertas, from Tecolote and from the Tessier.

LAND OF ENCHANTMENT

S pring in the Sangre de Cristos. The change in the light, the hints of green on the scrub oak and aspens. The local farms and gardens were being prepared for planting. In the towns and villages, the "gente" were ready for the warmer weather. Winters are mild but it can drop down to freezing from time to time. The many homes heated with wood stoves made sure they had a plentiful supply of firewood or coal.

Spring is also the season that brings Holy Week. That sacred week when Christians follow the life of Christ from Palm Sunday to Easter Sunday. A time for deep religious feelings and deep emotions. northern New Mexico has a long history with the Catholic church, dating back to the arrival of the Spanish and their missionaries...but within the church there are factions with differing thoughts about the way to worship.

One such faction is the Hermanos Penitentes. Dating back to the sixteenth century, this extension of the Third Order of St. Francis has long been a part of the southern Colorado and northern New Mexico Hispanic culture. The society primarily consists of men who, to atone for their sins, perform rituals that include self-flagellation, self-mutilation and other practices of pain and suffering to identify with the sufferings of Jesus. By doing this, they feel they have paid their penance and are purged of their sins. At least for the previous year.

Around 1850, because their rituals had risen to such an extreme level, the Archbishop of Santa Fe ordered them to abolish these practices. The Penitentes did not obey. They became more secretive, meeting in isolated places, the acts of repentance becoming more barbarous. It was well known that if one came upon the group while they were worshiping, their desire to repel outsiders made them dangerous. People were injured... on occasion their desire for privacy could be fatal to an unfortunate hiker.

The fraternity local to Las Puertas was one of the oldest in the area. The "Hermano Major" or chief officer lived on the north edge of San Miguel County, near Rociada, a small settlement on the edge the Santa Fe National Forest near the Pecos Wilderness. His name was Gaspar de la Madalena.

The Hermano Major held office for life. His group was organized with lieutenants, in this case the Hermanos de Luz, and other subordinates...as with other secret societies. Gaspar held his office fanatically. He attended church and prayed all year long as any other religious individual would. But it was Holy Week that he looked forward to. The week when his followers, and any new recruits, would be under his authority. When he would help them all rise up in the eyes of God and atone for their sins. He would lead them, imposing the pain of His holiness on them with ever more intense rituals.

Each year, on the Saturday before Palm Sunday, the men of Gaspar's brotherhood would start to arrive at his ranch outside Rociada. He solemnly welcomed them as they entered the "Morada", a large metal barn building behind his house. For the next week, they would spend the nights in the barn. The rituals would begin at sunrise on Good Friday. There were about one hundred men, most were long term members. This year, there were two new initiates.

Gaspar would greet each of them. "Welcome my brother. Soon we will begin our penitence in the eyes of our Lord. We will climb the mountains, as he climbed the Stations of the Cross. Out there, in God's virgin land, we will give ourselves over to Him. When we come home, we will be cleansed, forgiven of our sins..."

§

Late March, early April brought the melting snows. The Caballos River was swollen and overflowing throughout Las Puertas. The water had reached both piers on each end of the bridge. Some of the homes on Valencia Street and along the river all the way to Mills Avenue were watching the water creep toward their back door. It wasn't the first time...

many of the houses had been there for hundreds of years. This would pass.

Sheriff Joe Lujan was cruising the streets around the river, checking on folks who might need some help. The river comes very close to some of the houses on Delgado St. He thought he'd better check in on them.

But the water was welcome. This was springtime in northern New Mexico, and it was a time for fickle weather, possible flooding and slippery dirt roads. Joe expected to hear his radio spark up at any time with some emergency or other.

Joe knew there would be other incidents, other occurrences that happen in the Spring. Local farmers would start planting crops and there would be ongoing disputes over boundaries and water rights. Ranchers would be keeping a watchful on their herds, knowing it was calving season. The helpless calves were easy prey for coyotes and wolves. Things got tense. Joe, and his deputy, Roberto Castillo, would be busy breaking up fights and cooling tempers.

And there were the Hermanos Penitentes. The men would pass through Las Puertas on their way up to Rociada. You could sense when someone was in the brotherhood. They had a distant look in their eyes...on their way to salvation. Some were from inside the county. Joe knew many of them. They lived and worked in the nearby communities.

Then there were the others, coming from all over the state. Lured by the charismatic personality of Gaspar de la Madalena. Joe knew Gaspar... all too well. He was the most influential jefe in New Mexico. He was also the most powerful Hermano Major. His barn was the largest morada in the state. Next to the district's politicians and Joe, Madalena was the most powerful man in the county. His influence spread into Mora County as well.

Joe and Gaspar had a deal. Joe would avoid the gathering unless someone from outside of the brotherhood was victimized, in one way or another, by members. Then the deal was off. In turn, Gaspar would restrict his members from leaving the group, for any reason, and that they would hold the majority of their rituals in the morada or in the otherwise isolated areas of the Pecos close to Rociada. Local residents knew well to avoid them during Holy Week, keeping to themselves.

At any rate, Palm Sunday was a few weeks off. It was later in the Spring this year and the weather would be warmer. Joe knew that things would be relatively ordinary until then. With any luck, the Holy Week would pass without incident.

His radio crackled. It was Gabriella Rendon, Gabby…She was holding down the fort at the office while he and his deputy, Roberto Castillo, were on patrol.

"Sheriff, are you there?"

"Seguro, Gabby, What's up?"

"There's some flooding up by Montezuma, some debris blocking the river and the road. The folks need some help while they clear things up." She paused, "Shall I let Roberto know?"

"No. I'm on the north end. I'll go. I was heading that way from here anyway. Give the road crews a heads up. They need to get up there." He pulled out of Delgado Street and onto Gonzales, then over to Hot Springs and accelerated, lights flashing but no siren.

§

Mike O'Farrell made a living as a house painter in Rhode Island. He lived in a tough neighborhood on the outskirts of Providence and ran with a group of blue-collar tradesmen, mostly Italians and Irish in their twenties. They drank every night and partied hard on the weekends. Although they were good friends, getting loaded and into fights at the bars with others like themselves, or even with each other, was a given. They worked hard, making good money, but pissed it away on parties, pickup trucks and fast cars. Home was usually in one of those typical New England triple deckers built during the late nineteenth or early twentieth century.

Tall and lanky, curly black hair, Mike had known most of his friends since childhood. They were all very close and they lived that gritty lifestyle, tolerating the fact that Mike was both a house painter and a dedicated artist. New England lent itself to his ambition to become an accomplished landscape painter. When he started painting in junior high, nearby Narragansett Bay offered endless potential subjects for him, virtually in his own back yard. Once he started driving, he would go out on Cape Cod or up to Acadia National park for new vistas and greater challenges. Vermont and New Hampshire were also close enough for him to find bucolic views of farms and receding panoramas of the Green and White Mountains.

Mike chose to go part time to the University of Rhode Island and study art while still earning a living as a housepainter. He focused his studies on 19th and 20th century American landscape artists and discovered that many of them had been drawn to New Mexico, attracted to the unique colors of the high desert, the adobe houses and the Native American pueblos. He left University in his third year, feeling that the pull of the southwest outweighed the need for a degree. A friend of his, Jane Meyers, was attending university in some town called Las Puertas, near Santa Fe. Throwing his paints, brushes and a minimal amount of possessions into his old van, he spent a last night with his friends and headed west on a rainy weekday morning.

§

Other than around New England, Mike had never been west of Connecticut. I-95 was crowded with fast moving cars and erratic drivers. The New Jersey turnpike was a nightmare. By the time he hit the Pennsylvania turnpike he was drained. His hands were cramped and he figured he had better pull over at the next rest area and take a nap.

Unexpectedly, out of nowhere, a large pheasant flew across the road in front of his van, barely missing him. "Jesus! That was really cl..."

The impact was sudden. The loud smash of a second pheasant hitting the side of the car caused Mike to panic. The van swerved and he almost lost control when he hit the gravel on the shoulder. Still shaking, he pulled to a stop off the road and slowly released his tight grip on the steering wheel.

"Jesus Christ! What the Hell was that?" He pushed the door open...it creaked, resisting him due to the damage. He got out to check things out.

There was blood and feathers on the fender and part of the windshield. The side mirror was gone. "Just fucking great." Looking back down the road, he saw the body of the large bird on the roadway. The first pheasant had landed just past the road. It seemed sad and confused. There was the sunlight glinting off three or four pieces of chrome and glass near the corpse.

Now, Mike was not a religious guy, but the incident made him wonder...was this a sign? Was something telling him to go back. He felt he was a spiritual person. How else could he impart a sense of wonder to his paintings, a sense of a timeless presence that would be transferred to the observer? Was the sudden death of this poor bird telling him to go on into the unknown or return to what he knew. The safety of the past versus the insecurity of the future.

He got back into the van. Lighting a cigarette, he inhaled deeply. He slid the seat back as far as it could go and closed his eyes. "Should I push on? What does this mean?" he thought. "Ah, what the Hell. I'm on the road. No turning back now." He adjusted the seat, started the engine, and cautiously pulled back on the highway, heading west.

§

The rest of the trip was uneventful. He had to stop in Washington, Pennsylvania to buy a new side mirror. Other than that, he only stopped for gas and to grab short naps in the rest areas. He drove across the Midwest at night, few cars on the road, truckers sleeping in their cabs at the truck stops. A pack of Pall Malls on the dash.

He picked up Route 66 in St. Louis, or at least the remnants of it that had not been replaced by the Interstates. In Joplin, he blew a tire and bought a used one at a service station on the way out of town. The owner eyed him suspiciously, "Damn hippies. Wish they stayed back East." He made Mike wait for a couple of hours, putting other repairs ahead of him until, finally, it was done. It was after seven, dark, and the repairs had cost him almost a day. But he wasn't in any hurry. The mountains and mesas would be there, waiting for him.

Coming through Oklahoma and Texas on I-40, the land seemed dry and unfriendly. But when he crossed the border into New Mexico, the land suddenly rose up to the high desert. He pulled into a rest area and got out to stretch his legs. He noticed a path leading up to the top of a mesa and decided to hike up there and look around. The path led to the top of a rise where he came across a Geological Survey marker. Longitude 35N Latitude 103W. Turning to the east, he looked out over the vast central basin of the Central United States. It was surreal. The colors were browns and yellows and reds. The sky was pale blue with wisps of clouds. Coming from the New England coast, he had often surveyed the sea and wondered at the expanse of the north Atlantic. There the water is a deep blue gray. On a sunny day, the sky contrasted bright blue. On a gray day, the sky mirrored the dark, steely colors of the water.

On that mesa in New Mexico, he could almost see where the Cretaceous Inland Sea had once been. In his mind, the water covered the wide expanse, a great ocean with waves lapping at his feet where the former shoreline had been. He looked down and right there, at the edge of the existential ocean, was a fossilized shark's tooth. He picked it up and held it up against the breathtaking background. He knew he was where he should be. That his decision to come out west was right.

§

Leaving Interstate 40 just past Santa Rosa on Highway 84, he headed north. Coming in from the west, he arrived in Las Puertas late in the afternoon. He had Jane's address but had no idea where it was. The edge of town was less than inviting. Auto repair shops littered with broken down cars, small one-story run-down plastered houses with wash on the line. Abandoned metal buildings with bent and rusted roofs. A couple of blocks south he could see the tall cone of an old lumber kiln standing against the horizon. On the left was a rough looking roadhouse. "The Ringside," the sign said. "Live Band Saturdays, Friday Night Fights."

Mike felt a little unsure of himself. "Does Jane really live in this dump." Where are the charming Adobe houses with small gardens and picturesque cactus in the yard? Where are the mestizo girls dressed in colorful dresses and peasant blouses? The beautiful mission churches? He turned off the main drag onto one of the larger streets that looked like it headed into the center of town. Passing more houses and the odd liquor store, he chanced upon the central plaza. He pulled over and parked. He felt like he had landed in a time warp, a place unchanged for decades. A tired band stand in the center. An old hotel on one corner. Several abandoned store fronts and a shuttered bank building, a locked gate across the front.

"Jesus...I better ask someone if they know where to find Jane's place." He got out of the car and walked over to an old man sitting on a park bench. As he approached. He called out, "Excuse me, sir..."

The old man looked up at him and smiled. "Hola, amigo." He shielded his eyes from the sun. "Come, ¡siéntate!, sit down so I can see you."

Mike sat down a couple of feet away. The old man had a brown paper bag in his hand. "Have a swig." He handed it to Mike who cautiously took a drink from the bottle. "Got a cigarette?"

"In the car...I'll go get them." He went to the van and grabbed the pack off the dash. When he returned to the bench the old man looked genuinely pleased to see him. They lit up.

"Guillermo Jaramillo." He extended his hand to Mike.

"Mike O'Farrell." They shook.

"Looks like you just got into town. Where you from?" Gil smiled.

"I'm from Rhode Island. I have a friend who lives here." Mike pulled a paper from his wallet. "This is her address".

"You better read it to me. My eyes, they're not so good anymore. Getting a little ciego, blind." He took a deep breath. "Doc says its cataracts or something." Mike could see the cloudiness in his eyes. "It's okay. I can still get around. Don't need to drive anywhere. I live with my daughter and her kids. No está mal. It's not so bad."

Mike read the address to Guillermo. "She lives on 42 Lincoln Street. I think it's a big house turned into apartments. She talks about her neighbors a lot."

"Sure, sure. That's not too far. Nothing is very far in this town." Guillermo gestured at Mike's van. "You're headed in the right direction. Just go straight on up Bridge Street. When you cross over make your first right. A couple of blocks and make a left. That's her street. Numbers are not always easy to read but it's about two blocks, on the right. Big white house. Just south of the campus." He paused. "Goes to school here, does she?"

"Yeah. But she likes it so much here she settled in. She's an artist, like me."

Guillermo smiled. He patted Mike on the shoulder. "So, you came to capture the Espiritu, the soul of our land?"

Mike was stunned. "Exactly. I paint landscapes. For some reason I felt I needed to come here, to paint."

"Si. Seguro. The land...but it is the people that give it soul." A sadness passed over Guillermo's face. He gazed at the blue sky. "Remember that. When you are looking at the mesas, the pinyons, the arroyos...they are part of our being. You will find the essence of the land in the faces of our people."

Mike stood up, impressed. He gave Guillermo his cigarettes. "I guess I'll head out. Thanks for the drink and the directions."

"You're a good boy. I like you. Come and visit me. I'm here most days." He winked. "Bring your girlfriend."

"Oh, she's not my girlfriend..." He laughed. "Just a friend."

"Ah, yes." Guillermo held up his bottle, "One for the road."

"No, thanks anyway. I'll come by again, sometime." Mike headed to his van, the old man smiled and waved.

§

As he drove down Bridge Street, Mike noticed many boarded-up storefronts. There was a restaurant, El Palacio, and an insurance office. Not much going on. He passed the sheriff's office just before crossing the bridge. He made the right turn and drove past a laundromat and the St. Vincent De Paul thrift store. Turning left on Lincoln Street, he started looking for the big white house. "One house had the number 38 on it. Then two or three with no numbers. One was a large white house that looked right. A VW bug with Rhode Island plates was parked in front. This must be the place.

He checked the name on the mailbox and saw "Meyers" next to #3. The two doors on the front said #1 and #2. He walked around the side and found #3...knocked on the door.

It was about six. Footsteps approached, and the door opened. Mike was surprised to see it was a tall, dark-haired guy. He looked Mike up and down. "Yeah. What do you want?"

"I'm Mike O'Farrell. Jane's friend from back East."

The man smiled, kind of sly. "Yeah, sure. You're the painter. Come on in. My name's Ben, Ben Rangel"

Mike entered the hallway and followed the man to what must have been the living room.

"Jane's still at the library. She'll be home soon." He gestured at the worn-out sofa. "Grab a seat...you want a beer?"

"That'd be great." Mike sat down. The man went to the fridge that was, for some reason, in the living room.

"I'm Ben." He handed Mike the beer and offered his hand. They shook. "When did you get into town?"

"Just got here. I think Jane was expecting me."

Ben nodded. "She's looking forward to seeing you. Told me a lot about you."

"Are you and her...you know..."

Ben laughed. "Jane doesn't do boyfriends. You should know that." He looked askance at Mike. "I'm the roommate." He sat down next to Mike and took a swig of his beer. They sat in silence for a few minutes. "You going to do some painting?"

Mike face showed his excitement. "I can't wait. I don't believe the colors out here, the land. It's a different world. Back East everything is green, the sea is all around. The hills are green, rolling, bucolic." He paused.

"Out here, at least from what I've seen, the colors are reds, tans, yellows. The land jumps out against the bright sky, the mesas, the shadows, the mountains...it's wild, mystical."

"You've got it right, amigo. It's timeless." Ben was warming to this Anglo. "Why don't you bring in your stuff. I'll show you where you can set up. Jane's got it all figured out. By the time you're done she should be here."

Oddly enough, Mike suddenly began to feel at home. His new life had begun.

§

The small room in the back of the apartment was sparse. A bed, dresser and a straight back chair. There was a tiny armoire in the corner, but Mike didn't have much. He unpacked his clothes and put them away. He stacked his easel and painting stuff in a corner for easy access. He was eager to get out and start working.

When he came back into the living room, Ben was watching the local news.

"We're lucky to get one station here. There's only two out of Albuquerque. Sometimes you can get both, but the signals are really weak." He got up and walked back into the kitchen and grabbed two more beers. He looked out the window as he came back. "Here comes Jane now."

Mike jumped up and walked to the door as it opened. Jane was outside looking over his van.

"Nice wheels," she said sarcastically. "Looks like its lucky you made it...Hello Michael."

Mike came up to her and gave her a hug. She hung back a bit. Jane wasn't one for affection.

"Yeah, well I love your fancy digs. Reminds me of some of the places I rented in Providence." He paused. "I've seen worse."

"Come on in." They walked back inside. Jane put her notebooks and texts on the kitchen table. "Hey, Ben. How do you like our new roommate?"

Ben smiled and grunted his approval. "Seems okay." He turned back to the television. Jane got herself a beer and sat down at the kitchen table with Mike.

"What's the plan?" She asked him.

"I want to get started right away. I figure I'll start tomorrow. I think I have everything I need but I was curious...if I need more supplies. Is there a place in town I can get paints, canvases, things like that?"

Jane smiled. "Not here. The closest good art supply store is in Santa Fe. If you're not part of the art department, you're pretty much on your own. There's one place just off the plaza up there, calls itself a trading post, but that's where most of the artists here get their supplies." She got up and tossed her beer bottle into the trash. "If they don't have it, you'll have to go to Albuquerque...Welcome to Las Puertas, Mike. You'll be putting some miles on that van of yours."

§

The dawn on the Thursday before Palm Sunday was inspiring. It promised to bring another beautiful day in northeast New Mexico. Gaspar was already standing in front of his house, an adobe long house that had been in his family for generations. Next door, in the barn, the hermanos that had been arriving during the week were still sleeping. Gaspar expected many more today and even more tomorrow. All of his morada should be in attendance by Saturday. He walked over to the barn and entered.

"Despierto, mi hermanos. Despierto! Do not sleep away the day." He called out. "There is work to be done. Mucho trabajo!" He had a clay campana or bell by the door, hanging on a rope. "Despierto!" He rang the bell.

The men stirred, then sat up, startled. Gaspar walked between the rows of men, touching them on the head, a fatherly gesture. "Go out to the well. Wash the sleep from your eyes. There are beans and tortillas and coffee for you by the house. First pray, then eat. Clean the barn. Clean the yard. Build the crosses. There is lumber, and tools here..." he gestured to a work bench by the door. "I will be going to town for supplies. Each of you must contribute. He picked up a bucket and held it up. Por favor...put in whatever you can afford. If more of our brothers arrive while I am gone, show them what they need to know. I will return por la tarde. All must be ready by sunrise on Sunday. Bless you." He turned away.

"Via con dios, jefe." The men chimed together.

Gaspar went to his truck and drove off. Looking in the rear-view mirror he saw the men coming out of the barn and gathering by the front porch of his house. "This year will be un espíritu de júbilo, a triumph of the spirit. The hermanos will be closer to God than ever before." He reveled in the thought.

He was going into Las Puertas but he was going the long way, southwest, over the ridge between the Pecos Wilderness and the Santa Fe National Forest, then down through Piedras Blanca to Chapelle and the highway. He would make a stop and do a final inspection of some of the nearby but cloistered locations he had chosen for the upcoming rituals. After all, he had all day.

The roads through the national forest were barely roads at all. They were dirt tracks worn into the ground over many years. The few vehicles that passed through eliminated the vegetation where the wheels rolled and the climate defied any regrowth. Up near Wagon Mound, one could still see the tracks left by the trader's wagons that passed through the area one hundred and fifty years ago traversing the Santa Fe trail.

Gaspar had chosen the spots for his gatherings over the past year. Although close to the morada, some were surrounded by pine forests... others at the top of mesas with grand vistas both to the east and the west. The so-called main road followed the ridges and valleys. The side roads were old logging roads or paths made by the rangers. Others were wildlife trails that led to isolated clearings and the rare stream or pool of water.

He had made inconspicuous blazes on some of the trees along the trails. In other areas, he built small stone cairns to indicate where to turn. None were far from Rociada, making it easier to lead the brothers to the spot. The procession would go in a rough circle. There would be prayer sessions and meditation at each of the secret locations, mirroring the ten Stations of the Cross. They were private, isolated. Many of the hermanos' practices were both illegal by man's law and forbidden by the church.

He pulled over near the first of his holy places. It was one of his favorites. He left the truck and hiked the half mile down the deer trail and over the ridge to a flat mesa that rose treeless in the middle of an area of thick pine trees. He dropped to his knees and proclaimed to the sky... "I am the Hermano Major. I serve God. In this place we will share the passion of our Lord. Through sacrifice and pain we will come to you, bare our souls and be freed of our sins." He stood and raised his arms, "I will bring you my holy brothers and they will prostate before you and give you their lives if you so desire. This I swear to you." He fell to the ground. Shaking, as if having a fit. His face contorted into a mask of fear...his eyes teared up. He lay still for almost ten minutes and finally sat up. The day was cool, but Gaspar was sweating...exhausted from the presence of God within him.

At each of the places he had marked out for this year's gatherings he stopped and made his proclamation to God. By the time he had blessed all the locations, he was exhausted. At the last one high on the mesa overlooking the morada he prayed. He returned to his truck and rested, drank some water and gazed out over the land. The vista of God's beautiful country gave him the strength he needed to go on.

It was afternoon and he was hungry. Gaspar knew the trail well. He drove fast, wanting to get into town, get his supplies and get back up to Rociada before dark. There would be more brothers arriving. This would be the last time he would leave the morada until after Easter Sunday.

He started the descent to Piedras Blanca. Arriving at the little settlement he waved to the few folks who were out. Most of the people there knew him and they knew that the upcoming week was no time to go up into the Pecos. Unless you were ready to participate in the gatherings, you were not welcome. The brothers fearlessly protected their privacy. Outsiders were sometime held at Gaspar's ranch until after Easter, then released with severe warnings. Others were never heard from again.

§

"This is magical!" Mike thought to himself as he drove west from Las Puertas...down the frontage road of the interstate. It was just past sunrise. Jane had told him that there would be some great panoramic views if he took the frontage road and then the side roads to the north.

Mike noticed how the unmarked dirt roads looked rarely used. Though his van was running all right, he thought he better take one of the ones that seemed more travelled in case he did have car trouble. The one he chose was a little rough. It ran straight north rising gradually into the foothills.

After a mile or so he pulled over and gazed out over the landscape. The strong sunlight from the east dazzled one side of the mesas and cast dark, almost black shadows stretching across the valleys and scrub toward the west. It was mesmerizing. The yellows, reds, browns and greens were sharply defined, one from the other. The flowing yet irregular nature of the land created mystifying designs, distinct contrast of sunlight and shadow.

"This is where I was meant to be." He sat on a rock and surveyed the panorama, considering his strategy to begin painting. After a while, he went to the van, got out his easel and other supplies and went out into the scrub to start setting up. Placing a blank canvas onto the easel, he sat on his stool and began to sketch in the rough outlines of the vista. He had picked a sector that seemed to offer all the components needed to allow him to capture the unique nature of this new land...this new muse.

He rushed to get a good sketch before the light changed. When he was satisfied, he began to prepare his palette. He liked working with acrylics. The colors dried quickly, and he could easily begin to define the sharp contrasts he needed to properly represent what he was seeing. Cadmium yellow, burnt sienna, forest green...the colors he was seeing were as pure as the colors that came out of the tubes of paint.

§

As Gaspar came out of the foothills, he saw Mike's van by the side of the road. Pulling up behind the van, he noticed the out of state plates. It was a local practice to check out anything that was out of character. Find out what the strangers were up to. He got out and walked down off the shoulder.

Mike heard the truck coming and stopped working, waiting to see who it could be. He watched Gaspar looking over his van. Coming from back East where strangers often meant trouble, Mike thought he should see what this guy wanted. He went up to the road, still holding his brushes and pallet. When he got about fifty feet from Gaspar he called out... "Morning. Nice morning, isn't it?"

Gaspar looked over the tall, Anglo kid. "What's your business here, my friend.?"

Mike was surprised by the confrontational tone of the man's voice. "The name's Mike. I'm a painter...an artist. This..." He gestured to the wide landscape around him. "This is what I'm painting. Who are you?"

"You are trying to capture the work of the Lord on this puny canvas?" Gaspar walked over to Mike's easel. He looked closely at the painting. "You do not have God in your picture...I only see you! If you do not have the spirit of God in you, you will never be able to paint what you want to paint." Gaspar fixed his gaze on Mike, looking at him...but Mike felt he was looking right through him.

Mike was a Catholic. He was raised a good Irish Catholic boy. His friends were Irish or Italian so they grew up going to the same churches and the same Sunday schools. Home life included saying grace at meals and

Sunday dinners after church. Life was a blue-collar world and it revolved around family, friends, work, and church.

Mike's art made him the exception. He wanted to learn more about the great masters of landscapes and seascapes. He was the first in his family to apply and be accepted into university. As a freshman, he took the required course in philosophy. The professor covered both lay philosophers and those whose thoughts grew out of their religious beliefs. He was surprised to find that the great minds raised spiritualism out of the confines of the dogma of the institution to a higher, more enlightened level.

In his first year, he also took an elective course in art history. The great masters and the contemporary geniuses all evoked this sense of spiritualism from the viewer.

Mike had developed his own feelings about the mysteries of the universe, and they did not necessarily fit with the world he grew up in.

He stiffened at Gaspar's implication. "How do you know if I have the spirit of God in me or not? Who are you to make that assumption?" Mike grew up in a rough world. He wasn't ready to take any abuse from a stranger. The man was shorter than him...wiry, but no tougher than some of the guys Mike took on back in Rhode Island.

Gaspar smiled, his voice softened. "Rélajate, calma amigo. Maybe you do have some of the spirit of God in you. There is one way you can find out."

Mike was still riled, "And how would that be?"

"Is the Lord, Jesucristo, your God?"

"What business is that of yours. Who the Hell are you?" Mike didn't know what to think.

"Come over to my truck. I have something for you."

They walked back to Gaspar's truck where he reached in and found a piece of paper. He scribbled something on it and handed it to Mike. "My name is Gaspar de la Madalena. I am kind of a lay priest. Palm Sunday is coming up. I will meet with my brothers, Los Hermanos Penitentes, at my chapel in Rociada early that morning. Ask anyone how to find my place."

"I'm not much of a church goer. Sorry." Mike relaxed. Gaspar's attitude had changed from confrontational to concerned.

"No, no, no. This is not going to church. This is joining my brothers and I in a conversation with God. We are living in the blood and body of Christ. In the Sangre de Cristo mountains. Our prayers are heard by the mesa, the pinyons, the arroyos. If you come and hear our prayers, join our prayers…God will answer them through the firmament you are trying to paint. With us you will be able to strengthen your spirit and your art will radiate the God who made this beautiful land. Please come."

"I gave you a map. Come to my chapel, my morada. It is in the bosom of His land and He will speak to you there. Then your work…your art.. it will lose the pride of man, your pride. It will truly show only the spirit of Our Lord." got into his truck. "Come my friend. You and your work will be blessed."

Mike stood by the side of the road. He watched as Gaspar's truck disappeared in the dust cloud and moved down toward the highway.

§

Later that day Mike returned to the house on Lincoln St. Neither Ben nor Jane was there, so he grabbed a beer from the fridge and went to his room. He lay on the bed and sipped the beer.

The spirit of God…That's why he came to New Mexico. To capture something extraordinary, something mystical, something divine in his work. He pondered the sequence of events. The old man in the plaza, Ben and now Gaspar. It only reinforced his desire to learn more about the people who lived in this surreal world. That without more of the essence of the people, his paintings would never reach that higher level. The level that inspires the viewer to immerse themselves and perceive the power of great art. The human element.

Landscape art was found in Eastern art as early as the fourth century AD. There, the human element was a bridge over water, a farmer carrying a bundle of sticks in the distance. Introduced as a genre during the Renaissance, great artists like van Ruisdael and Cuyp, Lorrain and Poussin, included something of the human element in their work, a worker in a field, a distant windmill. It gave the image perspective. French Impressionists like Monet, Pissarro and Sisley often included a human presence in an otherwise pure vision of nature. American artists Bierstadt, Cole and Beers often did the same. Why not O'Farrell.

This invitation from Gaspar piqued Mike's interest. What better way to learn more about the people in this unique region than to be a part of a religious or spiritual gathering. He got out of bed and went out to his van. He found the road map and spread it out on the seat.

"Rociada, Rociada…" he ran his finger over the map in a spiral out from Las Puertas. "Here it is." It was about thirty miles north of town. The only way to get there was up Highway 518 through Sapello and then west through Cañoncito on the state road A26. Rociada was at the end of the road, tucked into a corner of the vast Santa Fe National Forest called the Pecos Wilderness. New territory for Mike. New vistas...new people. He decided he would take Gaspar up on his offer.

§

"I am the voice of God!" Gaspar screamed out the window of his truck. He was just turning off the interstate at the first Las Puertas exit. "If I can bring a gringo, an Anglo into the brotherhood...the Word could spread beyond Atzlan. To the unholy East."

He turned off Grand and headed down south Pacific to the plaza. He had medical supplies on order at Plaza Drugs, knowing he would be needing them during the upcoming holy week. He parked on Gonzales near the drugstore.

Sheriff Joe Lujan was coming down the plaza heading toward his office when he saw Gaspar leaving the drugstore, carrying two boxes of merchandise. Instead of heading down Bridge Street he swung over to Gonzales and gave a yelp with his siren. Gaspar saw him and waved. Joe pulled over behind Gaspar's truck and got out.

"Hola Joe! How goes it?" Gaspar walked over to Joe and shook his hand. "Any flooding down here? Saw some heavy clouds over Hermit's Peak."

"Yeah...Caballos Canyon got blocked up, but the boys up there got things squared away pretty quickly. How about up by you, any problems?" Joe watched Gaspar's face closely.

"Problems. No... the storm was south of the peak. Didn't get a drop. We could use it, though." Gaspar knew Joe. They didn't get along. If Joe had a way to do it, he would try to stop the Brotherhood's rituals. Over the years there were many emergency room visits by some of the members, weak from blood loss or dehydrated and exhausted. There were the phone calls from people trying to reach a relative who they knew to be in the area but did not know where. There were incidents in town...confrontations by members with locals, berating them for their lack of piety.

"I saw some of your friends coming through town on their way up to your place. Looks like you got a pretty good turnout this year." Joe looked Gaspar in the eye. "You'll let them know that there are no gatherings in the

National Forest without the proper permits, right? Some of them might not be aware of that...I don't want to have to go up there just to keep some of your 'guests' in line."

"Seguro, Joe. No problem. I always make it clear that those are the rules. Your rules. And that they must abide by them. Be assured, Sheriff, all will be as it should be. Por todo lo que es santo." Gaspar smiled a mocking smile. "Now I have much to do so hasta luego, Joe. Dios esté contigo!" He turned and entered the drug store for another load.

Joe stood on the sidewalk. His gut told him there was going to be trouble. Each year Gaspar became more extreme about his beliefs and what he and his brothers would be expected to do to be touched by God. Joe believed in God, but not a God that would ask his disciples to abuse themselves to the point of near death. He would notify the Park Rangers and the National Park Service that in his opinion, Gaspar was going to make this a banner year. From the looks of the supplies he bought, there must be at least a hundred or so brothers in attendance. Los Hermanos Penitentes would be a danger to themselves and others. Best to keep an eye on them. As he drove off he saw Gaspar loading another two or three boxes into his truck.

§

After picking up more supplies on Mills Ave., Gaspar headed out of town on Seventh Street. Just before the edge of town, he turned and parked in front of a neat, small adobe. It was David Rangel's place. Though too old to attend the rituals, David was a long-time disciple of the Hermanos and the first contact for new arrivals, looking for directions to the Morada. The front door opened, and David stepped out. Gaspar got out of his truck and walked briskly up to David.

"Mi hermano." They embraced.

"Come in, Mi hermano. Come in."

They went into the kitchen. David's wife, Adelina was at the sink. David's son, Ben , was sitting at the table. He was not happy to see Gaspar. "Hola Adelina, Ben. May the lord bless you both." Gaspar directed this at Ben. Ben said nothing.

"Good morning Gaspar. Please, sit down. Would you like a cup of coffee." She gestured to the chair across from Ben. Although she could not quite understand David's devotion to the Hermanos, she could not object to her husband's desire to be closer to God. She was a devout Catholic. But the local church and Mass on Sundays was enough for her.

"That would be most welcome, Adelina." He sat down and Adelina brought him a cup. "This will give me a nice pick-me-up, a real tónico."

Ben sneered. "I would think God would get you there without any help."

Gaspar looked sternly at Ben. "My son, someday God will open your eyes and see that what your father and I do is the only way to help the gente. The people. For our penance, what we give to God, it will only help all of his children." He turned to David. "I met a young man this morning, an Anglo. He is a painter and I think he has gotten in touch with el alma, the soul of this land. He seemed to want to know more about being in touch with the land...por tanto, Dios."

Ben kept silent. It was almost certainly Mike that Gaspar was talking about.

"I have invited him to join us for Holy Week." Looking at David, "I think he will come."

David agreed. "The brotherhood must reach out. The power we feel must be given out to everyone."

They continued talking. Ben got up, "I got to go. Bye, Mom." He kissed her on the cheek. He nodded to Gaspar and his father and left the house.

§

When Mike woke up the next morning he found Jane and Ben already at the kitchen table drinking coffee.

"Morning. You guys are up early." He walked over to the stove and poured himself a cup. He came back to the table and sat down. Ben was quiet.

"Going by Piedras Blanca again today?" Jane asked, her voice sounded concerned.

"Yeah. Sure. I've still got a couple of mornings up there to get the light right." He noticed her tone. "Why? Is there something I should know?"

"Ben's dad, he's with a group of religious guys. They're called the Hermanos Penitentes." She paused. "Ever heard of them?"

Mike was stunned. "Yeah, sure. A guy stopped by out there when I was painting and mentioned they were his group. He even invited me up to a meeting, in a town called Rociada. Have you ever been up there?"

"Was the guy's name Gaspar?" Ben asked.

"Yeah. He was pretty weird about my painting. Got into this religious take on art."

Ben sighed. "Listen, Mike. Gaspar stopped by my folk's house yesterday. I grew up in a house where my father went to these meetings, these gatherings, every year. He's been with Gaspar and the Hermanos as far back as I can remember. They're very serious about their religious beliefs." He got up and looked out the kitchen window. "Gaspar told my Dad that he met a young Anglo that morning and thought he might be able to get him to join. He was very excited, going on about how this could spread the reach of the Hermanos Penitentes further out, even back East. I think he's got plans for you." Turning back to Mike, he went on. "My Dad would be gone from Palm Sunday until a day or two after Easter. He was always exhausted, couldn't move very well. His back was cut up and his legs were badly bruised. Each year he was in worse and worse shape. The past few years he would have to take an extra week off work to recover... My Mom would take care of him, nurse his wounds. We're fairly sure we know what goes on up there but the lately it's become very intense. My Dad can't do it anymore but it he spends most of Holy Week praying... sometimes locked in the bedroom, whipping himself."

"I don't understand. Gaspar just said it would be an inspirational experience. That it would give me insight into the land and the people. It's something I was thinking I could use anyway...to give my art greater depth." He waved off Ben's concerns. "I'll just go up for the day. It's not far and from the map it looks like there might be some great country up there. If they start getting too weird, I can just leave."

Jane and Ben exchanged knowing looks.

"I think you should just read up on those guys before you go up there," Jane said. "The people I know around here give Gaspar and his group a wide birth during Holy Week. He and his brothers isolate themselves for the whole week. Things go on that they don't want other people to know about. I've heard they can be fanatic, even militant, particularly about what they do and where they do it." She seemed genuinely concerned. "You can ask around, but be careful, diplomatic. Everybody around here is very closed mouth about Gaspar and the Hermanos."

"That's why I don't live at home." Ben added. "My Mom put up with him but dreaded the whole thing. She was afraid that someday he might not have come home. Things can get pretty crazy. Gaspar might have something special for you in mind."

"Okay." Mike relented. "I'll check into it." Religious inspiration, suffering, holiness...the spirit of God. These are all themes that have helped to inspire art since the first cave drawings. He felt even stronger about going to Rociada. To him, it was an opportunity to experience the spiritual power that led many artists throughout history to achieve greatness.

"I better get going, I don't want to miss the light." He finished his coffee and gathered his materials. "I'll see you guys later. And don't worry, I'll give this some serious thought."

§

The call came in at about four in the afternoon on Saturday. There was some trouble up at Pino's Truck Stop. Joe was at his desk writing up the report on the canyon flood. It was a state highway so the state police needed a write up.

Gabby took the call. "Hey Joe. Pino's having some trouble with a couple of the Hermanos, I think. He said they won't leave the restaurant until Pino promises to close for the week. They say he's not listening to the voice of you know who."

Joe was not amused. He often found Gaspar's people to be intractable about their beliefs. Once they had made a judgement it was very difficult to dissuade them and move them along. He figured there would be at least one or two incidents like this.

"Roberto should be over by Robertson High. Tell him to meet me up at Pino's as soon as he can." Joe stood and unstrapped his weapon. He put the gun into his desk drawer and took out his extension baton. "I don't think I'll need my gun and tell Roberto to leave his weapon in the car when he gets there."

"If you think that's best." Gabby sounded unsure. "Things can get pretty hot with those alborotadores."

"I'm just going to break this up and send them on their way. If they give me trouble I'll tell them I'll be sure to go up to Rociada and tell Gaspar. They know he certainly doesn't want me nosing around up there." He put on his hat and headed out the back to his truck.

Pino's was a mile or so from the west end of town. Joe turned on his lights and sped down south Pacific out to Grand. Then, with sirens, he raced down the frontage road to Pino's. When he pulled into the parking lot by the restaurant, a crowd had gathered at the front windows. Joe got out of the truck and approached the crowd. They were mainly truckers and tourists.

"Okay, folks. Let's move away from the window. We're not selling tickets here."

Joe moved between the crowd and the front door. Just then Roberto pulled up in the squad car. Joe waved him over to his side.

"Hey Roberto. Let's get these people away from the building." Joe opened the door. "I'll see what's going on here."

Pino was standing by a booth occupied by two men. One was young and wearing gray coveralls. The other was older, maybe in his fifties. He was dressed in blue jeans and a worn-out sports jacket. He had a dress shirt under the jacket, a bolo tie with a gold cross.

Joe walked over to them. "Hello Pino." He turned to the other men. "Hola, amigos. Can I buy you a cup of coffee?"

The older man looked up at Joe. "Seguro, my friend. This man..." he gestured at Pino, "He would not serve us. He does not understand that we act only in his best interest. Tomorrow is the day God came to Jerusalem. We only wish to help this man to cease his worldly actions and walk with God."

"We heard him say that he was tired, discouraged," the young man said. "Our brotherhood allows us to throw off the shackles of this life.. at least for a time. If he will not come with us, he can go away from this, his burden, and find peace in his church or his home. This place only brings him misery."

"What the Hell is he talking about." Pino looked puzzled.

Joe couldn't help smiling. "So, Pino. You've been complaining again. About the café. About making ends meet."

"Maybe so. But this is my place. I can complain if I want to." Pino looked at the two men. "There's no place I'd rather be than here. No place."

"Why don't you go get us some coffee." Joe gestured at the booth. "Mind if I sit here?"

The younger man slid over and made room. Joe sat and folded his hands on the table. "My name's Joe, Joe Lujan. I'm the sheriff around here."

"Much gusto, jefe." The older man held out his hand. "I am Cedro Macias. This is my son, Ignacio."

Ignacio nodded to Joe. "Are you going to tell us we can't do God's work here?"

"No. Para nada." Joe feigned surprise. Pino brough over three cups of fresh coffee. He remained standing by the table. "Thanks Pino. Put this on my tab... Invito." Pino went back behind the counter.

Cedro frowned, "Muchas Gracias, jefe, but we do not need your charity and you cannot tempt us with your false kindness."

Joe picked up his cup in both hands. "It is only a cup of coffee. I didn't want to drink alone. Just consider it a cup of coffee."

Ignacio picked up his cup. "Yes...Thank you, sheriff." He paused. "I think you would like us to leave. To leave this man to his sorrow."

"You heard him. This is where he wants to be. He may complain, but he is only human." Joe took another sip of coffee. "I think he has heard your message. Now it is between him and God."

"As it should be." Cedro leaned toward Joe, "Man needs discipline. He must make sacrifices. This man should stop his earthly life from time to time, to give penance. Then he will find God's answer."

Joe looked sternly at Cedro. "It is between him and God. Finish your coffee and allow me to buy your lunch. Only as a new friend. Then I think Gaspar is waiting for you and it's getting late. When you talk about discipline, Gaspar is much stricter than I am."

The lateness of the day surprised the men. "Que hora es?" asked Ignacio.

"Dios mio, it's after five." Cedro took another sip from his coffee and gave Pino a firm look. "You are in the hands of God. We will pray for you. For all of you."

They walked out of the café and to their truck. Joe waited until they drove off. Roberto came in and he and Joe sat in the booth.

"Let's hope that's the last we hear from Gaspar and his brothers." Roberto took a fresh cup from Pino. "By tonight it should all be happening up by Rociada. Then it will be up to his neighbors to let us know if things start getting out of hand."

Pino sat next to Roberto. "God could not want his children to be so ready for a fight, so aggressive."

Joe leaned back. "Holy week," he said aloud, but more to himself. He stared out the window and watched as cars passed on the highway.

§

Palm Sunday services used to start at about nine-thirty at Mike's church back East. So, he had packed his van with enough gear to last him until Tuesday or Wednesday, just in case. On the map, it looked like it would take him at most an hour to get to Rociada. Then he would have to find Gaspar's place. He was on the road by seven going north.

He cut through the university and took 7th Street. It turned into the road to Storrie Lake. Thanks to the Spring runoff and the unusually heavy rain, the lake was nearly full. With the sun in the east and no wind, the lake was mirror smooth, with the sharp the reflection of the foothills on the surface. When he got to Sapello, he took the State Road 94 northwest. The scrubby foothills caught the morning sun as the country became more mountainous.

About halfway to the Rociada turnoff, Mike came upon a small cemetery. He pulled over and walked to the iron gate. In the arch above the entrance it read "San Isidro Cemetery". He entered and moved carefully between the graves. Montoya, Aragon, Martinez...Several military graves. Dates going back to the 19th century. Some headstones crumbled. Others illegible from the years of exposure to wind, sun, and rain. The old church stood against the stark sky. Clouds forming in the distance gave it an ominous look.

He knew he would have to return. This journey made him realize that to truly transfer this magical country to canvas he must learn about the history, the topography, the people...He felt like he would burst. His enthusiasm filled him with energy.

"Coming up here was my destiny." He thought.

It was almost 8:00 so he drove down road 105 through the valley. He turned off onto 276. A narrow road that led him right into the tiny village of Rociada. The Catholic Church was on the left as he entered town. Locals were driving up to the church, whole families piled into the back of pickup trucks. Others were walking toward the church. All carried pine branches or other green plants. It was Palm Sunday.

Mike stopped near the church and waved at an elderly couple walking on the shoulder nearby. "Good morning. Buenas dias."

The man stopped by the van and leaned on the passenger side window. "Good morning, young man. How can I help you?"

"I'm trying to find Gaspar de la Madalena. I think he called it his Morada? Can you tell me how to get there?" Mike noticed a change in the man's pleasant attitude.

"The Morada." The old man nodded. "You must go on up 276 until you see a blue adobe house, it has a windmill near the road. That's the home of Beatriz and Blanca Iglesias. If you get lost, they know everything up there. Maybe a mile or so further up, there is an arroyo to your left. The dirt road that follows the arroyo leads you to the Madalena place." He looked into Mike's eyes. "You are sure you want to go there. You are not like any of the other Hermanos."

"Yeah, well...I'm just a guest of Gaspar's. Just kind of checking things out. I'm only up here for a day or two." Mike was now used to people having reservations about the Hermanos.

"Just a day or two." The old man glanced at his wife. She rolled her eyes. "You know it is Holy Week. Most of Gaspar's people stay the whole week."

"Like I said. I'm just checking it out." He started the van. "I better head up there...Looks like services will be starting soon."

The old lady shook her head. "Bless you, my boy. Bless you. If you need help, we have a phone. Come to the white house next to the gas station...if you need help. I am Jacinta Parra, y mi esposo Ezequiel." Her voice trailed off and they continued on their way.

Mike drove on. He was a little concerned now...about what he was getting himself into. But it is the life experience that makes the art. He came to the arroyo and turned up the rough dirt road.

§

After a mile or so he came to a gate. There were two men sitting on the fence. Mike rolled down his window and called out.

"Good morning. Is this Gaspar's place?"

One of the men jumped down and walked over to the van. "You know Gaspar?" He asked.

"Yes. I met him the other day. He invited me up here to the gathering. I think he called it the Hermanos. Is this the place?" Mike was surprised by the security. So far everyone he met was very welcoming. This felt different.

"You must be the artista." The man seemed surprised. "Gaspar was hoping you'd come." He went to the gate and opened it and waved him through.

The road was dirt, rough, steep and washed out. Mike drove slowly, avoiding any large ruts and maneuvering carefully to stay on the path.

When he came over a rise and started descending he saw what he thought must be Gaspar's ranch. About seventy or eighty pickups and cars were parked in the open area in front of the outbuildings and ranch house. A large, metal warehouse like utility building dominated the enclave on the left. Several smaller buildings were scattered along the perimeter and the half adobe half cinderblock ranch house closed the semicircle on the right.

About a hundred or so men were milling about, drinking coffee and smoking. Mike parked alongside the other vehicles and got out of the van. He walked over to the group and their conversations stopped.

Cedro Macias, the man Joe Lujan had encountered at Pino's truck stop came up to him.

"Hola, amigo. ¿Quieres café?" He shook Mike's hand. "You must be Miguel. Gaspar said he met a Gringo, un artista, the other day and that we are to welcome you."

"Morning. I'm Mike O'Farrell. Yeah...I met Gaspar a couple of days ago. He said that you are all here on some kind of spiritual quest. I'm very interested in learning more about what you do. I know it is something that is a tradition. Something that goes back many years."

"It is much more than that, my friend. Mucho mas. I am Cedro Macias." He took Mike by the arm. "Come. Let's get a cup of coffee. Prayers will be starting soon."

They went into the morada where a side table had been set with a large, restaurant style coffee maker, paper cups and bowls, a platter of warm tortillas and a large pot of pinto beans. The hermanos were standing in small groups, talking, waiting...Many of them seemed uneasy about Mike being there. Outsiders were not to be trusted.

Cedro poured Mike a cup. "Drink it quickly." He advised.

Outside the morada, a loud, high pitched, shrill squeal pierced the mutterings of the hermanos. The sound was eerie...like an animal being tortured.

Cedro threw his coffee onto the ground and tossed the cup into the garbage. He gestured for Mike to do the same. "It is the pito. It is time to welcome Christ on his return from the wilderness."

In a corner of the morada there was a stack of pine branches. Each man picked up two branches and took his place in a long column of twos. Mike stood opposite Cedro. The men threw one branch on the ground and held the other branch up high over the path, the branches making a military style gauntlet. The pito sounded again, this time closer to the building.

Gaspar appeared in the doorway followed by the Hermanos de Luz and the pitero. They walked through the colonnade, over the branches, to a small raised dais at the other end of the morada.

Mike leaned over to Cedro and whispered, "Where is the priest?"

"There is no priest for us. The Hermano Major will lead our prayers."

"Is he a lay priest?" Mike was a Catholic. He wondered, "Where is the priest?"

"¡Cállate!, be quiet. There is no place for a priest here." Cedro waved him off impatiently.

Gaspar held up his arms over his head, he stared up at the branches, but his gaze was focused beyond, at the heavens. He seemed to be in a trance and spoke clearly, loudly. He spoke in English and, occasionally, in the ancient Spanish dialect of northern New Mexico. Many of the hermanos were not fluent in the dialect, fortunately for Mike.

"Welcome and bless you all." Gaspar brought his gaze down to the men gathered in front of him. "Welcome to our Lord Jesus who joins us here in our humble morada, where he returns from his time in the wilderness. This day, we begin the Joy, the Sorrow, the Pain, the Ecstasy and the Suffering of Our Lord." He gestured to the pine boughs. "These branches welcome our Lord with joy and triumph. They are not Palms. No. They are blessed because they are from the very wilderness where Jesus walked... From the wilderness that is our home...From the wilderness where we will go soon to stand with the Lord Jesus. To follow his path to Domingo de Resurrección."

The hermanos murmured "¡Gracias a Dios!... Amén"

The sermon went on. But it was not really a sermon. It reminded Mike of the televised evangelical revival meetings he had seen on the religious channel. Gaspar prompted the hermanos with responsive phrases. They began to answer, louder each time. Some began beating their chest like the 'mea culpas' he knew in his church in Rhode Island...only these men really beat themselves. Cedro hit himself so hard that he seemed to knock the wind out of himself. His knees buckled and he started to fall.

"Are you all right?" Mike went to grab his arm. To catch him.

Cedro threw him off, "No me toques. Leave me alone." He collapsed on the floor and began convulsing. Other men were also acting strangely. Soon the entire congregation was enraptured. Gaspar again reaching for the heavens, his trance deepening. His words more often in that unique ancient dialect. Then, suddenly he stopped. The Hermanos de Luz closed in around him. The pitero again made the shrill sound, the shriek that brought the mass, if one could call it that, to an end.

The men slowly recovered from their rapture. Cedro also recovered and accepted Mike's hand as he struggled to stand up. Gaspar managed to regain his composure. "Jesus is here, with us. Go now. Spend your time in prayer and meditation. Tomorrow, we will cleanse ourselves and the morada, Tuesday we will prepare ourselves for what is to come, Wednesday we will curse the soul of Judas Escariot and rid ourselves of our worldly goods. And Thursday...I will be as he was, a humble man who will wash your feet and welcome you to a last supper before we begin the journey to the Cross and the Resurrection." He led the Hermanos de Luz and the pitero back along the path of pine boughs and out the door.

The men began talking to one another." God is here." ... "We are with the Lord." ...They embraced. Shook hands forcefully. Stared into each other's eyes.

Ignacio and a group of two or three men came over to Cedro and Mike. "Are you with God now, Miguel?" Ignacio asked.

Mike, realizing discretion would be best, nodded. "How can I not be. This place is filled with the Holy Spirit. You men are truly amongst the righteous."

That seemed to satisfy Ignacio although Cedro did not seem convinced.

"Come and eat with us. Will you be staying through the week?"

Mike had had about enough for now. He needed to process the day's experience. "I wish I could. I have some work in progress that I have to get back to. But I can come back on Thursday. It would be an honor to join you for the final days of Holy Week."

Cedro smiled. "I will speak to Gaspar. We will let you know before you leave."

They went over to the side tables where the hermanos were bringing out food for lunch. Everyone was quiet, somewhat exhausted, and eager to continue with the quest for salvation.

§

Gaspar's morada was at the end of the arroyo, nestled in a canyon that led to the national forest. The afternoon light came down the ridge into the canyon, casting long shadows on the morada, the ranch house and the outbuildings. Mike drifted away from the men gathered in the yard and got his sketch pad and charcoal from his van. He walked back down the road and then climbed the north wall of the canyon and found a place high up to view the buildings, the men, and the surrounding terrain. It was a landscape opportunity to not only depict the countryside, but also the presence of the people...gathered as they were for this holy ceremony.

He thought of paintings like Bruegel's 'The Harvesters' and Bierstadt's 'Emigrants Crossing the Plains'. Even more so, "Roasting the Christmas Beef" by Remington. He studied the light and began a sketch, making notes of the colors, the shadows, the tiny figures of the hermanos. He became engrossed, concentrating on his work, glancing up only occasionally to refresh the image. He did not realize that someone was approaching until he noticed Gaspar at the base of the slope, looking up at him.

Mike waved. "Hello Gaspar! I'll just be a moment." He quickly added some last-minute strokes and started down.

Gaspar was smiling. "Our Holy gathering has inspired you?"

"Very much." They shook hands. "Your sermon was moving. I can feel the bond your hermanos have for each other."

"We are here to give ourselves to God. To experience Him." He paused. "As I said...the Joy, the Sorrow, the Pain, the Ecstasy and the Suffering of Our Lord. May I see your work?"

"Of course." He handed the sketch pad to Gaspar. "I felt the land and the people were one. Joined by the spirit of God." Mike hoped he sounded convincing. He wanted to be able to return, not so much for the gathering as for the opportunity to continue his work.

Gaspar looked at the sketch. "You need to be here again. You need to be here while the Lord is with us. Otherwise, this will not be a true representation of the power that you are trying to render. "He handed the pad back to Mike. "Cedro told me you are leaving today. That you want to come back later. This is not in your best interest. All the brothers must participate in the daily meetings. This will prepare you for the importance of the Crucifixion, of the Resurrection. For the true salvation you can have here with us."

"I will be sure to come back on Thursday. It's important. I want to work more on what I have seen today."

Gaspar was nodding his head. "I am sorry that you will not be here. The brothers may not be as understanding as I am. I will speak to them." He looked Mike in the eye. "You may go. But do not forget what you saw here today. What you felt. You will need to bring that with you when you return. The Lord will expect you to be prepared for the sacrifice you must make. Come back on Thursday. The true sacrifice to God starts early on Good Friday. You must be here and be ready."

With a final stern yet benevolent stare, he shook Mike's hand firmly, turned and walked back to the morada. He signaled to one of the brothers standing nearby. It was Ignacio. He came over to Mike.

"Gather your stuff together...get your van. I'll ride with you back to the gate and let the hermanos there know that you can leave. Gaspar must think your work is important, otherwise there's no way he would let you leave during Holy week. I'll wait here for you." Ignacio was not happy.

Mike went back to the morada and found his jacket and backpack. He got into his van and went back up the road to where Ignacio was waiting for him. They drove down the arroyo and stopped at the gate. The two brothers who were manning the gate came up to the van. Ignacio got out and spoke to them in a low voice. They grudgingly opened the gate and waved Mike through. This was obviously something out of the ordinary. Mike drove off but he could feel the glares of the men on the back of neck. The hair there rose slightly.

"Tough crowd!" he said to himself. He wanted to return, but he felt uneasy. For now, his curiosity prevailed over his sense of unease. This was a great opportunity for his art. His life had become an inspirational adventure.

§

Monday morning Mike stayed in bed, waiting for Jane and Ben to leave. He was not ready to talk about the morada and Gaspar just yet. Ben worked and Jane had classes all day on Mondays. Once he was sure they were gone, he got up and went into the kitchen. There was a note by the coffee pot from Jane.

'Glad you made it back. Interested to hear about it.'

It was a bright day and Mike wanted to work on his sketches of the morada. He grabbed a cup of coffee, his pad and charcoal and decided to walk up to the plaza and continue his renderings.

He had not been back to the plaza since that first day in town and wondered if the old man, Guillermo, would be there. He walked up Bridge Street, passing the sheriff's office. He crossed over to the plaza by the Plaza

Drugs and saw Guillermo sitting on one of the benches near the band stand.

"Good morning, Guillermo." He stood by the bench. "Mind if I join you?"

The old man gazed up at him, "Well, well. The Irish kid from back East, right? The artist."

"Yeah, Mike... How've you been?"

"Bueno. Con la ayuda de Dios." He had his bottle with him, in a paper bag." Join me for breakfast? Tamales. From Duran's liquor store. His wife makes them. Muy bien."

"You sure?" He took the tamale. "Trade you for some cigarettes."

"Seguro. No problem." He took a couple from the pack Mike offered him. One went behind his ear. He lit up the other one. "Drink?"

"No thanks. I've got some coffee."

"Got your art stuff, I see." Guillermo pointed at the sketch pad.

"Yeah." Mike opened the pad to the full drawing of the morada. "What do you think?"

The old man looked at the drawing. Mike could tell he recognized it. "That's Gaspar de la Madalena's place, is it not?"

"You know it?"

Guillermo nodded. "You were there? When?"

"Yesterday. Gaspar invited me to visit. To meet the Hermanos. To join the ceremony" He felt a sense of pride that he was invited to such a well-known event.

"During Holy Week? I'm surprised they did not make you stay the whole week." He shook his head. "When I was a boy, un estúpido joven, I always went to church. I liked it. But week after week it seemed to be always the same. I had heard of the Hermanos Penitentes and thought joining them would be more enriching, and mucho mas excitante."

"Really!" Mike wanted to hear more. "What was it like?"

The old man's eyes saddened. "Gaspar's father, Zacarías, was the Hermano Major. It was truly a brotherhood. We would meet and pray and follow the steps of Jesus. We would punish ourselves, it was a little doloroso, painful, but sincere. In the old days, a brother's extreme devotion would lead to injury, sometimes death...for the older or weaker men. They died while in the eyes of God so they were blessed, taken home and buried by their family. Zacarías did not allow such extremes. He wanted us to return after Holy week strong, for our families, for the gente."

Guillermo took a long swig on his bottle. He lit up a cigarette. "Zacarías died about twenty years ago. Gaspar stepped into his shoes. He felt we were not being sincere, that we were not repenting enough to prove our faith in the Lord. He guided us back to the old ways...and again men were badly hurt, again some died. I left the brotherhood after two years. The first year was muy malo. But it was for the faith, so I joined in. The second year was much worse. Several brothers had to suffer their injuries for two full days until after Easter Sunday. One passed on Easter morning." He breathed the cigarette smoke in deeply. Drank a little more whisky. "I knew then that this was not my path. I left in the early morning. I knew they would not let me go until Sunday night. I knew I would be disciplined for wanting to leave. The village church was not my path either. ¿Quizás? Maybe that's why my days are now spent here. In the sun. The solitude...and the whisky" He winked at Mike, "And now a new amigo, Miguel O'Farrell."

Mike smiled at the old man. "Do you mind if I sit with you while I work?"

"Please, con mucho gusto!" He laughed. "I will be quiet...but I will be watching you create your great work. Gaspar must have liked what you do. ¿Si no?, or you would be still up there."

"Oh, I'll be going back up on Thursday. He wanted me to come back and be a guest over the weekend. I have to go anyway, to work on the actual painting. I don't think I'll have to participate. At least, I don't think I will." Again, he felt that strange sense of fear on the back of his neck. "I'm sure he'll let me leave if I don't join in."

"Sure, sure. Well...ya veremos. We'll see." Guillermo patted Mike on the back. "I'm sure it will all be well. God will be there to protect you. He will be there." He leaned against the back of the bench, took a sip and closed his eyes. In a moment he was dozing.

"He certainly does seem at peace." He thought. Turning back to his sketchbook, he worked with renewed vigor. "Gaspar likes my work..." He doubled his efforts to be worthy of that admiration.

§

The rain had passed, and Joe was doing the final paperwork about the flooding at Caballos Canyon. Gabby was back in the cells cleaning and Roberto was out on patrol. It was a quiet day, Jueves Santo, the day of the last supper.

So far Holy Week has been calm… without incident. Joe was glad that there was no news coming from up by Rociada. By now, the brotherhood was isolated and ready to begin their final secret rituals starting on Good Friday and lasting through the weekend. It was a rare to hear anything from them until after Easter, if at all.

Gabby came out from the back and sat by Joe's desk. "I'll take the sheets and pillowcases home and wash them." She let out a long sigh.

"Sure, that's fine, Gabby." He looked up from his work. "What's up?"

"It's time for some new linens. The ones we have a threadbare." She hesitated, "I think they are on sale at the Sears Catalog Store. Do we have the money?"

"You let me know how much." No one knew better than Gabby how much cash was in the pot for office expenses. But she always asked… and Joe always said he'd check the budget. It was a routine that always went in Gabby's favor.

She got up from her chair and looked out the window. A battered old pickup truck had just pulled up in front and the driver, a young man in his twenties, walked around to the passenger side and help an elderly woman out onto the curb.

"Joe…it's Beatriz or Blanca Iglesias. Down from Rociada." She gestured Joe to come take a look.

"I think it's Beatriz," Joe said. "Hard to tell quién es quién."

The young man helped the old woman to the office door. Joe moved to the door and opened it for her. "Buenos días, Señora Iglesias." Come and sit down." Joe helped her over to the chair by his desk.

Gabby came over. "Señora, would you like a cup of coffee? Agua?"

"No Gabriella, Gracias. You know my grandnephew, Fabián." She gestured at the young man. He was standing quietly by the door.

"Seguro. Hola Fabián. Have you and your father started planting? The rain must have helped."

"Gracias, sheriff. We are starting the chilis and the corn." The boy was not there for small talk. "The rain was good."

Beatriz tapped her finger impatiently on the desk. "Sheriff, I came to town to tell you something. It may be nothing, but Blanca and I thought you should know."

"¿Oh, sí?" Joe sat down. "You came all the way to town. It must be more than nothing."

"¿Quizás?" Joe knew nothing happened on highway 276 without the

Iglesias sisters knowing about it. He hoped it was nothing major. "Blanca and I were sitting on our porch, waiting for Fabián and his father to take us to church in town. It was Palm Sunday. We saw a red van going west. Looked like an Anglo fellow driving, heading up the road. It had out of state plates. I think it was Rhode Island."

"It must have been a turista." He knew she probably had the license number and there was more to come.

"I thought so. No one but a fool or an outsider would be on that road during Holy Week." She continued. "When we got to town we met Jacinta and Ezequiel Parra at the church. Jacinta and I are old friends and we got to talking."

Joe waited patiently for her to continue. Gabby was standing by the door to the cells, listening.

"Jacinta asked if we had seen a red van go by. She figured we would have seen it and there was concern in her voice." The old lady paused. She turned to Gabby. "Some café would be very nice, querida. My throat is a little dry and the trip into town seemed very long."

"De nada, Señora." Gabby brought her a cup. Beatriz sipped the coffee and put it down on the desk.

"Jacinta said the boy was looking for the morada. That he had been invited by Gaspar to visit and observe the gathering." She took another sip of coffee, waiting for Joe to respond.

"I see your concern. It is not usual for Gaspar to open the morada to outsiders, let alone an Anglo." This interested him.

"No. No. Never. But that's not the end of it." She shifted in the chair. "Puedes hacerme el paro? Do you have a cushion perhaps. My bones are not what they used to be."

Gabby went quickly to the back and brought out a pillow from the cells. Fabián came and helped Beatriz stand while Gabby placed the pillow on the chair.

"Gracias. Gabriella," she said as she settled back down. "Eso es mucho mejor ahora."

"De nada, de nada." Gabby went back to her place by the door.

"En todo caso, after church we went home. Later that afternoon, maybe early evening, we saw the van going back toward town." She stopped, waiting for this to have the effect on Joe she expected.

"I see." Joe knew this was out of the ordinary. No one, once at the gathering, leaves the morada during holy week. It is forbidden.

"I think the boy must have come from Las Puertas, or Santa Fe. If he did go to the morada, and was there all day...this is very strange. Maybe you should keep an eye out for him. Muy extraño."

"You were right in coming here, Señora Iglesias. It is very strange. If the van is in town, it should not be hard to spot." Joe smiled to himself, "Acaso, by any chance, did you get the license number?"

Beatriz opened her purse and handed joe a piece of paper. "Rhode Island, The Ocean State CV-194. There was a little symbol in the corner. I think it was like a hook, perhaps an anchor for a ship. The year tag was 1974, April I think."

Joe took the paper. "You have very good vision...this will be a great help."

"Oh Sheriff, it was Blanca's binoculars that helped. She always has them at the ready." Beatriz got up and called Fabián over to help her. "Thank you sheriff. I will let you know if there is anything else different going on this year. With Gaspar, there is always a chance something will happen. And often...cosas malas."

She and Fabián went out the door. Gabby and Joe watched them get into the truck and drive off.

"Let's hope this is not an indication of things to come." Joe turned to Gabby. "No one leaves the morada during Holy Week. Gaspar is up to something."

§

It was that same Thursday, Jueves Santo. Mike slept in until about ten o'clock. Ben and Jane were gone but there was still some coffee in the pot. Around noon, Jane came home and found Mike packing up his van for the weekend in Rociada. "So... you're going up there." She was not an emotional person, but he was her old friend and you could hear the concern in her voice.

"Absolutely. I wouldn't miss this for the world." He carried more art supplies to the van. Jane was standing in the doorway. Mike walked up to her, "I know why you decided to in New Mexico. This is another world. An alien landscape. Different from any life you could have had in Rhode Island. The people here are in this timeless place. The land itself radiates this, I don't know...this strange energy that comes from the red dirt, the amazing light, the mountains and the mesas. I am so grateful to you that you chose to live here." He gave her a hug. In a moment that was very out of character for her, she hugged him back.

"Just be careful up there. The 'timelessness' of this land can also mean hardship and violence. There is the beauty…but it hides the cruelty of the past, the rough edges of the present." Pausing, she held Mike's hand. "Just be careful. Make sure you can get away if you have to."

She went into the house to her room and closed the door. Mike stood for a moment, thinking. He shrugged his shoulders, finished packing up the van and headed out of town.

§

Later that afternoon, Blanca and Beatriz were sitting, as usual, on their front porch. Blanca had her binoculars and they were sharing a Tamarind Jarritos. Beatriz saw the red van coming up the road and Blanca used her binoculars to verify the license plate.

"Is it him…is it the same van?" Beatriz knew it was but she wanted Blanca to confirm.

"Seguro. It's him." She lowered the binoculars and took a drink of the soda.

Mike saw the two old ladies. He waved as he drove by. In his time in Las Puertas he had adopted the habit of waving to folks he passed. Another nice quality of the culture around there. The ladies waved back.

He came to the turn off by the arroyo and was soon at the gate. Again, two of the hermanos were there, with their rifles. This time, they recognized Mike and the van. One of the men nodded to Mike. "Pasar."

He drove through and they closed the gate behind him. When he arrived at the morada, chairs and tables had been arranged in the yard. A large table in front of the morada was set with thirteen place settings and thirteen chairs.

The men were milling around, and all eyes turned toward the van as it pulled up near the ranch house. Cedro came over to Mike as he was getting out.

"You came back." He shook Mike's hand. "You will soon have the opportunity to join us as we give ourselves to God." He took him by the elbow and they joined the group of men lingering around the head table. There was some murmuring as he joined the group. Ignacio, always pessimistic about the presence of strangers, nodded at Mike.

"Hola Gringo. You have come to show penance? To give yourself to God?" He came close to Mike, looking straight into his eyes. "Have you prepared yourself?"

"I think so. I want to know what the Hermanos are all about." He tried to be diplomatic. "I have a great deal of respect for your dedication. If you find me worthy, I hope to capture your essence in my art. As Gaspar said to me, my being here will help me capture the work of the Lord on my puny canvas. The spirit of God!"

Ignacio smiled. "Then we will make sure you will feel our penitence... our complete devotion to the Lord. To our surprise, Gaspar told us you have been chosen to be honored by the Hermanos. To be a true Penitente." He led Mike over to a table near the front. "Soon we will have our last supper and join the Lord in his suffering and his resurrection."

All the men gathered and took their places at the tables. As the sun started to set, twelve men and Gaspar came out of the morada carrying torches. They wore white robes and walked single file, placed their torches in holders behind the chairs and took their places at the head table. Gaspar sat in the middle and the others sat six and six on either side of him. It was a scene from the last supper...somber and sacrosanct.

Every table had been set with paper cups and a large bottle of cheap red wine. There were plates of tortillas and pots of hot refried beans. This was the final meal before penance began early the next morning...Good Friday.

Gaspar stood and raised his cup, "We drink to our Lord, Jesus Christ and place our souls, our lives, in his hand so that we may feel the joy of his resurrection to heaven. My brothers, mi hermanos...drink and eat. Pray with me and the disciples of Christ. The earthly food will help, but our true strength will come from Him." He drank his wine and sat. He prayed in the ancient language of the southwest. The men bowed their heads and prayed. Mike bowed his head as well, feeling the holy spirit all around him.

After prayers the men ate quietly. Sensing that conversation was not the order of the day, Mike ate his food silently. As the men finished their plates, they stood at their places and waited for the others to finish. It was all done in complete silence. Mike was one of the last to stand.

Gaspar resumed prayers...he raised his glass. "The blood of Christ!" he held his cup high, then drank it down. The hermanos followed suit. "I welcome my new friend, the artist Miquel." He spoke directly to Mike. "You are here to learn about our brotherhood. This is something that cannot be done from outside, separado. You must be one of us."

He came out from behind the table and walked over to Mike. "I believe that you are sincere. Hablas desde el corazón. To know the brotherhood, you must be as the brothers." He motioned to the men nearby and they gathered around Mike, pressing in. "I believe God wants you to be a penitente. I believe that your soul wants you to be a penitente. This is why he brought me to you that day by the road." He looked at the brothers surrounding them. Mike was getting nervous, concerned. The men had an intimidating air about them. Gaspar continued, "Your soul wants to be closer to God, but your earthly self...may not be so sure." He motioned to the men. "Take him."

The men grabbed Mike by the arms. "What the Hell... What the Hell is this Gaspar?" He struggled to get loose but there were too many arms holding him. They lifted him up and carried him into the morada. A set of shackles and chains were brought out. Mike tried to break free, but the men tightened their grip. They dragged him over to a main support post and chained him to it, hands behind his back. Gaspar came over with a basin, followed by the Hermanos de Luz. "Gaspar. What is this. I am sincere, but I can't work like this. I won't be a problem."

"No, my friend, you will learn...God will show you this is the only way your earthly self will endure the sacrifice. When it is done...you will truly be an hermano." He knelt before Mike. Two other brothers pulled off Mike's boots. Gaspar washed his feet and prayed.

After Gaspar departed, the men all came into the morada and found spots to pray. They removed various whip like objects. Some were made from the local amote cactus or pounded yucca leaves, frayed at the ends like a rope. Others had whips of leather or rope with barbed wire entwined. Some even had glass shards embedded in fabric. They removed their shirts and gently whipped themselves over their shoulders as they prayed. They started to bleed where the whips had landed. They sang ancient songs, the alabados. After a couple of hours, outside the ghostly sound of the pito signaled it was time to rest. The men settled down and the lights went out.

Mike sat chained to the post in the darkness. His head spinning, his heart beating rapidly. It was not the spirit of God that took him. It was fear and terror.

§

The next morning, Good Friday, the men began to rise, talking excitedly amongst themselves. Mike had not slept at all. He tried to free himself during the night but the chains held. Suddenly, they heard the wailing, high pitched scream of the pito. It was the signal for all the Hermanos to rise up and prepare for the procession. The suffering that Jesus endured as he passed the stations of the cross.

The men released Mike from the post. Leading him out of the barn, they gathered in the yard. They held their whips in their hands. Gaspar came out with the Hermanos de Luz, and the pitero. All the brothers removed their shoes and formed a line to pass in front of Gaspar. The Hermanos de Luz brought a large washtub of water and set it down by Gaspar who proceeded to wash the feet of all the men as they passed in front of him. When all but Mike were done, Gaspar had him brought over. "I will wash your feet as well. Then we will begin the procession."

"Gaspar, please. I'm not ready for this. I'll leave. Let me go!" Mike pleaded. "Or just let me observe. No need to include me in the ceremony." His mind was racing, 'What have I gotten myself into?' "I can't paint with my hands tied. You want me to put God into my paintings? Let me be free to do this."

Standing, Gaspar nodded to the two men. "The Lord will guide your hand, but first he must be within you. Soon he will fill you with his spirit. And afterwards his strength will let you paint his spirit and spread the sacrifice and holiness of the hermanos to your world." They took Mike to the front of the line of men that was forming in front of the morada. Most of them now had their whips in their hands.

Cedro came over to Mike. "Now you will have the opportunity to achieve salvation. Now you will know the suffering. Bring me la mochila."

Ignacio went into the morada and brought out a small backpack. It was filled with small pieces of cholla cactus. The plant has short needles but they protruded through the fabric of the backpack about one sixteenth to one eighth of an inch. Two of the hermanos untied Mike's hands and removed his shirt. He tried to squirm out of their grasps but they held him firmly. "What is that." He struggled to break free. "Get that thing away from me." Without a word, they slid his arms into the straps of the pack and let it settle onto his back.

"Jesus Christ, are you crazy..." he let out an anguished cry. The pain was pervasive. The tiny needles sank into his skin across his back. His eyes teared.

Cedro wiped a tear away on Mike's cheek. He held up his hand.

"Mira! The tears of Christ!" The hermanos murmured "Dios!" and "Alabado sea jesus!" Gaspar approached Mike as the men retied his hands behind his waist.

"You will follow the crosses near the front of our procession. You will be closer to God there. He will give you strength." He walked to the west end of the yard. "Come my brothers, we go la primera estación de la cruz. Follow me. Three men in front of Mike picked up three heavy wooden crosses made from what looked like squared off trunks of trees. They strained under the weight as they hoisted them up onto their shoulders. Gaspar and the Hermanos de Luz led the march. The three men with the crosses followed, then Mike, being prodded to move by the men behind him.

Finally, all the brothers whipping themselves over their shoulders, across their back, murmuring prayers. One said, tears in his eyes, "Why did Gaspar pick the Gringo? I was hoping I would be picked for la mochila." Another answered, "Perhaps the Gringo will fail. Then you can pick up the mochila. Then you can feel the spirit."

The procession disappeared into the pine forests of the Pecos Wilderness.

§

Gaspar led them through the wilderness. He followed the marked trail that would take them to the clearings he had prepared for Holy Week. The paths to the prayer sites were laid out so the last one would be on that high mesa overlooking the morada. They would be there on Easter morning.

The first one was the isolated mesa that was Gaspar's favorite. His Garden of Gethsemane. The path climbed up the side of the mesa and although only about three quarters of a mile from the morada, the men struggled to get to the top. The three men carrying the crosses fell prostrate to the ground. Three other men ran up and took their place. Mike was weak from the constant pain and the loss of blood. He was glad for a chance to rest but the mochilla and his bound hands kept him from finding a comfortable position. His mind raced, desperate to find a way to escape from this madness. By now, all the hermanos were bleeding from the wounds and cuts made by the whips. Gaspar and the Hermanos de Luz had been flagellating themselves as well, yet they did not seem as tired as the rest.

Gaspar raised his arms to the sky and prayed out loud. "Jesus, we are here, following your steps, joining you in your sacrifice. Give us the strength to continue...to reach your last earthly presence among us...to be resurrected from our worldly existence and join you in the glory of heaven, free of our sins." He bowed his head and prayed in the ancient language. The men struggled to sit up, to stand, to join in the prayer. Some sang alabados to strengthen their spirit.

After about half an hour, the pitero signaled the men with another high pitched wail. Gaspar spoke, his voice strong and forceful. "Rise up. It is time that our Lord calls us to the next station. Rise up. Let Jesus fill you with his spirit. We will be with him."

§

The pain did not stop. It transformed. Mike had been blessed with the mochila for most of the day and into the late afternoon. Gaspar led them in a wide circle, from clearing to clearing. At each one they paused, praying...singing...moaning in pain from the whips and the relentless march.

They prayed at the betrayal, the arrest. They prayed at the denial, the trial, the scourge. Each clearing held one or two stations. As they approached the final clearing, Gaspar stopped the procession while still in the forest. He came to Mike who was weak and exhausted. The mochila caused hundreds of pin pricks in his back, but the small wounds half healed during the day. It became more like a horrible painful rash. It was why he was still able to walk.

"Miguel, I will now let you be our Simón. You will help Silvio with the cross." He gestured to Cedro and Ignacio to remove the mochila from Mike's back. They secured his hands in front of him and brought him over to the first heavy wood cross, resting on Silvio's shoulders. Silvio was obviously ready to collapse. Ignacio tied Mike's hands to one of the crossbeams of the cross and they let the weight down on his shoulder. It felt like it weighed a thousand pounds.

"I can't do this...I can't." His lips were parched. "I have the spirit. I have it..."

Gaspar smiled at him. "Seguro, seguro. And this last effort will assure you of a place near Dios por el resto de su vida. You are helping our Lord bear the weight. You and Silvio. Now go, march forward and soon we will join him in the ascent into heaven." He gave Mike a sip of water, then Silvio. The pito sounded and they continued up the hill to the high mesa overlooking the morada. Once at the top, the men bearing the crosses laid them down near some previously dug holes near the edge of the plateau.

Mike and Silvio laid their cross down and then crumpled into an aching pile of flesh and bone. By then, all the penitentes were drained, exhausted and weak from some loss of blood. Gaspar and the Hermanos de Luz still moved with strength. Gaspar walked over and stood by the crosses. "Not yet my brothers. Not yet. Come, gather your strength. I want a brother from Santa Rosa for His cross. A brother from Jemez and one from Chama. You will be on the thieves' crosses. We must do this now!"

The men got to their feet and gathered together, sorting themselves out. The brothers deferred to those who plead the strongest case to be honored, blessed in such a coveted manner. Over the years each man would have or have had the great honor to be that much closer to God.

They assembled around the crosses, the man from Santa Rosa was tied to the central cross. Mike, prostrate nearby, watched as they secured him to the rough wood and picked up the cross, standing it in the pre-dug hole. The same was done to the two men on the thieves' crosses. The sun was setting. The men on the crosses gazed at the sky, tears streaming down their faces. It was not pain…it was ecstasy. The brothers came over to Mike and sat him against the bottom of the central cross, tying him securely. They all gathered in a semi-circle near the crosses, facing the sunset.

Gaspar stood in front of the central cross. "Estamos en el Gólgota. We will hold our vigil until the Lord rises on Easter morning, Mañana de Pascua, when we will turn our faces to the sunrise and our souls will be shown the doors of heaven. Pray now." The sun set slowly…the men prayed and sang and slept.

§

Saturday's passing seemed like forever to Mike. The hermanos had lowered the men from the crosses. They laid them on beds of pine boughs and Gaspar anointed them with an herbal rub. It smelled like piñón pine. The men applied salves and poltices to each other to heal their torn skin. They prayed and held vigil by the three men as the followers of Christ did on Calvary. Some of the men were prostrate, obviously in need of medical care. Mike was going in and out of consciousness. He was still tied to the base of the cross. His back was irritated...it itched furiously but was too raw to scratch. He had sores where the cross had chafed his shoulder. His feet were blistered. His back was driving him crazy. He had a fever and chills.

'Did no one care? Would they let someone die and no one do a thing?' Mike's thoughts were a jumble...nothing made sense. When he asked someone if they were getting a doctor, medical care...for him, for the others who were in as bad or worse shape than he was, the response was always, "They will get help but only after the Lord has risen. We will see to our brothers and Dios will let them stay with us or take them unto himself."

Mike squirmed at his bindings. His endurance was limited, he was exhausted after only a minute or two. He yelled at Gaspar. "Motherfucker! This sucks! Let me go Gaspar...Let me go for Christ's sake!" He ran out of breath.

Gaspar came over to him. "Miguel, the sun will rise tomorrow morning. God will ascend to heaven, and you will be a Brother of Light... an Hermano de Luz. This is a great honor." He turned and gestured to the hemanos, prostrate, in pain. "You're here with us. Anyone here would die for this honor. But I have seen something in you, in your art. If the Lord does not take you to his bosom, al seno de Dios...tomorrow, after mass, I will personally nurse you back to health...give you the power to do God's work." He raised his hands to the sky. "Dios, dale la fuerza para hacer tu trabajo."

Mike felt hopeless. The pain surged. A darkness passed over him and everything went black.

§

Saturday night passed. When he was aware, all he heard was the droning prayers of the hermanos. The only light came from torches and a low burning campfires. When dawn came, Mike was untied from the cross. They carried him to a place in front of the a dias that had been set up at the base of the crosses. Gaspar and the Hermanos de luz stood in front of the crosses facing east and watched the Sun rise. They turned to the congregation.

"See this my brothers. See our Lord rise into heaven. See the face of God." He knelt and the Hermanos de Luz followed. Everyone fell to his knees. They had all fasted during Saturday's vigil and to a one, they were weak and in pain. Gaspar's Mass was very basic. First the liturgy of the Word and then the liturgy of the Eucharist. He quoted scripture that he knew by heart. His sermon was simple, assuring the group that the sacrifices they made were the only way that they would receive the Lord's blessing and expunge all their sins. They prayed together for the salvation of all men. The Eucharist was a small piece of tortilla and The Blood a sip of cheap red wine. When the last of the men received his offering, Gaspar went over to where Mike was laying. He knelt next to him and lifted his head. "My son, the Body of Christ." He broke off a piece of the tortilla and slipped it into Mike's mouth. Mike was in a haze. His fever had worsened. The infections had flared up overnight. Gaspar held a cup of wine to Mike's lips, "My son, the Blood of Christ." He sipped it but had trouble swallowing. Wine dripped down his chin. "Now I will take you into my house. The Lord will help me bring you back to health. You are an Hermano de Luz. God's strength is in you."

The pitero blew his whistle. The shriek was the signal for the men to rise up and begin the march back to the morada. Mike and several others had to be carried. The men took turns bearing the severely injured since they too were very weak and fatigued. It was a tortuous journey.

When they finally arrived back at Gaspar's ranch, they barely had the energy to place the infirm on the beds of pine boughs. Gaspar had Mike taken into the house and laid him on a cot. He was the most important penitente to God and Gaspar was intent on helping him recover. He was Gaspar's mission, a vessel to take the message of the Hermanos to the world.

§

Sunday afternoon, Blanca and Beatriz were again sitting on their front porch. They watched as the trucks and cars of the Hermanos came down the road on their way to their homes. They checked off each car as if they had a list in their heads of every one that made the trip to the morada over the last week. By nightfall, they made a mental note that they had not seen the red van from Rhode Island.

Back in Las Puertas, Jane and Ben started to worry. They expected Mike back that evening but when he did not show, they assumed he was staying up there for the night.

Beatriz and Blanca Iglesias continued to see vehicles going down the canyon from the morada. There were fewer than yesterday. Some of the pickups had one, sometimes two individuals on makeshift cushions, bandaged, with another man sitting in the back, tending to them.

There was no sign of the red van.

Blanca turned to Beatriz, "If that poor anglo doesn't show up by tomorrow night, we call Joe." Beatriz nodded in agreement.

Jane and Ben were genuinely anxious. Mike had gone to a place where rumors of injured men caused an uptick of emergency room visits after Holy Week. They too decided that if they hadn't heard from him by Tuesday night, they would let the sheriff know about their concerns.

Tuesday brought no news. Beatriz and Blanca saw no red van. For Jane and Ben, Mike never came home after dark. "I'm going to go over to my dad's, see if he's heard anything. Some of the penitentes probably stopped by his house on their way home."

Jane nodded. "I'll go to the sheriff first thing tomorrow."

§

Wednesday was Gabby's day off. Deputy Roberto Castillo arrived at the office on Bridge Street at 6:30AM. He parked out back and let himself in through the back door by the two cells. Once in the front office he put the coffee on and checked the answering machine. The message light was flashing.

"Hola Joe." It was Beatriz Iglesias. "I must let you know that the red van, the one the joven from back East drove. We have not seen it coming back from Gaspar's ranch. Most of them have left and some had what looked like wounded in the back of their trucks. That boy might be in trouble. I expect to see you here sometime today. Adiós"

Roberto couldn't remember a year when there was not some problem at the morada. This sounded different. He was distracted by a knock on the door. He walked over and saw David Rangel's son Ben and a young Anglo woman at the door.

He unlocked and opened the door. "Morning, Ben."

"Ese, Roberto." They shook hands. "This is my friend Jane Meyers. We need to talk to you, and maybe Joe."

"Seguro. You want a cup of coffee. Just made it." He picked up a clean cup.

Ben shook his head. "No, gracias. Thanks anyway. Jane and I are worried about a friend of ours. He might be in some trouble."

He gestured at the answering machine. "Got a message this morning. About some kid who got mixed up with Gaspar and the Hermanos."

"That's him. Mike O'Farrell" Jane nodded. "He went up there for the weekend. He's an artist...a pretty good one, and he wanted to immerse himself in the local culture. I think he was lured into something that might be more than he expected. I don't know much about the hermanos, the penitentes, but I've heard that they can get a little crazy up there."

"I asked my Dad if he knew anything about it" Ben joined in. "He used to participate in Holy Week but since Gaspar took over it got a little too rough for him...at his age. Gaspar and some of the brothers usually stop by our house to see him. Last week there was some talk about an Anglo kid who was getting pretty involved. I asked my dad last night if he knew anything about Mike. A couple of the brothers had stopped by on their way home. They told him that the kid was in pretty bad shape. Really bad, actually. Nada seguro. Gaspar was tending to him."

"If he's really hurt, is Gaspar a doctor or anything?" Jane asked.

Roberto shook his head. "No. He's nursed some of the brothers when they are recovering from the wounds, but he's no doctor. The guys in bad shape mostly end up in the hospital here in town. I can check with them, see if your friend ended up there."

"We already checked," Jane said. "He's not there."

Roberto looked up and saw the Sheriff's truck pull up in front of the office. "Here's Joe. Let's get with him and see if he knows anything. He'll probably want to go on up there and check things out. He's been dealing with Gaspar for years."

Joe came into the office and greeted them. "Morning Roberto. Hey, Ben." He nodded to Jane. "Hello young lady. What's going on?" All three started talking at once. "Más despacio, por favor. Not all at once."

Roberto explained why Ben and Jane were there. He told Joe about the phone messages. Joe went over to the answering machine and played them.

"I guess we'll be going up to Rociada today. I wouldn't want to disappoint Beatriz." He turned to Jane and Ben. "There's enough going on that concerns your friend Mike that's got my attention. He could be in trouble...or he might be fine. I don't believe Gaspar would be forthcoming over the phone. The Iglesias sisters might have more to tell us, but Roberto and I will go to the morada and check with Gaspar in person. Bueno. You two go home. Leave an address and phone number. Ben, check in with your dad now and then, in case he has another visit.

To Roberto, "Call Gabby and tell her we'll both be up at Rociada most of the day today. Maybe she can come in and watch the phones and the radio...and give Chief Flores a call. He'll have to get off his ass and have his local boys cover for us.

Jane and Ben thanked Joe and left. Roberto made the calls. "I explained things to Gabby and she says she'll be in in a half hour. We should go. She's got her keys. I left a message for Flores with Débora at the front desk. She expects him in..." He filled the thermos with coffee.

Joe shrugged his shoulders and took down the 12 Guage from the gun rack. "Might need a little respect from Gaspar. We'll both ride in my truck, the roads get rough up there...¡Qué pendejada!" He muttered as he walked over to the window and looked out on Bridge Street. "And I thought we made it through Holy Week without an incident. Let's hope it's just a wild goose chase and the kid's all right."

§

When Joe and Roberto arrived in Rociada it was mid-morning. They stopped at the little gas station and bodega by the church. Joe gassed up the truck while Roberto went inside and bought a couple of burritos for their breakfast. They headed toward the canyon and soon arrived at the Iglesias place. As expected, Blanca and Beatriz were sitting on the front porch.

Joe pulled up to the front yard gate. Fabián, the grandnephew, came over and opened it for them. Blanca remained seated. Beatriz stood and stepped down off the porch.

"Still no sign of the red van." No nonsense. Her attitude was that of a landowner, more concerned that something out of order was happening on her estate...not the misfortune or bad luck of a trespasser.

Blanca announced from her chair. "By now, all the extranjeros are gone. We only see the trucks of the Mendozas, old man Ramos or the ranch hands who work at Gaspar's. The mandamás, the acólitos sometimes remain for a few days...and the Hermanos de Luz."

"The young anglo is none of those things. If he is there…it is muy poco usuales, very unusual." Beatriz was also merely stating a fact. But the sisters' need to know everything going on in and around Rociada was of the utmost importance. Then, remembering the tradition of hospitality, she asked, "Perdóname. I have some coffee on the stove. Would you like a cup?"

Joe smiled. "No. No Gracias Señoras Iglesias. I think we should go to Gaspar's and see if we can find out about the boy."

"That would be best. ¡Buen día, Sheriff!" Blanca stated from her chair. Beatriz nodded to Fabián.

He walked over to the gate and opened it. Joe and Roberto knew the audience was over. As they were leaving, Fabián followed them out to the truck.

"Jefe. Would you like me to come along. I can help."

Joe glanced at him. "Three is better than two. Is it all right with sus tias?"

Fabián laughed. "My work here is done. I am their grandnephew. Not their hired hand. I'll let them know I'm leaving and follow in my truck. They will be happy to have firsthand chismo about Gaspar.

§

A man was standing at the gate to Gaspar's ranch. Another was sitting on a rock by the side of the road. The sheriff's truck pulled to a stop, Fabián's truck behind them.

The gate keeper walked over to Joe's window. It was Cedro's boy, Ignacio. "Hola Sheriff. Why are you here. The procession is over. There was no trouble. All the hermanos have left."

"But you are still here…" Joe gestured at the gate. "If it is all over, why is the gate closed and guarded? Is Gaspar expecting trouble?"

Ignacio seemed caught off guard. "It's…it's because of the livestock. Some horses…" he stammered. The other man came over. He was an older man.

"Hola Sheriff. I am Marcelino Espinoza. I work for Gaspar." He held out his hand.

Joe shook it. "Bueno. Ignacio says you've had some problems with livestock?"

"Si. We had some horses wander off while we were in the morada.

Just by chance there was a tear in the wire, or someone left the gate open... not sure which." He took a sideward glance at Ignacio. "Asi no, Ignacio?"

"Sure, sure. That's it. Gaspar wanted us to make sure they didn't get out this way." Ignacio was a very bad liar.

"Well, I hope you find them. Haven't seen any coming up here." Joe smiled, "Now, let us through. I have business with Gaspar. Fabián too."

Marcelino hesitated. "Gaspar is busy with the Hermanos de Luz. They are in prayer and discussions, about the events of Holy Week." He paused. "It was a very good year. God has blessed us all. Perhaps you could come back later."

"Marcelino, I am up here from Las Puertas on official business. Gaspar will have to spare us a few minutes." His voice hardened. "Open the gate."

Ignacio and Marcelino exchanged worried looks. "Seguro, sheriff." Marcelino nodded to Ignacio to open the gate. Joe and Fabián drove through, and the men shut the gate behind them. In his rear view, Joe saw them move quickly to their truck and begin to follow.

He turned to Roberto, "When we get to the ranch, go tell Fabián to grab his rifle, just carry it, casually. You both wait by his truck while I see if I can find Gaspar. Keep an eye on things."

"Claro, Jefe." They came to the ranch house. Joe parked near the house. Roberto took the shotgun and got out. he signaled to Fabián to park near the barn...the morada. Fabián got out and they both stood by his truck, Fabián with his rifle resting on the stock.

Joe went up to the front door and knocked. By then, Ignacio and Marcelino had also arrived. Other ranch hands, maybe four or five, drifted into the yard. They gathered by the corral and stood silently.

The front door opened. It was Inéz, Gaspar's wife. "Hola Sheriff Joe. ¿Cómo estás?"

"Hola, Señora de la Madalena. Bien, bien." Joe took off his hat. "Is Gaspar home. It is very important that I speak to him...May I come in?" Joe gently pushed past her into the front room.

"No, no. Señor. Por favor. Gaspar is busy with the Hermanos de Luz. Could you please wait outside?" She was nervous, a little frightened.

"I think I will wait here." The front room was sparse. A couch. An armchair. Some end tables. A large Royal Oak potbelly stove on the outside wall. Joe sat down in the chair.

Inéz was visibly upset. "Si debe permanecer. I will see if he can come out."

Joe scowled. "I will be here until he does.

She left the room going through the kitchen to the back of the house. Joe could hear voices. Angry voices. He got up and peered down the hall to the back bedrooms. One door was shut. In the bathroom at the end of the hall, there were bloody towels on the floor. Some assorted bottles and bandages were barely visible on the shelf above the sink. He walked over and looked in the kitchen. A large pot of water was heating on the stove and there were various bowls of pastes and poltices on the counters. More bandages.

Inéz was a curandera. A yerbera. An herbal healer with the knowledge of traditional remedios. She had obviously been hard at work preparing various concoctions to treat someone with severe problems. Joe returned to the chair.

When she returned she was very worked up, anxious. "Gaspar will be here in a momento. The Hermanos de Luz will be joining him. Please sit."

"Con su permiso. Senora. May I use the bathroom. It has been a long ride from Las Puertas." Without waiting he started for the hallway. Inéz tried to block him but once again, Joe just eased by her. When he got to the closed door he called back, "Is this it here?" He grabbed the doorknob.

She rushed down to try and stop him. "Senor, no, please, no." But she was not quick enough. Joe opened the door.

The smell of death hung over the room. On the bed, a young man lay on his stomach. He was nude and covered with festering, oozing sores...made worse by the stench of the various remedies and concoctions smeared over his wounds. His face was pale and covered with sweat. He was trembling, obviously in shock.

Joe went over to him. Checked his pulse. It was very weak. Inéz was standing in the doorway. Tears were streaming down her face. "Oh, Sheriff Joe. I have tried everything. Gaspar said he is now in las manos de Dios."

"He's in my hands now. Where is Gaspar?"

An angry voice came from behind Inéz. "Lo siento mucho, Sheriff. "He must stay in the hands of God."

§

Gaspar moved Inéz out of his way and came into the room. "Sheriff. You are trespassing. You are trespassing against God. This boy, he is a messenger from God. He must remain in His hands."

Joe could see the others behind Gaspar... the Hermanos de Luz. "No Gaspar. The boy must come with me. He'll go septic unless we get him to the hospital. If he is God's messenger, then he must be alive to spread the message. ¿No es verdad?" He slowly placed his hand on his belt, above his holster. "Inéz. Please be so kind as to go and ask my deputy, Roberto, to come in."

Gaspar scowled. "Inéz, go to the kitchen. See if the la medicina is ready." Inéz scurried away. Gaspar approached Joe and suddenly he smiled broadly. "Joe, mi amigo, we are the Hermanos Penitentes." The other men entered the room. "We are servants of the Lord. If it is God's will that this joven is to join him, then his message was meant only for us. If he is blessed with life, then will he have the power to spread the word of God through his art." He walked over to the bedside and touched Mike's shoulder. The boy's body shuddered; his breathing became labored. "You see...there is life in him. Some would have already passed into His hands. But he is alive. He will become a great artist and pass the holiness of penitence to the world. I knew this the first time I saw his work." He stood between Joe and the bed. "Sorry, Joe. He must stay." He nodded to the hermanos in the doorway. They moved into the room and formed a semi-circle around Joe. "Please go now. Or we will keep you and your friends here until Miguel either recovers or goes to his bosom."

Joe looked Gaspar in the eye. "No Gaspar. That's not the way it will be." He drew his weapon and held the gun in front of him. Looking at it.

"Joe, you will not shoot any of us. You are a man of the law and a child of God. How can one life be protected by the death of others?" He held out his hand. "Give me the gun. Go. Let God resolve this."

Suddenly Joe fired the gun into the ceiling. He again held it I front of him, not pointing it at anyone.

Outside, Roberto and Fabián heard the shot. Roberto grabbed the shotgun and they ran toward the house. A few ranch hands moved to block them, but Roberto waved them away with the 12 Guage. When they entered the house they saw the crowd down the hall. Telling Fabián to wait in the living room, Roberto pushed his way through the crowd to join Joe in the bedroom.

"Madre de Dios. Is that O'Farrell?" He looked at the young man suffering on the bed.

Joe's shot had startled Gaspar and the Hermanos. They backed away.

"Joe, are you crazy." Gaspar looked up at the ceiling. "You shot up my house."

"No se moleste. I'm not going to kill anyone. But some of you might lose a toe or two if you don't let Roberto and I take this boy with us now." He gestured to Roberto and together they carefully lifted Mike and held his arms over their shoulders.

He groaned as they lifted him. "No. Please. I see God. Please. No more…"

Joe kept his gun out, at the ready.

Gaspar and the brothers slowly backed out of the room and made way for them to leave. When they got to the living room, Joe passed Mike over to Fabián so that he and Roberto could take him out to the truck. Joe remained in the living room, his pistol in his hand.

Gaspar had his hands clasped. "Por favor. Joe…it is God who must decide the boy's fate."

"As he will…but not here." He backed up to the door. "If the boy recovers, he and God can discuss any future he might have with you and the hermanos. I'm sure he will have much to think about. If he dies, you and your brothers will be facing involuntary manslaughter charges. Then man and God will decide your fate." He turned and looked out into the yard. The ranch hands were milling about, blocking the way for Roberto and Fabián holding Mike up between them…waiting for instructions from Gaspar. "Tell your boys to clear away."

Gaspar reluctantly went outside and signaled his men to clear a path. Joe followed Roberto and Fabián to his truck. They spread out some blankets and lay Mike carefully across the back seat.

Joe found Mike's car keys in his pocket. "Roberto, you drive the kid's van. Lead the way. Fabián follow me." He turned to Gaspar. "I'll make sure we close the gate. Don't want any of those horses getting away."

Gaspar looked confused… "Horses?"

With Mike's red van in the lead, they slowly went back down the road toward the highway.

§

The Iglesias sisters were still sitting on the porch when Blanca spotted the red van coming along the road. The sheriff's SUV and Fabián's pickup followed behind. They all stopped in front of the house and Fabián got out and walked over to the sisters. Joe called out from his truck.

"Muchas Gracias, Señoras. We have the joven and will let you know how he is doing." He nodded to Fabián. "Your sobrino, he is a good man."

"Seguro Joe. He is *our* sobrino." Blanca assured him.

Joe took the lead, lights flashing. He left Roberto in the dust, Mike's van not able to keep up. He had radioed Gabby and told her to have the medics ready at the hospital on Legion Street. They were waiting for him when he arrived. They placed Mike on a gurney and rushed him into the emergency room. Dorotea Guzman, the hospital administrator, came over to Joe. "What's the story, Joe."

Joe just shook his head. "Another Holy Week story for you Dot. This one's pretty serious. How many this year?"

Dorotea looked sad. "Seven. This makes eight. Nothing this serious."

"The hermanos...They are close to God, but why cruelty, suffering... There's enough of that without their help." He got back into his truck. "Keep me posted. I've got some follow up to do. Let's hope God is on this poor kid's side."

§

Jane was Mike's first visitor at the hospital. She sat by his bedside for a few hours every couple of days. When he regained his senses, she happened to be there.

"I kept your room clean for you." Were her first words to him. He nodded. "The sheriff dropped off your van. All your stuff was still in it. Ben and I put it in your room."

Mike nodded again. His voice was horse. "My sketches, they're all there?"

"From what I could tell. Looks like you got a real taste of New Mexico. Some real inspiration." She paused. "You are going to continue your work, aren't you."

"Do I have a choice. I was at the mercy of fate...of God. I'll be out there again. I'll have to try and capture the land with another light, more than the sun and stars... "He faded into unconsciousness.

Mike was released from the hospital by the end of the month. He would bear the scars of Holy Week for the rest of his life. The Hermanos and Gaspar were blinded by their love of God, driven by that love and inspired by the traditions, misguided by the past. Mike did not hate them. He felt no anger. He knew that the pain and the rituals would forever influence his spiritual being.

He rested for several days. The wounds and the lasting pain made the desire to begin painting again stronger. After a few days resting he was ready to go back out. Back to where he started his first painting on the road to Piedras Blanca.

When he arrived at his spot, he held up his first piece. It looked dull, incomplete. Leaving it in his truck, he took his gear and set up down by the rock where he had been working before. The sun still cast the shadows, lit the reds and yellows. But now, for some reason, he saw a glow, a brightness that he had not seen there before.

He began to paint furiously. Inspired by the land...and possibly some other power.

www.ingramcontent.com/pod-product-compliance
Lightning Source LLC
Chambersburg PA
CBHW011648010726
47495CB00011B/2957